SILVERCREST ACADEMY

FALLING SHADOWS

KC KEAN

Falling Shadows
Silvercrest Academy #1
Copyright © 2023 KC Kean

www.authorkckean.com
Published by Featherstone Publishing Ltd

Cover Design: DARK IMAGINARIUM Art & Design
Editing: Encompass Editing
Proofreader: Sassi's Editing Services
Interior Formatting & Design: Wild Elegance Formatting

Falling Shadows/KC Kean– 1st ed.
ISBN-13 - 978-1-915203-40-3

To Heather,
Making memories with you is always a gift I will treasure
forever.

ELIVEN REALM

AMBERGLEN

SI

SHADOWMOOR

E

HAVEN COURT

CREST
EMY

PINEBROOK

WASTELANDS

DALE

LICA REALM

Follow your heart, find solace in the shadows, and take down the dawn.

PROLOGUE

Raven

Wind sweeps through my curly locks, dusting around my neck as tears stream down my face. I don't know why I'm crying. I just know that the sound of Mama and Papa arguing hurts my heart.

Sniffling, I wipe my nose on the cuff of my dress as a rumble of thunder sounds in the air. Mama is mad. The thunder bites like that every time she gets a twitch in her left eye.

Another tear rolls down my cheek as I stand on the porch of our home, helplessly looking up at my older brother. I'm four and he's six. I've never seen him smile, but maybe he's just never smiled at me. Maybe he does it when I'm not around. Maybe he's happier then.

"Seb," I start, but he quickly dismisses me with a shake of his head and his finger pointed in my face.

"Shut. Up. Raven."

I squeeze my eyes shut, my bottom lip trembling once more as the front door bursts open and I startle, blinking up at Mama. The wrinkles around her bright blue eyes, almost onyx in color, are more pronounced than usual as I hear my papa call out her name.

"Evangeline, listen to me." His tone is cold, his arms folded over his chest as he glares at her, completely ignoring Seb and me.

"I've listened enough, Abel. It's not going to change, *you're* not going to change, and if the consequence is a lifetime in Shadowmoor, then so be it. At least there, I'll know where I stand and what I'm up against."

Her hands vibrate at her sides with pent-up magic, a duffel bag hanging from her shoulder as she heaves with every breath. I reach out to touch her without realizing it, her fingers long and dainty compared to my own as she peers down at me.

A soft, sad smile touches her lips and I try to give her one back but fail miserably.

"Mama?" I ask gently, and she sighs, grabbing me under my arms a moment later and lifting me onto her hip.

I nestle into her side, resting my head on her shoulder as another rumble of thunder ripples through the air. "Forget it, Evangeline. She remains here. They *both* remain here."

Mama scoffs. "What, so you can destroy them too? I

don't think so." Her arms tighten around me and I cling to her collar. The smell of her familiar scent cocoons me as my sobs slowly subside.

Everything is always better when I'm in her arms, where I'm safe from Papa's wrath and Seb's…anger.

"You don't get to make all of these decisions, Evangeline," Papa bites, but Mama takes a step back.

"You've made enough decisions for the entire family without considering anyone else but yourself. You don't get to pass judgment, Abel. I'm done with all of this. Consequences be damned."

My eyebrows furrow as I squint between them both, even chancing a glance at Seb, but he's glaring at Mama as he stands beside Papa. Papa's jaw ticks and Seb reaches for his hand.

Lines have been drawn, solidarity among the Hendrix family torn apart in a matter of breaths.

Not another word is spoken.

Not as Mama puts me in the car, not as I glance out of the window and watch as we leave them behind, and nothing at all for the next fourteen years.

Yet it somehow still feels too soon.

Pain at the hands of family, in the name of love and pride, even without physical harm, can destroy you.

How do you come back from that?

ONE

Raven

The crowd roars with triumph as I keep my back plastered to the wall. The bloodbath in the pit below holds everyone captive as the referee counts down to zero and calls the fight. The winner throws his hands above his head, celebrating his victory, while healers swarm the man at his feet in an attempt to save him.

Resurrection is against The Monarchy's law, so it's no surprise when the healers call time on the man's life, sending another ripple of applause around the underground setup. We cheer at the loss of a man's life. That's what everything has come to. There's no hope here, no blossoming gut feeling of a future that equates to more than this.

Shadowmoor.

Filled with shadows and...*moor* shadows.

Nothing more, nothing less. It's in the name, but when

we came here fourteen years ago, my mama and I, I didn't understand. Yet day after day, week after week, it has drained my perky step and cheery smile and turned me into just another one of them.

I lurk in the shadows, hiding from the sun's glare as if threatened by its rays. I don't know why I'm here. I do this every week, watching the brutality before my eyes, but I gain nothing. There's not much else you can do here, though, and the four walls I call home were consuming me. This was the only alternative that didn't involve a mistake at the end of it. More specifically, a guy. Any of them. Shadowmoor produces bad people and even worse lovers.

Sighing, I throw my hood up and stuff my hands into my pockets as I slink away from the pit. I avoid the larger crowds, focusing on putting one foot in front of the other until I step through the side door and find myself in the forest again.

I purse my lips as I glance back at the tree trunk I just stepped out of, expecting something...*more* to happen, but, as usual, nothing does. Keeping my hood over my face, I head for the clearing that is the fastest way home.

After only two steps, I halt at the sound of a snapping branch. I know it wasn't me. The noise came from my left. I was hoping to avoid this tonight, my knuckles still busted from the beginning of the week, but there's no rest for the wicked.

"Is that little Raven out all alone? Whatever will we do with her?"

Disappointment washes over me. I know that voice. The man behind it is why I've sworn off men. Again. It's not *my* fault his pencil dick didn't make me want to stick around. His asshole complex definitely didn't help either. Now it seems his ego is here to rear its ugly head. Delightful.

Pulling my hood off, I turn to face him, not at all surprised to find him lurking in the shadows with his two closest friends flanking him. Alone, he was needy, whiny, and a raging fucking pussy. With his friends? He's just an asshole with an inflated sense of self-importance.

"Are we really going to do this, Wyatt?" I ask, bored as hell with the inconvenience, and he sneers at me.

His head tilts to the side as he steps toward me. The only light comes from the moon, but it's enough to make out his features. Not that I need the illumination, I can envision him from memory, from the crook to his nose and the scar down his left cheek, to those thin lips that were so gross against mine.

"No one will care about another dead shadow. There's no one to protect you and you can't defend yourself. You're. Nothing. Just like all of the others. Especially since you have no magic to even put up a fight, Void."

I resist the eye roll threatening to take over my face. I've known this guy all through school. He lives on the next road over from my house. I've never been shy nor meek and I'm pretty sure when he was dick deep inside of me, he proclaimed my badassery was a turn-on. Now? Not so much, it seems.

The sting of the truth on his lips burns my veins, though. I don't have powers. He's right. Nothing manifested on my eighteenth birthday, not even a flicker of energy, which is why I'm here and not preparing to attend Shadowmoor Academy. There's no use for me there, not when I have nothing to offer. I refuse to let him see how much his dig hurts, however. He doesn't deserve it.

Unzipping my jacket, I drop it to the ground, my adrenaline keeping my arms warm against the wind whipping up around us. "Let's get this over with. I'm tired," I grumble before charging toward him. The grin on his lips quickly dissolves as I throw my shoulder into his stomach, knocking him backward as his friends laugh.

"Fucking stupid bitch," he grunts before we tumble to the ground. His friends quickly rip me from his body and I'm relieved they're using their bare hands. It means I haven't thrown myself into the deep end against guys with highly-graded powers. Not that anyone in Shadowmoor has substantial gifts. It's like our magic is as sullied as our lifestyle. Rotting in the pits of Hell taints our abilities.

Not in my case, obviously. This place took them away entirely. Just like it enjoys taking everything else away from me. It sucks everything from my body and soul without ever offering anything in return, and it won't stop until we're all drenched in the same darkness it consumes us with.

Each of them grabs an arm but I still kick my legs, smashing Wyatt in the face with my boot. I grin when he dramatically falls back again, his attempt to stand squashed beneath my heel before I turn my attention to the two goons he brought with him.

Gripping the guy on my left by the arm, I dig my nails deep into his flesh and pull him toward me, smashing my skull into his with a precision that I know will leave him worse off than me. His hold on me drops instantly, his groan like music to my ears as I turn my slightly-dazed attention to the final fucker.

Before I can consider my next move, he lets me go, cursing under his breath before he takes off running. I frown, trying to catch my breath, my chest heaving as I glance down at the fallen attackers at my feet then back to the one who got away.

I might chase him down any other night to put him in his place, but Wyatt's jibe at my lack of power is causing more of a stir in my chest than I'd care to admit. I just want to go home and nurse my bruised ego.

Reaching for my jacket, I zip it up and hover over the fucker who thought attacking me would be a good idea. "What I lack in power, I make up for with strength because I refuse to be left vulnerable to motherfuckers like you," I bite, ready to kick him while he's down, but I think I've already proven my point.

"Void bitch," he grunts, hand cupping his bloody nose. I kick that fucker where it hurts before offering him a two-finger salute and getting the fuck out of there.

Once I'm out of the forest and onto the road, I slow my pace but remain alert, avoiding the gazes of everyone I pass with my hood firmly back in place. Curiosity always gets the better of me, leaving me wondering if any of these people are Void too. Are they proud of what they can do if they *are* gifted? Do they take pride in where they come from? Is their home complete, or broken like mine?

I don't know what it's like in the rest of the realm, but here in Shadowmoor, being a Void is more common than not. The second your magic doesn't manifest on your eighteenth birthday, you become even more of an outcast than before. We're already residents in the worst part of the realm, but to have no magic as well? It's game over.

No magic means no entry into the academy, where you can at least try to better what the rest of your life looks like. Which means meddling in the fighting pits and salvaging some kind of income to survive is all I'm left with. I shouldn't react so hard to being called a Void, but I can't fucking help it. It's still fresh, and all you can do in Shadowmoor is hope and dream that your magic will help set you on a better path. So, to have nothing to be thankful for but your every breath is soul destroying.

Every day is even more of a battle than before. I wish everyone wore a sign proclaiming what they are or what they can do. At least then I would know what I was up against the next time someone tried to attack me. It's a common occurrence in Shadowmoor. I don't think I've gone a week without someone swinging their fists at me since I turned thirteen. Even before then, it still happened. It was just less often.

It's not how I remember my life before I came here, but it all feels so vague now that I can't be sure. It's just me and my will to survive. Along with Mama when she deigns to make an appearance.

Turning onto my road, fourth house down, I notice the front light isn't on, which is a sure sign that Mama isn't home yet. Disappointment twists inside me like it always does but I quickly squash it down and roll my neck, telling myself that I'm the independent badass bitch I pretend to be and her presence doesn't make a difference.

We left our home together, standing in solidarity that I didn't understand, but we have grown apart as the years have dwindled on. Yet she's been my only constant for the longest time. Even if she's never home, there's always a roof over my head and food in the cupboards. It may be sparse some days, but it's there all the same.

I take the key hidden under the plant pot and let myself inside. It's safer than carrying it on me in case someone successfully brings me to my knees. Plus, it stops me from using it as a weapon, which got me into trouble a year or so ago.

Kicking the door shut behind me, I sigh, hating that this is what my life has become. Shadowmoor is one giant pit of pain, hatred, and dishonor. Just how The Monarchy likes it to be. Separate us, tell us we're bad for long enough, and we'll just start to believe it. They live their best lives in Haven Court, where the sun gleams brightly and gold touches most surfaces the light kisses, and we survive in squalor among the darkness.

My head falls back with a thud and a floorboard squeaks from the kitchen a moment later.

Fuck. My. Life.

I would really love to catch a break right about now.

I wonder if I mention my head is pounding and my knuckles are still red from the previous run-ins I've had this week that whoever it is might fuck off, but a second creak sounds in my ears and I know I'm shit out of luck.

Holding my breath, I square my shoulders and curl my hand around the key I'm still holding. I give myself to the count of three before slamming my hand against the light switch to illuminate the room.

A figure stands in the doorway leading from the lounge to the kitchen and I freeze in place. I must have hit my head harder than I thought because I sure as shit can't actually be seeing what I think I'm seeing right now.

"Oh, good. You're finally home."

His voice is the same crisp ice I remember in my nightmares. The only thing different about him is the scar across his chin and the gray peppering his temples.

"Abel," I croak despite myself, refusing to refer to him by anything other than his given name. I've hated him all my life and craved his approval and presence more than I can bear to admit, but how he looks at me hasn't changed. He still has the ability to leave me standing here feeling like I'm…less than.

A flash of memory from the last time I saw him flickers in my mind. The smell of rain in the air, the wind in my hair, the tears running down my cheeks, and Mama's grip around my body as we left.

"This isn't quite the warm welcome I expected, Raven."

I'm still rooted to the spot, shock leaving me weak as irritation quickly cuts through my veins at his comment.

"I don't recall inviting you here, so I'm struggling to see why you would be welcomed, let alone warmly," I grunt, hands flexing at my sides as he simply smirks at me.

"Nonetheless, I've come to claim you."

My eyebrows pinch, confusion warring inside me as I try to process what this crazy man is doing in my home.

Wetting my lips, I ignore him momentarily and throw a question of my own back at him. "Where's Mama?" He rolls his eyes, waving a dismissive hand at me as he steps toward me. "Where. Is. She?"

"Really, Raven? Is that how I raised you to speak to people? Especially your elders. Where are your manners?" he asks with a raised brow and a look of disdain on his face.

"I was raised in Shadowmoor, in the pits of Hell. What would you know about how *I* was raised? You weren't there, Papa! Now, where is Mama?" I hate that I address him with a title he doesn't deserve, but my emotions are getting the better of me.

He takes two further steps toward me before responding. "Waiting for you back home."

"I am home."

He looks around in disgust but I don't follow his line of sight, refusing to see this world through his eyes. I'm sure he can't see in the dark as well as we can, or guess the curves of the shadows that mend at will with every step he takes. No. He's used to the light, I'm sure.

"I played your mother's little game and allowed you to hide away in Shadowmoor, but now it's time to step back into the real world, Raven."

"What's that supposed to mean?" I fold my arms over my chest, anger bubbling inside me as his grin widens, spreading from ear to ear, leaving a sinking feeling in my stomach. He will take great pleasure in his following words and leave me furious. I can already sense it.

But even my gut feeling couldn't prepare me for what he says next.

"It's time to get ready for Silvercrest, Raven. The most prestigious academy in the realm is awaiting your arrival."

TWO

Raven

I hold the duffel bag tossed over my shoulder in a death-grip as I stand rooted to the spot, staring up at the house I once called home. I barely remember anything apart from the night we left it all behind, and standing right here in front of it again makes me feel two feet tall.

Squinting, I take in every detail, committing it to memory but failing to compare it to the last time I was here. Everything I have known is tainted by that dreaded night. The pain I felt and the confusion it left makes me wonder if the exterior walls were always that sickly, pale gray. Were the window frames always black? The front door so boldly onyx too?

I can't even tell which was my room from here but, as soon as I start to consider it, I quickly shut it down. Those are attachments we have zero care for.

It feels the same, yet completely different all at once. I don't know whether that's because it's so foreign to me now or because I've grown since then, but now it's just brick and mortar. It doesn't hold any more value than that.

"Come now, Raven. You insisted," my father demands, waiting on the porch, but my feet still refuse to move.

I agreed to pack up my bag, the very one my mother brought with us when we left here, and follow his word if it meant I could see Mama first. There was tremendous reluctance on his part, but he eventually agreed.

Now that I'm standing here, I wish I hadn't pushed the issue.

This place isn't good for me. Amberglen was supposed to be the beautiful home where I would grow into a sweet girl, running through flowers and being carefree, but the hand I was dealt led to a completely different life. This place is just as haunting as Shadowmoor now.

Pursing my lips, I look to the window to the left of the porch and instantly see Mama's silhouette. I know it's her without question. Her petite frame, arms folded around herself as she looks down at the ground. As if sensing my eyes on her, she inches closer to the window and meets my gaze.

The pain is there, the disappointment at the situation. Whether it's for me or herself, I can't tell, but it's thick in the air as I gulp.

"Raven, Silvercrest is a prestigious academy for highly gifted and respected families. I agreed you could come here on the way because I assumed it would be a quick visit. If you insist on dragging this out I can change my mind and take you straight there," Papa grates in irritation, folding his arms over his chest and stretching the Monarchy-issued suit across his sizable frame. That's what is most important to him. His job, his role in what he believes to be the greater good.

I don't recall what that is anymore, but I remember the raised voices in the house. It was always about him, his job, and Mama's lack of understanding.

Mama never gave me a full explanation of why we left, but over the years I've come to assume it's because of Abel and the corruption within The Monarchy. Him summoning me back and demanding I change my life may as well be law. I can't outrun him and I refuse to try, it would only make me look weak.

"You know I'm a Void, right? She's told you that?" I match his stance, leaving my duffel on my shoulder as I fold my arms.

"It's not possible for you to be a Void. Now, will you move this along, or shall we skip this little reunion and proceed to the academy? You're going to have to do something about your hair too."

Pompous asshole. He irritates every damn bone in my

body. No one is touching my hair. It's pink because I chose for it to be that way. The center part I wear, though, is there to fall on either side of my face and hide the shadow markings I gained when I first stepped into the darkness. The small black star by my right eye is a stark reminder of where I've been and what I've escaped.

Escaped.

Rolling my eyes, I don't let him stray from the point I'm trying to make. "There is no point in me attending a gifted school when I don't have a *gift* to wield," I point out, not moving an inch.

"I didn't create a Void and neither did your mother. It's not possible. It will all be taken care of at the academy. Now, what shall it be?"

Growling, my teeth grind with frustration. I fucking hate the way he says '*now.'* That's one thing I do remember as a child. Back then, it made me afraid that I was in trouble. *Now* it makes me want to *start* trouble.

I look up to see Mama through the window and find her leaning closer this time, her eyes fixed on mine as she shakes her head. *'Go'* she mouths, cracking the ice wall around my heart as disappointment burns through me.

I don't know what I expected coming here. It's pitch-black but still not as dark as it gets in Shadowmoor, and, once again, I'm being sentenced to a life I didn't ask for. Do I want to return to the troubled shadows back home?

No.

My knuckles ache, my skull still vibrating from the headbutt earlier.

Could Silvercrest be any better? Surely it can't be worse. Either way, it beats the bullshit I'll get if I stay here any longer. I have nothing going for me, nothing in this life that feels any more substantial than the shadows I've become so comfortable in.

I look at the house, Mama, and the man I'm supposed to call my father before looking back at the car parked behind me.

Settling my gaze on Mama again, the pain is apparent in her eyes as she mouths, '*I love you.*' My chest tightens, confusion rippling through my veins. I know we're not the closest these days, but shit… she wants me to leave without a word. What the fuck is that about? As if sensing my frustration, a rumble of thunder vibrates across the sky as her eye twitches and tears stain her cheeks.

A calmness washes over me, a decision made in my mind.

"I'm done here."

"I've told you, Raven, you—"

"I said I'm done," I repeat, louder this time, as I point over my shoulder. "Take me to Silvercrest."

His grin instantly spreads across his face, the lines marking his forehead disappearing as pride settles over him. Fucker. "And your mother?" he asks, pushing, just like I remember.

I take one final look at her through the window, a sad, teary smile on her face, before I look back at him.

"You have us both at your mercy with whatever bullshit this is and I get the sense she wants me as far away from you as possible. So the distance works in my favor. *Now*, am I going or not?"

The driver doesn't utter a word as I sit alone in the back of the car, and I lose myself in my thoughts as I stare down at the pamphlet in my hands.

Silvercrest Academy.

The font practically fucking shimmers in my hand, like golden lava running across the page.

My dearest *papa* barely spared me another look after I agreed, waving me into the car without another word before he strolled inside the house. I have no fucking clue what's happening, but when have I ever? I grew up living on the cusp of knowing and drowning in the world around me.

Leaning back in my seat, I watch the scenery go by through the window. We've been driving for well over two hours now. I'm sure my father knows someone who could portal me to the academy, but this is probably a life lesson or some other bullshit.

I've tried to nap to no avail, despite the twilight hour having come and gone, giving way to a dark sky and an endless, inky blackness.

It's not until the rays of sunlight pierce through the clouds, sunrise breaking through the air, bringing a shimmering life to everything it touches, that we see anything other than trees and shrubbery in the distance. The driver takes a right and I know, without a shadow of a doubt, that the vast building propped on the mountain range ahead is our final destination.

The charcoal-gray peaked roofs and ivy-covered walls are unmistakable, even from here.

Turning the pamphlet in my hand again, I take a peek inside.

Welcome to a future like no other.

Silvercrest Academy is renowned throughout the realm for fostering those with gifts vital to our world—the protectors of our lands, and the saviors of our people—and honing those gifts so that our students may rise to unimaginable heights and preserve our way of life for generations to come.

Our core values—determination, composure, and results—guide the hands of our faculty and staff and form the foundation of our world-class curriculum at every turn.

The only academy endorsed by The Monarchy, Silvercrest guarantees you a prosperous future, honored by all.

Trials and tribulations may come your way, but overcoming them confirms your rightful place in this world and your importance to our people.

Follow the sun, destroy the shadows, and survive another dawn.

—

Professor Burton - Head of Silvercrest Academy

Oh, great. It looks like I've got more pompous shit to deal with. I bet he's just like my father. This is going to be wonderful. I fight back an eye roll as I turn the page, glancing over the list of proffered classes; everything from herbs and potions to combat classes and magic training courses. Not that the latter will be of any use to me.

The car rolls to a stop as I hear the crunch of stones beneath me and I glance out of my window again to find the building now looming right in front of us. The first glimpse I got of it did it no justice. I'm sure you could fit the entirety of Shadowmoor in the grassy area surrounding the academy.

I climb from the car before the driver can get the door,

which earns me a grunt, but I'm too engrossed to care as I take in my surroundings and the morning chill makes me shiver. There are multiple buildings on the property, none as big and grand as the one directly before me, but the place feels like it goes on and on for miles until you meet the cliff edge in the distance. At least if I want to take a run and jump off of it, it's not too far away.

Flowers adorn the walkways and birds chirp in the distance, all of it otherworldly compared to the bleak darkness of Shadowmoor. I feel like I've left the land I was raised in and traveled to an entirely different dimension. If this is what Silvercrest looks like, I dread to think how spectacular Haven Court is. Everything seems to shimmer and shine, from the stained glass windows to the golden statues that line the tops of the academy's towering pinnacles.

Maybe I'm in over my head. Perhaps I'm more suited to staying put and fighting it out in Shadowmoor. This… feels like it belongs to someone else entirely and I don't even know where to begin navigating it all.

The thump of my duffel bag as it lands at my feet pulls me from my thoughts and I look at the driver with a frown.

"Your guide will be here in a moment, Miss Hendrix. Good morning, and goodbye." He slinks back into the car without another word, leaving me riddled with the creeps at the only words he's spoken to me this entire time.

Reaching for my measly belongings, I gulp down the uncertainty that threatens to consume me, roll my shoulders back, and try to exude confidence. I can face this place just like I faced Shadowmoor. The point of attack and defense will be different, but I'll survive it nonetheless.

I don't know whether to stand and wait or head toward the circular door ahead, but it doesn't take long before curiosity gets the better of me and I slowly make my way toward the door. Three stone slab steps lead up to the entryway and I'm halfway up them when I hear a guy's voice from inside. It's loud and obnoxious, irritating me immediately.

"Give me two minutes to deal with this fucking brat and I'll be right with you. Make sure to save some of that early-morning pussy for me, would you?"

Barf.

My gut tells me *I'm* the "fucking brat" being referenced here. I want to be mad about it, but I've been called far worse.

Like "Void."

Bracing myself for some asshole to walk through the door, it swings open a moment later, leaving me dead in my tracks for what feels like the hundredth time in less than twenty-four hours.

His eyebrows wrinkle, his nostrils flaring as his jaw tenses.

"Raven?"

My name on his lips sounds like more of a curse than a blessing and I'm already regretting being here—well, being here without asking some obvious questions beforehand—but it seems information was withheld on both sides, not just mine.

Sighing, I steel my spine, ready for the onslaught.

"Sebastian."

My brother. Fourteen years and he doesn't look any different. His eyes still glimmer with mischief, his angry, snappy tone all-too-familiar, and the sneer on his lips remains the same as the day we left all this behind. Nothing has changed.

"What the fuck are you doing here, Raven?"

THREE

Raven

Istand in shock, staring at my brother, the grown version of him not far from the boy I remember. Confusion clouds my brain, the familiarity of him wanting to warm my senses, but his wrath, which haunts my memories, still lives in the sneer on his lips.

If anyone was born to be an only child, it was him. Until now, he'd had his wish, it seems. My forced presence here appears to be pissing him off more than it does me.

His navy-blue and gold uniform reminds me of our warriors' outfits upon their return from battle. Except he's wearing a crisp white shirt and polished black shoes with a matching tie perfectly centered at his collar.

Glancing down the length of me in my baggy pants, oversized jacket, and combat boots, the stark difference between us is clear. That's just the exterior version, though.

I'm sure the interior would be just as drastic.

"Well?" I blink at his words, watching his nostrils flare and his pupils widen with annoyance. "What are you doing here?"

Hiking my duffel bag up my shoulder, I sigh. "Abel sent for me."

His face scrunches as he takes a step toward me, our height difference becoming noticeable, but I don't retreat. "You mean Papa?"

"I said what I meant." I cock an eyebrow at him.

He huffs before swiping a hand down his face in frustration.

"You're not attending here." It's a statement, not a question, and when I smile, he frowns.

"Excellent. That's exactly what I told him as well, but it seems I don't get a say in anything that happens to me within this family. So, despite my refusal, here I am. But if you think you can change his mind, I'm all for it," I offer, more than happy to be out of his hair.

Sebastian purses his lips. His jaw is still tight as he looks at me in disgust. I catch his gaze lingering on the mark by my left eye before he nods, but he doesn't get a chance to speak before a bell chimes in the distance.

He curses, exhaling harshly as he assesses me. "It's going to have to wait until after this," he states, spinning toward the door with a stomp.

"I'm sure it doesn't. The quicker you speak to him, the quicker I'll be out of your hair."

He stops, glancing back over his shoulder to sneer at me. "If that's what you think, then I don't need to worry because you won't survive a day here." Without another word, he continues inside, not looking back as he forces the door open.

Uncertainty worms its way inside me as I consider chasing after him or hightailing it out of here, but when I glance back, I realize the car is gone.

Great.

With a sigh, I rush toward the door, following after my long-never-lost brother, thankful he didn't have time to lock it from the inside before I could decide. I guide the door closed behind me, not having more than a second to note the cream and gold-laced marble surfaces in the entryway as I spy him rushing down the hall to the right. There aren't any other people in sight as I skid across the floor to keep up. Arched alcoves and golden beams soar above me as I rush after him down the long corridor.

I slow as he takes a left through a pair of glass double doors and attempt to catch my breath as I take in the scene before me.

Hundreds of students fill the open courtyard with stone benches and an arched walkway bordering the fountain in the middle. The early morning sun basking down on the space makes me squint, but even that doesn't take away from the beauty of the world I've stumbled into. There's nothing like this back in Shadowmoor, not even the damn benches, and I instantly feel entirely out of my depth.

Sebastian still doesn't look back as he heads through the crowd toward a group near the front. A guy slaps him on the back in greeting and the girls preen at him, desperate for attention, and my gut twists. At least one of us managed to land on our feet and find somewhere they matter.

That fact instantly makes me dislike this place a lot more than I did on the way here. Shit, I'd almost convinced myself that it might be good. As usual, I was wrong. Possibly even cursed at this stage. Nothing seems to work in my favor.

A small bell rings and the murmuring around the courtyard halts. Everyone turns to face the open space that leads out into a meadow. Deciding to lay low, I move to the side, staying under the canopy of the arch at the back of the space as a man suddenly appears in the air.

Projection.

It's only faint, but I can tell it's not a natural person with how their shoulder flickers on the left. I recognize the man, though. He was in the pamphlet I read on the way over here. It's—

"Students," he calls, garnering a tandem response from every student.

"Professor Burton."

Chills run down my spine at the snap of obedience. It's palpable in the air as I gulp.

"We'll be brief today. We lost two pupils in the early hours of this morning to an attack in the northwest of Ashdale." My heart lurches, confusion washing over me. "They believed they had the strength to fight among men, as I'm sure many fourth years do. Let their deaths be a lesson to you."

What the fuck?

I gape at him. His words blur as he rattles on about knowing our place, paying closer attention, and learning from those offering their aid if we want to live longer than our peers. I'm left reeling from the flippant delivery of such impactful information.

Students just...died?

What attack?

Ashdale?

It's clear there's a lot I don't know from being isolated in Shadowmoor, but do I even want to find out?

"That's all for today. Strength testing will commence in three weeks. Follow the sun, destroy the shadows, and survive another dawn." His voice booms through the space and I gape as every student present repeats the latter statement back to him in chorus.

Just like that, he's gone again, but my eyebrows are

still drawn in bewilderment.

Everyone disperses, bustling around me in groups as they head off, making it hard to keep track of Sebastian. When it's clear he's not coming back and the courtyard dwindles down to just a handful of people, I curse.

"Motherfucker."

I tap my boot against the pillar beside me, annoyance getting the better of me. Someone clears their throat to my right and I turn to see a girl standing with her arms folded nervously over her chest.

"Are you okay there?" she asks tentatively, her round blue eyes blinking at me as her button nose twitches.

"Uh…" I pause, hating to ask for help, but what alternative do I have right now? "I have *no* idea where I am, and my br—my guide seems to have disappeared," I admit, tucking a loose lock of pink hair behind my ear.

She offers me a reassuring smile, glancing around us before fixing her gaze back on me. "If he happens to be called Sebastian, then there's no way in Hell he's coming back. I don't know how he became a prefect, but he has no interest in anyone but himself. Please don't expect him to recognize or acknowledge you for the remainder of your time here," she says with a chuckle, and I grin in response.

If only I could guarantee he would fuck off and pay me no mind, I would dive into my time here with relish, but something tells me I won't be so lucky. Not unless he manages to get ahold of Abel and organize my departure. I'd more than happily hear from him then.

"I like you already," I say, taking a deep breath as I try my luck. "Do you mind helping me out?"

"You shouldn't," she murmurs, adding to all the confusion I'm already handling.

"I shouldn't what?"

"Like me. Nobody does." Her words ripple in my soul, her pain evident in every word.

I want to say "me too" or "girl, same," but that would diminish her feelings right now, and that's not my aim. Things are shit, and *people* even more so.

"I'm not nobody," I state in an attempt to reassure her. "I'm Raven." I watch her rub her lips together nervously as she twists a piece of blonde hair framing her face.

"I'm Leila."

"It's nice to meet you." I feel like a fraud. This level of nicety is not the norm for me, but I'm not usually so out of my depth either.

She clears her throat, standing tall as she smiles. "I'm free first period. I can show you to the office if you like."

"Thank you," I breathe in response, relieved I don't have to navigate this place alone. I fall into step beside her, the courtyard completely empty now as we step inside and head back down the long corridor. When we're back in the entryway, the cream and gold-flecked marble glistening around us, Leila pauses before a stone door to the left.

"I hope you're ready for this," she mutters, pushing it open and stepping inside.

I'm never ready for anything life throws at me, but I've made it this far.

What on earth could an academy like Silvercrest put me through that I haven't already experienced?

FOUR

Raven

Leila rapped her knuckles on the door and hightailed it out of here before a voice sounded from the other side for me to enter. Now I'm faced with sharp eyes that meet mine as I swing the door open.

A woman sits behind a mirrored desk, half-moon glasses perched on the bridge of her nose as she assesses me. Her white hair is slicked back into a bun at her neck, and she's wearing a pristine white skirt and blazer with a golden silk shirt underneath that matches her heels.

She practically blends in with the marble back in the foyer and her glare is anything but welcoming.

Avoiding her stare for a moment, I glance around the room that glows with the sunlight filtering in through the golden-stained window panes. It's light, airy, and prestigious here, a stark contrast to the surroundings I'm familiar with.

All that sits in this large room are the lady, her desk, and the chair beneath her. A pen scratches along parchment before her, but instead of watching it, she remains focused on me.

"What are you doing here?" Her tone is as sharp as her gaze, threatening to plunge me right back to where I came from.

"Uhh…" I pause, pointing at the door as I glance back at it, wondering if I should have avoided it altogether, but I'm here now. Yet the answer to her question isn't so simple. "Honestly, I don't know."

Her eyes narrow and her nose wrinkles. "Then don't waste my time."

Rude much? Despite the instant irritation thrumming through my veins, I take a deep breath and try again.

"No, I mean, uh, I was dropped off here this morning and I don't know—"

"You don't know what?" Anyone else would bristle at her tone, at her interruption, but I simply glare openly at her. Dropping my bag from my shoulder, I tilt my head as I observe her.

"Are you okay?"

"Excuse me?" She bristles like I didn't just ask a normal question.

"I said. Are. You. Okay?" Her eyebrows furrow, but I

push on, annoyed enough with her to get my point across. "I was led here by someone because the first guide that met me at the front doors disappeared." I intentionally redact the fact that it was my brother. "I have no idea where I am or what I'm supposed to be doing. I'm already on edge with all the changes I've been through in the past... shit, none of that matters, but your attitude is grating on an already irritated nerve."

The pen pauses on the parchment and she rears her head back, mouth wide as she gapes in horror at me.

"How dare you," she hisses, placing her palms flat down on the desk and spreading her fingers out.

"Right, of course, how dare *I*. But could we skip this bullshit and get to the part where you tell me where I'm supposed to go because Abel gave me no further instruction." My niceties are gone, any inclination to attempt remaining civil down the drain. I need a damn nap and she's getting in my way of one.

To my surprise, she shrinks in her seat, jaw moving a few times before words actually pass her lips. "Abel as in Abel... Hendrix?" Her voice is barely more than a whisper and I spy a slight tremble to her fingers.

"Yes."

"H-he sent you?"

I nod. "Yes."

"He sent you here?" What more confirmation does she

need for the same question?

"Yes."

She sits tall in her seat, nervously rubbing her lips together as she continues to eye me. "And your name is…"

"Raven Hendrix."

Her skin practically turns to ash as her eyes widen and her hands fly to her chest. She's dipped in fear, laced with poison, and on her way out. I'm sure of it.

"I'm so sorry, miss, I…" her words trail off as she rises to her feet, glancing around all flustered, and understanding slowly dawns on me. My eyebrows pinch together in a mixture of irritation and disappointment and I take a step toward her.

"Don't do that."

"Don't do what?" she asks, peering at me with worry etched into every feature on her face.

"Fear a name," I state, and her head rears back, eyebrows pinching as she frowns at me.

"I'm sorry?"

"If you're going to be a raging bitch, then be a raging bitch. Don't hide your true colors out of fear. That's more distasteful than my dirty boots on your untouched floor."

She visibly gulps, shaking her head at me slightly. "You say that like your father isn't—"

"He isn't my father," I interrupt, my bite snappier than I expected or intended, but I don't take it back.

Her eyebrows knit together even tighter as she gapes at me. "But—"

I wave my hand, interrupting her as I make myself clear. "I don't care what the paperwork may say, it doesn't mean anything. How about, I won't mention your attitude if you only refer to him as Abel. Agreed?" My heart pounds in my chest, but she slowly nods her head and relief floods my veins.

"Agreed."

For the first time since stepping through the door, I smile. "Perfect. Now, I really don't want to be here, but when my alternative was surviving another night in Shadowmoor, I decided to take my chances. Can we skip to the part where you help me out because I've been traveling for what feels like forever and I need a nap and a shower. I'm not fussy about the order."

"S-shadowmoor?" she stutters, hand clutching the collar of her silk shirt as horror darkens her eyes. "Why on earth—"

"It doesn't matter," I interrupt, again, but she's trying to delve into things that really don't hold any significance right now. "The past is the past unless you decide to make it the present, and I'm really not loving that idea." *Brother and Papa included.* Just because they're both suddenly present in my world, doesn't mean I have to act like they exist in it. Far from it.

I watch as the woman's shoulders slowly relax back, the tension drifting from her as her eyes continue to pierce mine. "Do you always have such words of wisdom?"

A laugh passes my lips before I can stop it. "If you were raised in the depths of Hell, you'd have some mantras to live by as well."

I'm almost certain a sad smile touches the corner of her mouth but it's gone before I can confirm or deny it. She snaps her fingers and a manilla folder appears on the desk. "You're going to need this," she says, pointing down at it, and I move closer to take a look.

It's no surprise that it's a golden folder with my name cursively written in white ink. It matches the rest of this place. Everything is white or gold, and spotless. Whereas everything back home was black, gray, and tarnished. The contrast is unreal.

I run my finger over my name on the folder, the intricate calligraphy making me warm inside, as she continues to speak. "Everything you need will be found in that folder." I want to ask what *everything* entails, but it's as if she senses my thoughts and expands. "The details on where you will need to go to have your uniform fitted are in there as well as a list of the items you need. While you're there, you may want to take the list of books you'll need for this semester as the stores are nearby in the on-site facility." She barely comes up for air as she rattles everything off, leaving me to nod at her. "There is also your schedule and all extracurricular activities that may be suitable for your powers." I freeze, almost interrupting her again, but I decide mentioning I'm a Void really isn't going to get this over with any quicker. "You'll also find your assigned housing on the map, along with your key. Your housemates will be in classes at the moment, but that will work out well for you as you'll only be given today as grace to gather what you need before everything starts tomorrow."

When I'm certain she's finished, I quirk my brow, collecting the folder as I wave it slightly. "Is there anything *not* in the folder?" I ask, smirking, since it seems the entirety of my new life is all contained in here, but she doesn't grin back. If anything, her face drops further and her eyes look grim.

"How to survive this place."

I wasn't expecting an honest answer, or one so dark, but I force the smile to remain on my lips as I nod. "Perfect. Thank you…" My words trail off as I realize I don't know her name.

"Lyra."

"Thank you, Lyra."

Grabbing my bag, I make sure I have everything before turning for the door, but I don't get far before she's calling my name. I look back over my shoulder to see her nervously wringing her fingers as she rubs her lips together.

Whatever is playing on her mind seems to settle as she points at me. "Since you've offered me so many words of wisdom, would you like some in return?"

"I'll take what I can get," I reply, intrigued as hell.

"Keep your head down and avoid any trouble. Especially when it comes to your brother."

My hair is damp with sweat, clinging to my face and neck as I take another turn, hoping like hell I've finally figured this fucking map out. There are multiple pages to the damn thing, a fact it took me two wrong turns and a hot minute to realize, but the tag on my room key reads *King Phillian House*, and the sign up ahead says the same.

My pace picks up, hope blossoming in my chest as I, once again, retrieve the key. *Third time's the charm*. Taking the pathway to the right, a single story building comes into view.

It's not grand or excessive, but the view it offers as I get closer is breathtaking. It's by the far end of the cliff, water lapping in the distance while the coastlines of surrounding towns fade off on the horizon.

Please let this be where I'm supposed to be.

Twirling the key in my hand, I squeeze it tight as I come to a stop before placing it into the lock. The latch that sounds makes me squeal, excitement buzzing in my veins and relief flooding my senses at finally finding the building housing my latest accommodations.

Without wasting a moment, I step inside to find a completely open living area, dining table, and kitchen, with doors leading off on either side, but my attention is focused straight ahead. Floor to ceiling doors offer a panoramic view of exactly what I'd been admiring outside. It makes my heart lurch in my chest. It's so open, so majestic in a light and airy way, that I don't know where to look first.

Little critters scurry over the wooden furniture in the yard as birds fly high overhead, dipping and diving in pairs over the cliff edge as the light breeze outside flutters the flowers.

I feel like my eyes are wide open, my retinas burning from all of the brightness.

Shuffling further into the room, I place my bag down on the pale gray chair closest to me. The seating area is situated prominently in the middle with a huge dining table running the length of the right-hand side and a kitchen bigger than my entire house back home filling the left.

I'm sure there was another key in the folder for my specific room and a quick glance inside reveals the smaller key labeled *five*. Squinting at the doors framing the room, I count each one until I find the fifth, matching my key.

Grabbing my things, I tiptoe through the room toward

the right, like I'm not supposed to be here, and quietly unlock it. I think I need to punch myself in the face or, at minimum, pinch my arm because this surely can't be happening right now.

A queen-sized bed sits against the left wall, nightstands on either side, and a pale white drape hangs over it; a desk is tucked in the corner, a leather chair pushed against it and a walk-in wardrobe beside it; a private bathroom leads directly to the right and the window offers a pretty view of the flowers in the garden.

Nowhere, not even the richest parts of Shadowmoor, would have anything like this. Knowing this is how Sebastian has likely lived all his life makes me instantly want to hate it, but it's impossible.

Placing my bag on the bed, I take a seat beside it and exhale, giving myself a second to catch up, but it's not going to happen yet. Or at all, for that matter. Opening the folder, I pull out all of the documents inside and organize them by what's important now, and what can be read later.

I prioritize my uniform and book information, saving my schedule and extracurricular details for after. Despite my need to pass out and gorge on any food I can get my hands on, I decide to get this shit over and done with first. I make sure to grab both keys and the lists before locking up after myself and following the map.

I'll be curious to see my housemates later. I'm not

really a people person, but I guess I'm going to have to adjust a little. Not too much though. I'll be able to hide away in my room as much as possible.

Finding the right page in the map book, I hurry toward the on-site facilities. I don't know what I'm expecting to find, but it's not rows of stores, restaurants, and bistros. This is madness. Since most people are in classes, I get to move around without interruption. It's only when I step inside the uniform store and the assistant comes over to help me that I stutter.

"How am I supposed to pay for this?" I ask nervously as she immediately starts taking my measurements.

She looks up at me with an inquisitive glance but chuckles. "Your presence here is an honor to many. No student pays for anything here."

"Nothing?" I clarify and she nods.

"Your favor will be returned in one of two ways, as will everyone else's."

Confusion knits my eyebrows as she takes a step back and waves me toward the dressing room. "How?"

She grabs one of each item before coming to a stop beside me. "You'll pay with your life. Either failing to survive the trials and tribulations of the academy, or on the battlefield, defending your people."

"What battlefield?" Back in Shadowmoor you chose to be a soldier. It wasn't forced upon everybody.

"Oh, well, I'm not really sure, but I guess the realm is always under attack from others and Silvercrest is where the elite are trained to protect us."

She presents the information like I should know this, like it's a basic fact. Which it might be for everyone else, but apparently citizens of Shadowmoor aren't provided with the same basic information offered to others.

Her words repeat in my head non-stop as I leave the store bagless. She scanned my room key, promising my items will be there upon my return. The same thing happens in the book store. I triple check I have every item on the list before they do it, but my mind is still fixated on the words the assistant so casually shared.

I'm here to die? Is that the case?

I mean, I know we all die eventually, but this feels way more brutal. I really don't have a clue what I've gotten myself into. Or more exactly; what *Abel* has gotten me into.

More and more students appear around me and I assume it's the end of classes for the day, which only serves as a reminder that I still haven't eaten. Using the cashless positivity that comes with unwillingly putting my life on the line, I grab a coffee from the vendor, along with a deli sandwich and cupcake, before I head back to my room.

I'm completely lost in thought as I somehow make my way back by memory without the map. No one seems to pay me any attention as I head down the trails and spot the sign for my house. But that all changes as I push my key into the lock and open the front door.

Four sets of eyes whirl around in my direction, annoyance, anger, confusion, and surprise greeting me as I smile mildly back at the four hot guys filling the space.

"I guess this is our new housemate."

FIVE

Raven

I don't know where to look first with all of the testosterone up in here. Did someone turn the heat up? Fuck.

Observing the tallest of them first, I'm met with muscles on top of muscles. His cropped brown hair and broad frame as he stands with his arms folded over his chest make him look almost daunting but, if anything, I find him intriguing. Especially his eyes. One's brown, the other green. It's alluring. He's dressed in a white loose-fit tank and a pair of gray shorts with a scowl on his face as he assesses me.

Swiftly moving on, the guy beside him rakes his fingers through his tousled brown hair, blue eyes piercing into my skin as his chiseled jaw flexes for the briefest second before a wicked grin touches his lips. He's in the same uniform as I've just been fitted for, the gold accentuating his olive skin as he looks me up and down.

There's a moody one and a flirt. How original.

Continuing around the group, inquisitive onyx eyes meet mine. He tucks his black hair behind his ear as he purses his lips. His face is completely expressionless, making it hard for me to get a read off him. With his hands tucked into his pants pockets, he seems happy to just observe what's going on around him.

Unlike the guy to the right who announced me as their new housemate. Hazel eyes are framed with black-rimmed glasses and his blond hair sticks out in every direction as if he hasn't stopped tugging at the ends. He's wearing a band tee with worn jeans and an almost-knowing smile on his face.

They're all easily over six feet tall, making my five foot seven feel short in comparison. Do they only accept giants around here or something?

I'm not quite sure how I feel under their intense stares. It's clear I'm stepping on their territory, but their reaction is still yet to be decided.

"She's *not* a guy," the brown haired one with the wicked grin assesses.

The tall brute beside him shrugs. "That's obvious, man."

"Aren't housemates supposed to be all the same sex?" Mr. Band Tee questions, and I shake my head at them.

"I'm standing right here, you know." I toss my hair over my shoulder as if that will somehow make me more corporeal.

"Oh, so she speaks," Band Tee Guy retorts, a snort following swiftly after.

It's on the tip of my tongue to give him a piece of my mind, but Onyx Eyes waves his hand. "He doesn't have a filter, so you're going to have to sit back and let him process this out loud with us." He makes it sound like it's a common occurrence, but I'm not sure why the responsibility falls to me too.

Reluctantly, I nod, letting the front door shut behind me as they all continue to watch my every move like I'm from another dimension or something. "Can I take a seat while this happens? I'm exhausted and my legs are aching." I point to the chair they're all hovering by and the quiet guy nods, taking a step back.

The second my ass hits the seat, the four of them adjust their stance to face me.

"Who are you?"

"Raven."

"Raven who? I don't know a Raven," Mr. Band Tee states, and I smile.

"Now you do." He completely ignores my sass as he points to himself.

"I'm Zane, this is Creed, Eldon, and Brax," he

introduces, waving his finger at his friends too.

Creed is Mr. Quiet with the onyx eyes, Eldon with the wicked grin, and Brax the muscle man.

"I'm confused how you're here. You don't have a guy's name so it's not like there could be any confusion," Brax grunts, and I shrug.

I might be here, but that doesn't mean I have any answers. Shit, I've got more questions than them at this point.

"When did you get here?" Creed asks, remaining further back than the others as his gaze locks on mine.

"About two hours ago."

"Where are you from?" Zane interjects, happy to keep bombarding me with questions.

"Shadowmoor."

He pauses at that. All of them do. Their brows furrow together in sync, heads tilting slightly to the left as they stare me down.

"That's not possible," Eldon counters, his wicked grin still in place.

I look down at my lap, then to my hands, before lifting my chin again. "I mean, it must be because I'm sitting right here."

"The fuck?" Brax grunts, nostrils flaring. "There's no one from Shadowmoor here."

"I don't know what you want me to say to you, and

honestly, I'm cranky as shit. I've barely slept since I was pulled from my home, the drive here wasn't the best, the shit I've had to deal with since getting here is only making me more irritated, and I really did come from Shadowmoor. If you don't want to believe that, then it's cool, but can I step out instead of wasting everyone's time?" I ask, pointing toward my bedroom door and the deluxe bed I know is on the other side begging for me to take a nap.

Four sets of eyes stare at me, silence washing over the room as they each assess me before Eldon takes a step toward me. "Is that what the marking is on your face?"

My fingers run over the mark I know sits at my temple. "Yes."

"Is it there by choice?" Zane quizzes, nose scrunching with a hint of distaste.

"No."

He's in my personal space in the next moment, thumb knocking my hand away as a warmth radiates from his touch. Before I can question him, he's moving away, a pleased smile on his face, but the lingering heat from the brush of his skin against mine remains.

"All better."

Creed must understand the confusion I'm feeling because he explains. "It's gone."

"No fucking way," I gasp, running my hand over the spot again like I'll be able to feel a change. When I realize it's not as simple as that, I jump to my feet, taking two steps toward my room before a handheld mirror is held out in front of me.

Eldon offers me a knowing smile as I peer at my reflection. My hair is straggly, my eyes tired, but there's not a single sign of a marking on my face.

"Holy fuck." Zane chuckles as I look at him, even more pleased with himself as I stare at him in awe. "Thank you, honestly," I breathe, shaken by the relief flooding through my veins.

"No problem. I don't know why you haven't done it yourself."

I avoid his gaze as embarrassment heats my cheeks.

"I didn't know I could." Running my hands over my pants, the clammy feeling doesn't leave. "Was that your gifted power or just casual?" I ask, hoping to distract from myself and it works.

"Just casual." He smiles, taking the bait, but I don't miss the fact that he doesn't offer what his gifted power is. *Good.* That means we shouldn't have to expose the fact that I'm a fucking Void.

"So, since we're diving into the deep end here and it seems as though we're going to be sharing our space, what's your surname?" Eldon asks, and I bite back the sigh threatening my tongue.

They're going to piece it together eventually so I may

as well be honest.

"Hendrix."

"As in Sebastian Hendrix." Brax's disapproval is clear with the way my brother's name burns his tongue. I don't know whether I was expecting them to fawn over him or something, just like the students did in the courtyard, but to my surprise, they're all wearing scowls.

"Yeah," I rasp, and Brax huffs. "I can't read what your anger means. If you hate him too, then—"

"Wait, you're Raven Hendrix, as in Abel Hendrix's daughter that's been in hiding for the past fourteen years?" Creed catches me by surprise with his knowledge. I don't know whether to confirm or deny since only half of that statement is true. The looks I'm getting from the four of them tell me some form of explanation is going to be needed anyway.

Clenching my hands, I exhale sharply. "Yes, *that* Abel Hendrix, but I technically wasn't in hiding. I was living in Shadowmoor, remember?"

"No way," Eldon huffs, eyes narrowing at me. "My mother was friends with Evangeline. I would know if you were in Shadowmoor."

"Did he miss the marking on my face?" I direct my question back at Creed, my eyebrows raised as he shrugs in response.

"I'm standing right here," Eldon interjects, and I turn a

wide smile his way.

"It doesn't feel too great, does it?" My lips twist, preparing for him to lay into me, but he just rolls his eyes and waves me off.

"None of this makes any sense." Brax glares at me, even as I nod in agreement with his statement.

"You're telling me. I have shit to figure out and classes to attend tomorrow and I don't know anything, so if we're done here, I have a lot to wrap my head around."

I take a backward step toward my assigned room, and when no dispute arises, I take another, and another, until the door handle is in my grasp.

"We'll be eating in two hours. That's how long you have to get a grasp on your seemingly-new reality." Eldon gives me a pointed look and I nod in agreement.

"Anything else?"

The four of them look at each other, something silently communicating between them before Creed takes a step toward me but stops short as he tucks his hands into his pockets.

"If all of this is true, Sebastian is going to make life hard for you, Raven."

"I thought as much. He's never made anything easy. But I've spent the past fourteen years in the depths of Hell, I can protect myself."

The extra curriculum sheet blurs in my hand as I try and fail to read it again for the fiftieth time. I got into the vehicle and came here of my own volition because I had no prospects, no future, but now? I don't know whether I like this as an alternative. The schedule is filled with everything. There's just too much.

Hand-to-hand combat, ordnance training, team building, and survival instincts are just some of the mandatory classes, leaving me worried over what will come. One thing is clear though: they're training us for war. A war I'm not entirely aware of. The lady at the shop mentioned that I would pay with my life, like it was a known fact and expectation. I don't recall anything like that being mentioned in Shadowmoor, but then I guess we were all fighting among ourselves there instead. The soldiers of Shadowmoor protected just that: Shadowmoor. They never actually left the perimeter.

Some of the other classes are more magic specific, but I don't really pay any attention to them since I have nothing to work with.

Stretching out on my bed, I squeeze my eyes shut tight before prying them back open again. The words seem to form a little better this time, but it's still overwhelming to digest. I drop the sheet of paper with a sigh, deciding that now just isn't the time for it, before draping my arm over my face.

A nap. I need a nap.

The second my eyes drift closed, a knock sounds at the door and I groan. Glancing at the time, I'm not the least bit surprised that exactly two hours have passed since I managed to slip away from my housemates.

When I don't respond quickly enough, another rap of knuckles vibrates, louder this time. "I'm coming," I huff, too intrigued by the prospect of uncovering more of their dynamic to argue.

Pulling the hair tie from my wrist, I quickly braid my hair back off my face as I head toward the door. The second I open it, I come face to face with the giant that is Brax with his fist poised in front of my door ready to knock again.

His eyes darken with annoyance as he takes a step back. "How nice of you to join us." He stalks off to the dining table to join the other guys, unpacking boxes of food to fill the table.

"I don't have to." I remain in place as I defensively fold my arms over my chest.

"Actually, you do," Zane hollers with a wide smile. "Maybe I should give you the housemate handbook to read after you've gone through all your academic stuff."

"The *what* now?" I ask, closing my bedroom door behind me as I move to join them, avoiding Brax's harsh stare.

I come to a stop at the end of the table and it looks like a barbecue exploded all over the damn thing with the amount of meats and sides there are. I gulp, completely out of my comfort zone. This is more food than I can process. This would feed me and Mama for a month back home, and here it is just effortlessly available.

"Sit here." Creed draws my attention as he pulls the middle chair out on the right. A small smile curves my lips as I mutter my thanks. My body tingles with anticipation as he takes the seat to my left and Eldon drops down on my right.

Brax sits across from Creed and Zane directly opposite me. Eight eyes are all aimed in my direction and I feel like I can't breathe. They really don't make them like this back in Shadowmoor. There aren't any niceties there. No one pulling your chair out or eating dinner together. It's cut-throat by comparison and a little bit jarring. So much so that I'm struggling to let my guard down.

They each dig into the food, loading their plates up with a bit of everything. Once they're all occupied, I reach for the plate of ribs in front of me, taking two before adding some of the potato salad as well.

Happy, I bask in the silence, refusing to look up at

anyone as I eat, until Zane clears his throat. Peering through my lashes at him, I note the confusion knitting his brows. "Aren't you going to have more?"

I finish the food in my mouth before reaching for a napkin. "More what?"

"Food."

"I don't know what you mean…" I tense under their scrutiny again as Brax huffs.

"You're going to need to eat more than that to survive the training. You're going to need to bulk up your slim frame too."

My nostrils flare at his judgment of my body and I glare at him, ready to give him a piece of my fucking mind when Creed places his hand on my arm and halts me. "I think what Brax and Zane are trying to say is that, starting tomorrow, everything is going to be full on. They put our bodies through the wringer time and time again, and that's only in the first class," he explains, alleviating the tension in me slightly, but not completely.

"What does that have to do with my *slim frame*?" I bite, pointing another glare in Brax's direction, but he doesn't seem fazed by my irritation.

"They'll make an example out of you. They'll enjoy breaking you, Sebastian especially. This place isn't for the weak," Eldon states, annoying me more.

"I'm not weak."

"Sure, but you're not trained to this level either."

He's not wrong, but that doesn't soothe me at all. I hate being underestimated.

"Food wasn't as easy to come by back home, so I can't eat more than what my body can handle." I return my attention to the food on my plate and do my best to ignore them. Thankfully, none of them say another word about it and I get to finish eating in silence.

I could definitely reach for another rib or a chicken breast, but out of principle, I don't touch anything else once I'm done.

"So, what's this roommate book I need to know about?" I ask Zane, and he smiles, snapping his fingers to produce a file in his hands. Holy shit, he wasn't joking.

"It contains all the rules and expectations of what you bring to the house." I nod at his words like it makes sense as I take it from him, but it really doesn't.

"I spoke with Professor Burton too. He's aware you've been located here with us and he's happy for this to be our arrangement, even though it goes against the grain." I turn to Eldon and the confusion must be clear on my face because he continues. "Usually, girls share with girls and guys with guys."

"Maybe I should complain, kick up a fuss so I can be relocated and not be an inconvenience." I direct the end of my offer to Brax but he ignores me as Zane shakes his head.

"Nope. Everything happens for a reason. You were meant to be here, it's as simple as that."

"You're good… for now, at least," Eldon adds, and I shake my head in disbelief.

When do I get a say in my life again? It's gone from zero to one hundred in a matter of hours and I need a breather.

"Just don't bring any bullshit to our door. We have enough on our plates already," Brax orders, not looking up from his food.

I can't decide if they're being nice or not. I'm so used to hostility that I find it in the smallest of gestures, and Brax seems far more irritated about my arrival than the others. That's enough for me to get the hell out of here, but where else am I supposed to go?

Nothing is going to happen by the end of tonight though, that's for sure. So I need to suck it up for now at least.

"Are we done, or does this file dictate the rest of my evening?" I ask, my snark clear as Zane cocks a brow at me, but he simply shakes his head.

"No. You're good."

I take that as my cue and stand to leave, but the second my chair scrapes back, a hand wraps around my wrist.

"Don't fuck this up, Little Bird. Just keep your head down and your gaze averted. You might not last the week, but don't fucking bring us down with you." Eldon's eyes shimmer with a rage that catches me so completely off-guard that any kind of verbal response is lost in me. It's a complete contrast to the carefree grin he offered moments earlier.

Actions speak louder than words though and I really don't take too kindly to being grabbed like that. Punching him in the gut, I'm met with tense muscles, but I still manage a dig harsh enough to make him grunt.

His groan echoes around me as I get the fuck out of there, slamming my bedroom door shut behind me as quickly as I can, too nervous to chance a peek over my shoulder as I go.

That was probably more aggressive than necessary, but he just reminded me that no one can be trusted. He needs to know I'm not a weak push over, an easy target, or someone that will effortlessly fall in line at his order.

I'm panting as my back hits the wood, prepared for some kind of response, but nothing comes except a short, sharp laugh, and I could swear it's Brax, but that's impossible. Right?

Nevermind surviving Silvercrest, I need to survive living in this goddamn house.

SIX

Eldon

Beads of sweat trickle down my spine as my muscles strain beneath the unforgiving rays of the early-morning sun. My hair drapes over my eyes as I lower my body to the ground once more, grunting, and lift myself back through the push up before doing it again.

"Ninety-two," Zane calls out. "Ninety-three."

"You're being a pain in my ass," I gripe, repeating the motion again, but my snark doesn't stop him from continuing.

"Ninety-four..."

I don't need him to count and he knows it. But he was out here earlier than me this morning, which certainly isn't the norm, and now he's grinning from ear to ear because he's gone through his exercises already.

Fucker.

It's not my fault. I couldn't help it. I woke before my alarm was due to go off, disappointment racking my veins as I gasped from the dream I was torn from. A dream which involved a naked Raven and my cock. Just as I was about to paint her with my cum, I woke up and had to finish myself off because there was no way in hell my solid-as-fuck cock would go unnoticed otherwise.

The memory of the vision infiltrates my thoughts once more, my dick stirring beneath my shorts, but I force myself to trample it back down. I can't remember the last time I had a wet dream, especially not over someone I just met, but it was so vivid. Her creamy skin beneath my olive palm, her bright pink hair fisted in my grip, and that sassy mouth of hers raw and red from the abuse of my cock.

She literally knocked the wind out of me last night when she unexpectedly jabbed me in the gut, but it seems that's a turn on.

"One hundred," Zane hollers, slowly clapping as he pulls me from my thoughts, and I stop, falling back to my knees as I take a breath.

Reaching for my bottle of water, I glance out over the edge of the cliff, mesmerized by the ripples of water in the distance and the charming way the sun cascades over the peaks. The view is too stunning for a place like this. We're unworthy of it, really, and I can't help but soak it up every day, letting the calmness attempt to brighten my darkened soul and tainted past.

It doesn't last for long though, reality always rearing its ugly head.

"Fuck off, Zane. Your clapping is pissing me off too," Brax bites from across the grass where he's working through some deadlifts. Zane shuts up, much to my annoyance since he completely bypassed my irritation but listens to him.

Creed flops down beside me, perspiration clinging to him as he closes his eyes and tilts his face up to the sky. "Remind me why we do this to ourselves again?"

"Because we have to do better, be stronger, and outwit these fuckers if we want to survive the year, and the next, and the next," I state. As much as I get a rush from the adrenaline, a nice dopamine boost from all of this, I'd much rather be curled up in my sheets with my dick in my hand. Unfortunately, it really is a matter of life or death.

"We probably should have woken Raven up for this too," Creed murmurs, and my lips purse.

"From the swing she took at me last night, I'd say she's not as weak as you think."

"Are you sure, or just too chicken to admit that you're soft?" Brax says with a chuckle, and I stick my finger up at him. He knows that's not the case, but he doesn't want to admit she's not as weak as he first expected. "Besides, she ran her mouth about the food last night, she needs a reality check today. She needs to see we're not fucking around and this is serious shit."

"And how does that look to you? Just walking her into the lion's den and letting her die?" Zane asks, his brows furrowing slightly at the words on his tongue. Brax shrugs, too accustomed to this life to offer any kind of empathy.

"Of course not," Creed mutters, still not opening his eyes as he sighs. "Ignore Brax. She's one of us. We protect her just like we would protect each other."

"Says who?" Brax barks, clearly not appreciating how this is going.

"Says life, Brax. Says me, says the fucking handbook. We're a group, you can't just pass her off to die because *you* see her as weak. We need to put the time and effort into getting her to our level," Creed retorts, his usually quiet demeanor shifting as he defends our new roommate.

Our hot new roommate who now lives rent-free in my fucking dreams. For once, I may side with Creed over the matter instead of going for the bleak stone-cold reality that I usually lean toward, like Brax.

"What do you think, Eldon?" Zane asks, playing with a blade of grass between his fingers.

Creed lifts one eyelid to look at me and Brax drops his weights to hear my thoughts while I slowly stand. Turning to glance inside the house, I startle when I see a flash of pink moving around in the kitchen, completely oblivious to the fact she is the hot topic of conversation.

"I think… our housemate is awake," I murmur, sweeping my hair back off my face as I head for the glass door.

Sliding it open, my gaze is drawn to her as she waltzes around the room in an oversized tee that falls to her knees. The sound must catch her attention because she whirls around to face me with a spatula in hand, ready to attack.

Her eyes are wide and her body is stiff as she looks at me. I slowly raise my hands in surrender and she exhales harshly before her body relaxes.

"Don't sneak up on me like that."

"Hey, I just opened the door, Little Bird. I didn't realize that was going to be an issue." I take a step toward her, giving myself the opportunity to rake my eyes over her from head to toe while she busies herself at the stove.

"You clearly never lived in Shadowmoor. A creaky floorboard, a snapping branch, a squeaking door hinge… it's all the same; defense-inducing stress." She doesn't glance back at me as she speaks. I lower my hands, letting her words drift over me.

There's a lot we don't know about this girl, that's for sure. From what I've seen so far, she's the complete opposite of her brother. Which, somehow, doesn't seem possible. Especially when they have the same father who is as much of an asshole as Sebastian.

"What are you doing?" Brax appears at my side with his arms folded over his chest and gaze pinned on the delectable wonder that is our new housemate.

"What does it look like I'm doing?" Raven barks back, cocking her hip and glaring at him.

"Wasting time and energy doing menial shit like this." Brax waves his hand at all the pots and pans littering the counter as Creed and Zane silently step into the room.

Raven rolls her eyes at him, which somehow only makes her look hotter, even though her pink hair is a rumpled mess on her head. No one should look that good with no effort at all. With a sigh, she turns to face us all head on, but stops dead in her tracks as her eyes slowly scan over each of us. From Zane, to Creed, me, and back to Brax.

Her cheeks tinge a deeper shade of pink with each passing second, her gaze locked on us below eye level as her tongue peeks out between her plump lips.

Is she checking us out?

Please fucking check me out.

My dick gets hopeful and I try to adjust myself as discreetly as possible, but it seems to cause a stir in her because she quickly remembers herself.

"Do you guys not own a shirt between you or something?" she grumbles, turning back around to the stove, and a grin spreads across my face.

"Why? Can't keep your eyes off what I have to offer, huh?" I say with a grin, taking another step toward her.

"Please, I don't know what you're talking about. I'm just saying, it would be completely different if I was to do the same." She cocks a brow at me from over her shoulder, trying and failing to act like she's unfazed.

"I'm all for it, actually. Need some help?" I offer, cutting even more distance between us as her eyes widen in surprise, pupils dilating eagerly, but Brax interrupts, side stepping so he's between us.

"We're still wasting more time than is necessary," he mutters, slowly dragging his hand over the eggs and bacon sizzling in the pans.

Raven gapes at the transformation before her eyes, watching her efforts turn into plated meals with no effort at all. The bacon goes from barely cooked to crisped to perfection, and the eggs scrambled just right, piled high on the plates. I can't decide if she's mad at him for taking over or killing her cooking vibe, but realistically, he's right.

"Grab a plate, Raven. We've got thirty minutes before we need to be out the door," Zane explains, reaching around Brax to grab a plate before heading to the table. Creed and Brax quickly follow after while I hold back, watching her lips purse and shoulders fall with a heavy exhale.

With her head down, she joins everyone at the table, and I'm two steps behind her, dropping into the same seat as last night beside her. Despite the thick emotion that filled the room moments ago, we all eat in comfortable silence. It's not lost on me that Brax piled her plate of food just as high as ours, and she eats a good three-quarters of it before slumping back in her seat.

"How long have you guys been here?" Raven's question cuts through the air as I place my utensils down on my empty plate.

"Two months," Zane answers, beating me to it.

Raven nods, digesting the fact as she rubs her lips together. "Are all the classes back in the main building?"

Understanding dawns on me. She has no clue what she's getting herself into today. At least when we came, we had each other to figure this shit out with, but it seems she's far from eager to actually ask for help.

"What are your classes today? We can try to help you," Creed chimes in, and I frown at him, irritated that he beat me to it.

Raven offers him a tighter smile, which could have been mine as she rises from her seat. "I'm not sure, can I show you once I'm ready?" Creed nods, relaxing back in his seat with no hint of an expression on his face, as usual. "Thank you," she breathes, tucking her chair under the table.

"Genie isn't going to be happy about this," Zane states, pausing Raven from taking a step away from the table as irritation worms its way under my skin at the mention of her name. Brax chuckles humorlessly at the statement and a ghost of a grin crosses Creed's face too.

Fuckers.

"Who's that?" Raven asks, tucking a lock of hair behind her ear.

"Eldon's ex."

Her eyebrows pinch together and her hands grab the back of her chair. "Is her issue going to be with me specifically or…"

"She's going to hit the roof. She's not over our man here at all, and you being here is not going to help that," Zane continues, a grin on his lips.

"Why would she have an issue with me being here in my own bed?"

"Because we didn't let her in at all," Brax says, and her eyebrows rise in surprise.

"And how long were you together?"

"Too fucking long," I finally add, injecting myself into a conversation that involves me. "She loves the drama too."

"Don't all girls?" Creed states matter-of-factly, and Raven shakes her head.

"I hate it. Almost as much as I hate… well, everything." She absently reaches for her plate before going to take Zane's from her other side, but Brax pounds his fist into the table, making her pause.

"What the fuck am I missing?" he growls, eyes turning to slits as he looks at Raven.

"What?"

"What's with all this handsy shit? Why are you doing things for yourself instead of just using your magic? And why the hell are your knuckles so banged up?" He points at the busted skin on both of her hands. It's not possible they came from the blow she landed on me yesterday.

"I don't know what you're talking about." She drops the plates and turns her hands so the damage can no longer be seen. *What's that about?*

"Why are you so hands on with everything instead of just making it happen like everyone else?"

Raven sighs, heavier than earlier as she steps back from the table. "I obviously don't know what life is like here, or wherever you grew up, but Shadowmoor is less about the magic, and more about the… brutality. Now, if we're done, I need to get ready." She rolls her lips, answering Brax's question yet leaving me even more intrigued than before.

They stare each other down for what feels like an eternity before Creed stands, scraping his chair across the floor as he goes. "We really don't have time for this. Raven, get yourself ready. I'll be waiting out here to help you."

She mutters her thanks before leaving the table, and I've never had my gaze so fixed on the sway of someone's hips before. Even if they are hidden beneath a baggy t-shirt, she's still fucking delectable.

Brax clears his throat, pulling my attention away from the view. As my eyes lock on his, the sound of her bedroom door closing vibrates around me. Fuck. "Eyes on the prize, Eldon," he bites, tapping his temple as a reminder.

It takes me a second to realize he doesn't mean Raven is the prize like I had hoped. No. He means living to see another day. If the fates allow it.

SEVEN

Raven

I fix the tie around my collar, hating the restrictive feeling instantly, while eyeing my reflection in the floor-length mirror propped in the corner of my room. I slept hard last night, harder than I expected, considering I'm in an entirely new place, but I clearly needed it.

After seeing all four of my new housemates topless, I was hoping to give myself some relief in the shower, but there was no time. Which means I'm going to be carrying this sexual tension around with me all day. I'm going to have to get used to it, though, because I don't imagine sleeping with one of them would end well.

It's just my luck that I'm rooming with four hot guys, all in their own right, who have chiseled abs, defined *V*s trailing down beneath their waistbands, and tight asses. I'm so screwed. I'm going to need all of the strength I can muster to get through the day. The reality of how long I'm actually going to have to cope is an issue for another time.

Brushing my hands over my blazer, I'm good to go. I look foreign to my own eyes in the navy and gold uniform. The polished black shoes and white socks finish off the look, while my navy skirt falls mid-thigh. I hope we have alternative clothes to wear during active classes because the skirt is far from ideal for that.

I've secured my hair in a ponytail on top of my head and done my usual make-up routine: light foundation, concealer, a touch of bronzer, and a coat of mascara on my lashes. Finished with a touch of blush and a swipe of my nude lip gloss. I reach for the bag I found on my bed yesterday and head for the door.

I startle when I find Creed leaning against the wall beside it but he doesn't even flinch. "How long have you been standing there?" I ask, hoping he missed me ogling him. The uniform is a stark contrast to the loose jogger shorts and no tee from earlier, but he's still hot as hell.

He shrugs. "Do you have your schedule?" Nodding, I dig into my bag to find it and he takes it from my hands before replacing it with another piece of paper. "We have most of the same classes together anyway, but that's a copy of my schedule so you know where I am," he states, returning my schedule.

"Thanks," I breathe, starting to feel the nerves of the

day thrumming through my veins.

"Are we leaving or what?" The sound of Brax's voice makes me whip my head around to the front door, where I find him standing beside Eldon and Zane. They're all dressed in their uniforms and I have to fight the urge to fan my cheeks.

What the hell is wrong with me?

"We're good," I muster, tucking the sheets of paper away in my bag before falling into step with Creed and the others as we head outside.

Silence settles over us as we take the path toward the main building and I notice a few other small groups of students heading in the same direction. Despite my best efforts, I don't miss the subtle glances our way, but I can't decide if they're eyeing me as the new kid or checking out the men surrounding me. My money is on the latter, especially if the soft giggle from the group of four girls in front is anything to go by.

"I didn't realize I was rooming with campus royalty," I tease, a grin tugging at my lips as I nudge Zane beside me.

He rolls his eyes dramatically as Eldon chuckles, glancing over his shoulder to peer at me. "What can I say, Little Bird? You're in the presence of greatness."

I wrinkle my nose as Brax shoves his elbow into Eldon's gut with a grunt. "Not when you say cringy shit like that."

"Sorry about Eldon, Raven. His ego needs deflating sometimes." Creed smiles, knowing his words are an understatement for the man leading the way. Eldon scoffs.

"My ego is just fine, but if you want to talk about something big, I can redirect our—"

He doesn't get to finish that sentence as Brax elbows him again. "You're making me cringe. Shut the fuck up."

Eldon pouts, looking back at me for sympathy, but I shake my head at him instead. I can't get past the contrast between the funny man before me right now and the guy who warned me not to bring trouble to his door yesterday. They're opposite ends of the scale.

The large arched entryway into the academy looms ahead and I tilt my head back as we step through it, staring up in wonder at the intricate carvings that line the stone walls. How can somewhere be this pretty when Shadowmoor is so…gloomy?

"What's the first class?" I ask, feeling a little anxious as we walk through the cream and gold marble hallway. The pathway isn't as clear now as more and more students linger around, but they seem to shuffle to the side slightly for my housemates and I'm just lucky to be in the middle of them. For first years, it's surprising they seem to have such a presence.

"The History of Silvercrest and the Eliven Realm," Zane offers, placing his hand on the small of my back as he guides me to the left when we reach the end of the corridor. Heat blooms at his touch, rising up my spine and sending a shiver through my core. His head whips to mine, eyes wide, and he looks as startled as I feel. A moment passes between us, leaving me breathless, before he quickly pulls his hand away.

I choke in a sharp breath, aiming my gaze straight ahead as I will my body to calm down from his touch.

"Hey, baby." A girl's sweet and sickly voice travels through the air over the hum of everyone else and Eldon stiffens in front of me. It's only slight, and if I wasn't standing right behind him, I'm sure I wouldn't have noticed, but it seems to ripple through the other guys as we stop.

He doesn't respond, just a nod as he turns into the room on our left and the others follow him. Creed swings his arm out for me to follow after Zane and only then do I see the pissy look on the girl standing by the door. Her brunette hair falls in perfect waves around her face, highlighting the green of her eyes, while her red-painted lips turn up in a sneer the second she lays eyes on me.

My back stiffens and my fists clench, ready to defend myself like I would have done back in Shadowmoor, but Creed nudges me through the doorway before I can make a move.

"Hey," I shout-whisper, glaring at him over my

shoulder, but his face remains as impassive as ever. "Why did you do that?" I push, still slowly stepping forward even though I have no clue where I'm walking.

"Do what? Save you from an unnecessary shit show?" He cocks a brow at me, irritating me even more, but the sound of my name distracts me.

"Raven. Hey." Leila stops me in my tracks as she smiles wide, offering a slight wave in greeting.

"Hey, can I sit with you?" I blurt, overwhelmed by the presence of my housemates and needing some space.

"Uh, yeah. Are you sure, though? I told you yesterday—"

"And I didn't tell you that people usually hate me on sight so, if anything, we're a perfect fit," I retort, interrupting her, but my harsh words only make her relax and she smiles with a nod.

"Okay, well, I usually sit—"

"You'll sit here." My forehead wrinkles as I glance over my shoulder to see Brax pointing at the table in front of the one he's at with Eldon.

Pursing my lips, I shake my head. "I appreciate you guys helping me out, but now you're throwing out orders and demands like I have to listen and I don't."

The room goes quiet around me, my gaze locked on Brax's as his eyes narrow.

"You will sit here," he repeats slowly, like he didn't

hear a damn word I just said, and I sigh.

"It's okay, Raven. Let's just sit there," Leila murmurs, linking her arm through mine and pulling me the remainder of the way to the table Brax is insistent on.

I want to argue and assert my independence and put the asshole in his place, but when I glance around the room, I realize everywhere else, bar one other table, is already taken. The table where little Miss Pissy from outside is standing with her friend beside her and they're both glaring in my direction.

Sinking my teeth into my bottom lip, I'm about done with all the judgment and orders being thrown my way, but the professor steps through the door and gains everyone's attention. Pissy One and Pissy Two take their seats, leaving me with no choice but to take my own. Leila quietly takes the spot to my right as I drop my bag to the floor.

"Who's that girl over there?" I whisper, leaning into Leila as she follows my line of sight.

"That's Genie. She's… awful." Leila quickly drops her gaze, busying herself as I glare at the back of her head for a second longer until Creed clears his throat. He's seated with Zane at the table to the right of Brax and Eldon, and when I look back at him, he's giving me a pointed stare.

I want to shove my finger up at him, remind him that they talked about this crazy bitch this morning, yet he wants me to do nothing to defend myself. I don't care if she hasn't actually made a move yet. The trick is to swing first before they get a chance. I prefer the upper hand, even if I am out of my depth.

"Good morning. If everyone wants to set up, we will be doing a heavy overview of the Eliven Realm and the different towns, cities, and surrounding areas today," the professor explains. "We'll be doing a comprehensive test in a few weeks and you'll want the information for review."

Thick brown leather-bound books appear on the desks in front of everyone, me included, and I jump in surprise. A feather-tipped quill appears beside it and I watch in a mixture of shock and awe as Leila runs her hand over the front of the book and it flips open to a blank page. The quill floats in the air, hovering above the parchment, just like in the receptionist's office yesterday.

Glancing around the room, I watch everybody else do the same thing and my heart sinks. How the fuck am I supposed to explain why I'm not doing the exact same thing too? Nothing yells "I'm a Void" more than not using magic to do a menial task like this.

My heart rate picks up, but I still reach for the book, which has *Raven Hendrix* etched in gold along the front, and open it up to a blank page. Avoiding the quill, I dig out the pen I placed in my blazer pocket before leaving my room and steady my hand over the paper, ready to write.

"As I'm sure you're all aware, Eliven Realm is

comprised of six main areas. Silvercrest is the most central point. North of here, you have Haven Court, Amberglen, and Pinebrook. Leaving Ashdale and Shadowmoor as our more southern regions."

"You mean the poor regions," Genie says with a laugh, and anger vibrates through my bones. A few other students chuckle along with her but, to my surprise, the professor doesn't join in.

"Actually, Genie, each part of Eliven plays an important role. If every part of our realm were the exact same, it wouldn't exist."

What does that even mean?

"Why?" Genie's friend asks with her face scrunched in disgust.

"That's what this class is for, Harper. If you two could keep your mouths shut for a minute, you might learn something." I bite back my own smile as the room rumbles with laughter again while noting everything he has said so far.

"What are you doing?" Leila asks, frowning at me and where my hand rests on the book.

"Oh, I retain information better this way, that's all," I rush, and although she stares at me funny for a few more seconds, she shrugs and turns back to the professor. I sigh with relief.

"Shadowmoor and Ashdale are the closest gateways

to the Basilica Realm. They remain dark, torn, and on the verge of breaking to protect Haven Court. Just as Amberglen and Pinebrook shield the capital."

My hand pauses, my mouth falling slack as I glance up at the professor. He says the words so casually, like there isn't death and despair ripping Shadowmoor apart, and it pisses me off.

"Why are they left in that state? What about the people who live there?" I ask, unable to stop myself. I may not have enjoyed my time in Shadowmoor, but nobody does. There's no way out, and it seems that's just how they like it.

Everybody glances at me, eyebrows raised at my question as the professor clears his throat. "Miss Raven Hendrix, correct?" I nod, finally taking him in for the first time as he stands with his hands gripping the lapels of his tweed blazer. Flecks of gray tint his otherwise dark hair and the stubble on his cheeks is at least a day old. "Well, Raven, the Basilica Realm continues to believe the rest of our realm looks like that too. It's how we've managed to keep them at bay for so long." The pride in his tone is apparent.

"But what about the people who live there? Why don't they see any benefits from that? They don't receive any reward for living how they do. That hardly seems fair, especially if they've played such a big part in defending our realm like that." I'm pushing, I know I am, and he's obviously not the right person to be asking, but the anger is gnawing away at me.

He fixes his glasses on the bridge of his nose. "I don't have the answers to that, unfortunately. All I have is the knowledge to empower you in your journey. What you do with it beyond this institution is none of my business." My eyebrows pinch together. That's not an answer to my question at all, but before I can breathe another word, he turns away from me and continues with the lesson. "Each part of our realm has outposts for us to defend our beloved home. They have played a successful role in fending off attacks and keeping any power-driven leaders from other realms from trying to take our lands. Another factor in our success is the well-trained students of Silvercrest Academy. Our investment in your training ensures the security of our borders."

What a load of bullshit. Instead of trying to blow air up our asses to inflate our egos, maybe he should explain in more detail why any of this is necessary. But what the fuck do I know?

I barely register anything else he says, too hung up on the fact that I was living that life for fourteen years, never truly understanding why things were such a struggle. The feeling of helplessness that claws at you is undeniable in Shadowmoor, and everyone else seems to be aware of it.

More than that, they're intentionally crafting it to stay that way in order to defend themselves and their beloved capital.

It's bullshit.

Straight. Up. Bullshit.

Not a single person here knows the Hell that place has become. I'm not saying they don't have their own demons, but they have a roof over their heads, endless food on the table, and above all else, they have a sense of hope that doesn't exist there.

A bell rings out, startling me from my inner turmoil, and I watch as everyone starts to stand. The books and quills are gone so I quickly drop my pen back into my pocket and rise to my feet.

"Are you okay? You seemed to space out there," Leila says, concern etched into the pull of her eyebrows as she looks at me.

"I'm fine, just lost in thought. I'm trying to catch up with all of this, that's all."

It's not a lie, but it's also not the entire truth. No one needs to deal with my wrath, especially not her, since she's been nothing but friendly to me since I got here.

"No worries. Do you have ordnance training next, too?" she asks, happy to leave it at that, and I smile. I love it when people don't push for information they don't require. It only makes me like her more.

"She does," Creed interjects, and I glare at him. I'm still annoyed about earlier. I don't need him inserting himself into my conversations too.

"Let's go then," Leila chirps, a grin on her lips like this is amusing to her or something. I freeze a little when she links my arm again, but we fall into step and head for the door.

Thankfully, Genie is nowhere to be seen as we leave, but a guy plants himself in my way before I reach the door. He has curly blond hair, crystal blue eyes, and a toothy smile that spreads wider when my eyes lock on his.

"Hey, Raven, right? I'm Finn," he offers, tucking his hands into his pants pockets as he rocks back on his heels.

"Hi."

"Are you settling in okay? I can be your unofficial tour guide if you like. Maybe I could show you around after classes. We could grab some food, go to—"

"Fuck off, Finn."

My eyes squeeze closed at the sound of Zane's voice cutting him off. When I blink them back open again, I find Finn and Zane in a glare-off. I turn further, hoping to get Eldon, Brax, or Creed to put a stop to it, but I only find them holding the same feral snarl on their lips too.

What even is my life right now?

Side-stepping Finn, none of them pay attention to me, so I use that as my opportunity to hightail it out of there with Leila chuckling as she holds on tight to my arm.

"I knew it would be exciting with your arrival after meeting you yesterday, Raven, but holy hell, the double dose of drama surrounding you is crazy."

EIGHT

Raven

It's almost reassuring that the locker rooms at Silvercrest Academy are no different in layout from those at Shadowmoor High. Coat hooks line the walls with oak benches beneath them, only breaking off for the exit and the opening that leads to the showers.

The main difference is watching each student press their thumb against the tip of the coat hook to reveal a set of shorts, a t-shirt, and a pair of sneakers moments later. Glancing at Leila, she nods for me to do the same, and I nervously wet my lips. The cool metal presses against my thumb and nervous energy has my pulse ringing in my ears but, to my relief, I'm treated to the same garments appearing in front of me.

Switching out my clothes, I'm not shocked that the shorts and t-shirt fit me perfectly, and the sneakers too.

"Please tell me why you have the Bishops glaring at anyone who looks in your direction?"

"Who?"

Leila shakes her head with amusement flickering across her lips. "The Bishops. Eldon, Creed, Zane, and Brax."

"The Bishops? Why are they called that?"

"Do you always answer a question with one of your own?" she pushes, cocking her eyebrow at me.

"No…well, maybe, but that's beside the point," I admit, both impressed and irked by the fact that she can call me out so quickly.

"Noted, but I asked you first. Why are they glaring over your shoulder at everyone that glances in your direction?"

I peer around the room, making sure everyone else is involved in their own business. Not that it makes a difference, I'm not about to tell her a deep, dark secret, but it's instinctive for me to cover my back. My gaze locks with Genie's for a brief second, who is glancing at me over her friend's shoulder with a deathly stare. She's not a threat from this distance, but that could easily change.

"Honestly, I have no idea. They're my housemates and—"

"They're your *what*?" she blurts, cutting me off as her eyes bug out, and I snicker at the comical expression.

"My housemates," I repeat, soft and calm, but it still doesn't change the sheer shock on her face.

"They don't mix—"

"Boys with girls. I know, but one of them spoke to Burton and he didn't change his mind." I shrug, not sure what else to say. "That doesn't explain the way they're acting, though. I'm getting whiplash from some of them, and honestly, I don't need the drama on top of everything else." It's a good thing they're hot as hell or I wouldn't be putting up with any of it. For now, though, they're on thin ice.

"Damn, no wonder Genie instantly has daggers aimed your way." I glance in her direction, expecting the physical kind, but it's the deathly glare that still remains on her face that Leila is referring to.

"People love to hate me. It's not a new thing." I fix my hair tie as Leila starts to follow the crowd out of the changing room, leaving our clothes hanging from the hooks. I keep in step with her and my body tenses as we pass Genie and her friends.

"How gross. Pink hair is *so* trashy." It's the same sickly-sweet voice from earlier. Genie. I want to teach her a lesson now before this continues, but Leila grabs my arm and yanks me out into the hallway.

"Pick your battles, Raven."

"I do. I choose all of them." I glance back to sneer at the bitch smirking at me with her friends.

I pull my arm free from Leila's hold, ready to make

good on my promise, when a hand grips my throat and I fly through the air. My back hits a wall and I grunt as the hand flexes around my neck, cutting off my air supply.

Through the rage that instantly consumes me, I blink to see Sebastian in my face. A red mist coats my vision, draping in the reddish Hell inferno he reminds me of. I have no idea if people are watching us now, but none of that matters. I have to keep my gaze fixed on him.

Even with me clutching his wrist, he doesn't relent, only inching me higher up the wall until I'm no longer touching the floor. Every breath is an effort, becoming more and more labored as each second passes. Digging my nails into his skin, he barely hisses as he snarls in my face.

"Why the fuck are you here?" he bites, his lip somehow curling even more as I choke in his hold. My head feels like it's going to burst and, as much as I swing my legs at him, it's no use.

I can't breathe, let alone answer his damn question.

How the hell do we have the same DNA running through our veins? It shouldn't be possible.

"Answer me," he growls, his tone dropping an octave or two.

Is this guy dense?

"How the fuck is she supposed to do that, Sebastian, when you're cutting off her air supply?" Leila hisses, her voice cutting through the fog. I still can't pinpoint where she is.

Her words somehow have the opposite effect of what I can only assume she was going for as he squeezes my throat even tighter. My vision starts to blur and my breaths are nothing more than short, shallow gasps until he suddenly releases his hold on me and I slump to the floor.

My throat burns with every rasp as I cough and splutter, gulping lungful after lungful of oxygen into my body. I lift my hand to my chest, willing the tightness to ebb as my head pulses with pressure. It feels like I'm inching my way closer to death before I finally get a handle on myself, and when I lift my head, I find my brother still looming over me with a pleased grin on his face.

My nostrils flare with anger as I force myself to my feet, refusing to lean back on the wall for support so I don't look any weaker than I already do. Swiping a hand down my face, I find dampness coating my fingertips. Tears must have spilled from my eyes with the intense pressure and struggle. That will definitely make Sebastian grin.

"I'm going to guess that Abel didn't listen to his favored child either and I'm here to stay, despite the fact that I'd rather not be." I look up at him, *really* look up at him. The irritation in his brown eyes, the quirk to his brows, and the way he naturally bears his teeth makes him look like a petulant child who didn't get his way.

"You won't be here for long, little *sister*. Sending you

home isn't the only way to get rid of you. Facing the trials will be your demise. I'll make sure of it," he rages, hands clenching at his sides, and I'm almost certain he's going to stamp his foot, but he manages to hold it together. "And you," he adds, whirling around to the left. "Keep the fuck out of shit that has nothing to do with you."

I follow his line of sight to find Leila with her arms folded over her chest. "Try me, asshole."

He creeps one foot toward her and I'm ready to pounce on him, but he surprises me by spinning in the opposite direction and getting the fuck out of here. I don't move a single muscle until he's completely out of sight. Only then do I slump back against the wall with a heavy sigh.

Fuck my life.

"Are you okay?"

"I'm good, thanks," I muster as Leila steps closer and squeezes my shoulder.

"Raven...please tell me, for your sake, that Sebastian isn't your brother."

I scoff, head dipping until my chin hits my chest. "I wish I could tell you that."

The sound of pounding footsteps echoes around us, getting louder until the floor practically vibrates beneath my feet. Expecting a herd of assholes ready to finish what Sebastian started, I stand tall again, bracing myself for a fight. Instead, Eldon, Creed, Brax, and Zane appear moments later.

"What the fuck did we miss?" Eldon barks, sweeping his hair back off his face as he casts his eyes over me from head to toe.

"Nothing," I grumble, relaxing at the fact that I'm not under attack.

"It definitely wasn't nothing," Leila argues, and I glare at her, but she's not looking in my direction anyway. "It was Sebastian."

Traitor.

They're already confusingly overbearing as it is. Why is she making it worse?

"The fuck?" The cords in Brax's neck tense as he scans his eyes over me, but I wave them off.

"I'm good. I need to get to class."

"We'll walk you," Creed offers, but even as I shake my head, Leila steps to my right side and the four guys seem to circle behind us in a protective stance.

"I'd rather you didn't."

"Why?" Zane asks, a hint of hurt to his tone, but that can't be possible. I don't even know these people.

"Because I have enough drama with my brother. You guys didn't mention you're known as the freaking 'Bishops' on campus, and even if I don't know what that means, it's causing more issues and giving me unnecessary attention. I'm strong enough without you. You have no idea what

I've already survived getting here."

Silence is all that greets me as I continue toward the open field where the rest of the students are all spread out and seem to be warming up. I'm almost sure they will take my statement and respect my boundaries, but I'm foolish like that.

A hand wraps around my waist, pulling me back against a hard chest as lips brush against my ear. "Get used to it, Little Bird."

Focusing is more challenging than I care to admit. The run-in—or hijack as I prefer to call it—with Sebastian has me on edge. It definitely, one thousand percent, has nothing *at all* to do with the way Eldon held me earlier.

At least in this lesson, the professor introduced herself to me. Professor Eleanora Figgins. A soldier, a warrior, and, as far as I can assess, a badass bitch. Her brown hair is braided back off her face, revealing the three claw scars that dominate her right cheek. She wears them with pride and a sense of honor that bewilders me. The realm is so much bigger outside of Shadowmoor. I don't understand the greater good we're training for, the sacrifices being made, the belief in the cause, and the integrity that some have.

I've only missed three ordnance classes since the term began, so everyone is still in preliminary training mode, which involves endurance, strength, and agility. Apparently they want our bodies to be weapons too before we can actually get our hands on the real deal. Luckily for me, you need all those things to survive Shadowmoor for more than a day.

"Excellent, now I want each of you to run the circuit three times, starting at a slow jog and building up so that the third time is as fast as possible. It's not about being the quickest. It's about training your body to maintain a steady speed, but harbor the energy to push hard and fast when necessary," Professor Figgins orders. A few groans ring out around the field from the other students. She has already had us lap the circuit twice, getting a feel for what everyone can do, and now she wants us to go again.

"Save me now, Raven. I'm going to pass out," Leila mutters, sweat beading at her temples at the mere thought, and I grin at her.

"You've got this. You just have to dig deep." My attempt at reassuring her fails drastically when she side-eyes me with a huff.

"When I call out your names, I want you to join the starting line. I'm matching you with those I think you can hold and maintain with. Let's see if we can make that possible."

"Yup, definitely separated then because you're crazy fast and I'm the little slow tortoise you hear about in old folklore," Leila whines before moving to the line at the sound of her name being called.

She glances back over her shoulder with a pout and I stick my tongue out at her, which only adds a glare to her disapproving features. Genie, two of her friends, and a handful of other girls step forward before Figgins shoots a flare gun into the sky. As we watch, they all set off at a slow pace, allowing me a moment of reprieve as I take a deep breath or two.

A shadow casts over me after a few seconds and I really should have expected it, counted down to it happening, if I'm honest. Glancing to my left, I find Creed, but he's not looking at me. He's watching the other students run the circuit. After staring at him for a solid thirty seconds, I realize he's simply standing beside me and not forcing a conversation. That I can handle.

The silence becomes more comfortable as Leila enters her second lap, the two of us standing side by side. His arm grazes mine occasionally and I try to act as unfazed as possible, but it's more complicated than it looks. Every nerve ending is on edge, especially after my encounter with Eldon earlier. I can't think when they're around, and it's a feeling I've never experienced before, which leaves me completely off-kilter.

All too quickly, the group reaches the end of their third lap and another group joins the starting line. I'm acutely aware that the Bishops, two other guys, and myself are the only ones not yet called. Leila doesn't mention anything as she comes panting to a stop on my other side, basking in the comfortable silence until the second group finishes too and I'm called forward.

"The seven of you come and line up. Now, for you guys, I expect you to keep a faster pace for the first and second runs, but I want you to push as hard and as fast as possible on the final circuit. Don't worry about staying together then. I want to see who gets to the finish line first. Understood?"

I nod in response as Creed keeps to my left and Zane slips to the starting line on my right. Another flare flashes red in the sky and we take off. It's a slow-paced run that everyone settles into and it's a good groove. I'm startlingly aware that I'm the only girl, which means I'll likely be under more scrutiny than the others, but I've never had a problem rising to a challenge.

As we round the end of the second circuit, I inhale deeply through my nose, ready to transition into an all-out sprint as I step over the white line. The grass rumbles underfoot as everyone takes off and I straighten my spine, angling my body to cut through the air with precision as I move my legs as fast as they will go.

Excitement pools in my stomach when the two guys I don't know drop back behind me and it only blossoms further when Creed and Zane hover behind me.

"The fuck?" The surprise in Brax's voice has me grinning like a fool.

Keeping my gaze fixed ahead, I round the final bend with Brax and Eldon two steps ahead of me. My lungs burn as I push harder, coming into line with them again, then a step forward, then two. Holy shit, am I going to…

"No fucking way," Eldon grunts, leaning forward and rolling over the finish line first.

Motherfucker.

I slowly stop, hands braced on my knees as I try to catch my breath. Brax stares at me for a moment, a flicker of wonder in his eyes before he dismisses me. He's quickly replaced with Eldon, who throws his hands up in the air like a champion. Asshole.

"Are you pleased with yourself?" I ask, instinctively reaching up to pull a blade of grass from his hair. I'm suddenly aware of how close we are, just like we were earlier, and my mouth goes dry.

"Hell yeah, I am."

"Creative, Eldon. Crazy, but creative," Figgins states as she moves toward us and I take a step back, finally managing to breathe again. "But I must say, Raven, you have me impressed so far." I turn to face her as she assesses me, eyes slowly trailing from the tips of my sneakers to my face. "I have a feeling you're going to shine like a star here, Raven."

I laugh, shaking my head at her. That's not the compliment she wants it to be. Not to me, at least. "The issue is, Professor Figgins, stars don't shine. They burn."

NINE

Raven

I flop down onto a seat across from Leila at the dining table with a sigh. The room around me is like a still image from years gone by. Everything is fancy, especially for a dining hall. It's nothing at all like what I had back in Shadowmoor. The tall, ornate ceilings, high-back wooden chairs, and the marble floor leave me nervous to touch anything. There are at least thirty tables set up, long oak slabs framed with eight chairs, and a large chandelier hanging above each one.

My stomach instantly grumbles with hunger, reminding me of what the guys had said last night. I definitely need to start eating more. As much as I enjoyed the exercise in ordnance training, it quickly took its toll on my body.

Glancing around the room, I try to figure out where I'm supposed to get my food from, but there's no one lined up. Despite my independent stance, I turn to Leila for guidance, only to find her swiping her finger through a hologram hovering before her.

"Leila?"

She peers through the transparent display before her, confusion marring her face for a moment until understanding dawns on her.

"Where did you go to school?"

"Shadowmoor."

Her eyes widen, but there's surprisingly no judgment there. Which is strange because my body instinctively assumes it's coming and stiffens, bracing for impact. Shaking my arms out, I try to alleviate the tension as she puts her hand through the projection to wave above a small circle carved into the table before me.

"And I'm assuming this wasn't how you ordered food?"

"Nope," I murmur, distracted by the display in front of me.

Thankfully, she doesn't push further as I tentatively reach a hand out to swipe away from the first option displayed. It moves seamlessly, offering a chowder as my second option, but I know I need a higher level of protein and I keep searching.

It takes a few extra swipes of my fingertips to reveal a chicken, vegetable, and rice option and I know I've found my winner. If only I knew how to select it...

"Hover your hand back over the mark. Like this," Leila states, and I realize she's been waiting for me to find my option before proceeding herself. Nodding, I do as she says, copying her movement, and the screen disappears as a plate of food appears in front of me.

I'm sure my eyebrows are touching my hairline at this stage, but if Leila notices, she doesn't mention it. While I've opted for the most practical option, Leila decided on the tastiest: pizza. She digs straight in, but I take a moment to observe the room again before I let my guard down.

Every table around us is now filled. My housemates, or the Bishops as Leila called them, are four tables over, surrounded by Genie and her friends. My lips purse, my eyebrows drawing together, and I'm unsure why. I lock eyes with Eldon, my body freezing, before I quickly glance away and focus on my food without another look.

We eat in comfortable silence, sipping from the glasses of water that also appeared with the food until my plate is empty and my stomach is full.

Leaning back in my seat, the swirl of chaos and mumbling from around us continues to hover in the background as my skin tingles with the feeling of eyes watching me. I ignore it, clearing my throat and meeting Leila's stare instead.

"I need you to catch me up to speed."

A soft smile curves her lips as she leans forward slightly, bracing her forearms on the table. "Where do you want me to start?"

Lacing my fingers together, I consider her question for a moment and opt for the most obvious one. "Back home, magic wasn't as prominent as it is here. Like, nowhere close. Even though power is in the air, I haven't seen a single student use their abilities yet. Is that normal?"

"As first years, we're only allowed to use our mundane abilities in our houses and our gifted powers in the specified classes, strength training, or any of the trials."

My eyebrows rise once more. If the wind changes, I'm going to look like this forever since they're permanently up there with the constant state of surprise and awe I'm in. "Does that change through the years, then?" At least the first year will allow me to fly under the radar somewhat with my nonexistent magic.

"Yeah. Second years can use mundane magic anywhere but must only use their gifted powers in a training capacity. Third years can begin using their strongest powers outside the academy grounds, and fourth years are on assignments before they reach the end of their final year and join the realm as adults."

I consider her words for a moment, completely baffled by the stark difference I grew up with. Here, they're trained to wield their power, grow stronger, and protect the realm in a capacity I didn't even realize was needed. While back in Shadowmoor, everyone is trying to survive each day as it comes, not offered the luxury of a future, no prospects at all. No matter what path I looked at, it always ended in survival. Unlike here.

Storing those details away for later, I glance out of the corner of my eye toward my housemates again. Eldon and Creed are sandwiched between Genie and one of her friends while Brax and Zane sit across from them, another two girls hanging off their every word. Not like either of them are speaking. No. The latter two are both glancing over in our direction.

Fuck.

Sucking my bottom lip into my mouth, I pry my eyes away from them again, already annoyed with the next question.

"What about them?"

"Who?" The mischievous glint in her eyes makes it clear she knows who I mean. She just wants to hear me admit it.

"Them," I grumble, nodding in their direction, but she cocks a brow at me. "Fine, the Bishops."

"I don't even know where to begin with them." It's my turn to give her a questioning look but it goes unnoticed as she runs her eyes in their direction.

"I've known them since I started school at the age of

six. Their presence has never changed. Girls flock after them, boys want to be them, and all the while, they're generally charming assholes." Charming assholes? I didn't realize that was possible. "Eldon is the leader, bossy to his core, while collecting ladies' panties as souvenirs. Brax is the grumpiest." I nod, understanding that assessment to a T. "He's probably who I know the least about. He's so standoffish. I don't think I've seen him speak to anyone other than Eldon, Creed, and Zane."

I can't stop myself from following her line of sight, taking them in through her lens instead of the limited interactions I've had with them so far.

"Creed and Zane?"

"The latter is the most amusing, especially when he goes on a tangent and can't find his filter. He's also a little nerdy, which some girls love. Creed, however, is quiet and observant, never showing any emotion and keeping the rest of the world at arm's length from all of them."

I nod, unable to deny that I've picked up on the same vibes as her assessment, but I need her to give me something else, something...more. "Give me some shit on the down low, Leila. I have no idea what I'm dealing with and I need all the help I can get."

"Brax was orphaned as a baby, taken in by Eldon's family, who are supposed to be the sweetest people in existence. Creed's father was a sergeant for Silvercrest's training army until they ran into an ambush where he died, along with twenty-six students and two other professors." Holy shit. "Zane's sister is a council member, and his father is a high ranking member of The Monarchy." That's an information drop, but still not what I'm looking for. It'll help me understand them, though, and hopefully survive living with them.

"Anything I can kind of protect myself from them with?" I push, and she purses her lips in thought before she slowly shakes her head.

"It's hard. They're the Bishops of campus, like Gods on land, but they keep everyone at a distance. They don't show any emotion past a snarl or a flirtatious grin, which is why it's strange as hell that they have such a protective stance around you, no offense, housemate or not. I won't be the only person intrigued by the fact, that's for sure."

"They're not anything with me."

She huffs a laugh. "Are you serious?"

"Of course I am. They're my housemates, sure, but apart from a little overstepping this morning, they're fine. I'm going to put them in their place tonight and everything will be *fine*," I insist, unsure if I actually believe it myself or not. That's a complete understatement. They're a fucking handful, but I don't need to admit that right now.

"Okay, let's see if that's true." Before I can even ask what she means, Leila yells at the top of her lungs. "Finn!"

It feels like the entire dining hall goes quiet, turning to look in our direction as Leila waves her hand for the guy in question to come closer. He's sitting three tables behind her, so I get the unhindered view of watching his grin spread with hope while his friends pat him on the back. Rallied to his feet, he tries to muster some swagger in his stride but he doesn't ooze the confidence he hopes.

"Ladies, what's up?" He smiles a toothy grin, just as he did earlier, his blond curls bouncing around his face. Finn braces his palms flat against the table, leaning closer to me than I would prefer, but instead of calling him out on it, I turn a deathly glare Leila's way.

"Finn, I was just telling Raven here that there's a party on Friday night." If she senses my frustration, she either loves it or doesn't care as she flutters her eyelashes at him.

"Yeah, out behind Silvercrest Memorial." His breath brushes against my cheek and I lean back, offering a tight smile as he grins at me.

"Right," Leila encourages. "So, what do you say if—" Heavy chairs scraping across the marble floor interrupt whatever she was about to say, but as she looks at the additional guests joining our table, she doesn't seem mad about it. No. That's a glimmer of victory in her eyes.

Dammit.

Finn slowly stands, nervously clearing his throat as he takes in the new arrivals. Reluctantly, with my heart pounding wildly in my chest, I turn to find four men who were being fawned over by other women only moments ago.

Creed is right beside me, Brax next to him, while Eldon and Zane sit beside Leila. None of them are looking at me or my friend. They're all glaring at the guy who is slowly starting to edge away from the table.

Kill me. Kill me *right* now.

As the chatter of the dining hall slowly reaches my ears again, I squint from one to the other until I settle on Creed. "What the hell? What are you doing?" I bite, hands clenching into fists as I try to act as unfazed as possible and fail miserably.

Creed shrugs, leaving the response to come from Eldon. "Making sure everyone knows you're off limits."

I splutter on my breath as I gape at them, feeling Leila's giddy smile without looking her way.

Swiping a hand down my face, I take a deep breath and repeat his words. "Why are you under the illusion that I'm off limits?"

Zane chuckles, shaking his head as I hear Genie hollering Eldon's name across the hall. He doesn't acknowledge her as he stares me dead in the eyes.

"You didn't read the housemate's handbook, did you?" Zane says with a snicker, making my eyebrows pinch together. Before I can ask what the hell *that* is supposed to mean, Brax slams his fists on the table, making the cutlery clatter as he garners everyone's attention.

Slowly turning to look at him, his nostrils flare as he works his jaw.

"Because we're the Bishops and we fucking say so."

TEN

Eldon

B rax's response went down about as well as someone slapping your mom across the face. I agreed with what he said without question, we *are* the Bishops and whatever we say goes, including anything in regards to our new housemate, but even I can't deny that his execution could have been a little…gentler.

If looks could kill, I would have sworn that was her magical ability. The way her eye twitched, the vein at her temple throbbing with anger as she glared at each of us, had me ready for a scolding from the little bird. Yet I watched in complete bewilderment as she slowly rose to her feet, hitched her bag over her shoulder, and stormed from the dining hall with Leila hot on her heels.

Despite her silence, her rage was evident as we followed her through the halls, sat behind her in the last class of the day, and stayed close by as we stepped from the main academy building to head home. She's maintaining a cautious step ahead of us, shoulders tense and bunched together as she dips her head closer to Leila, who murmurs something into her ear.

I've never wished for enhanced hearing before, but I would do just about anything to listen in on what they're talking about.

"Do you think Leila is a safe friend choice for her?" Creed asks, staring straight ahead as I consider his words.

"Who would you rather she lean on, Leila or someone like Genie?" Zane asks, making me shiver.

"Definitely not the latter." I watch Leila toss her head back with a laugh and my veins itch to know what's happening, but I'm left with these three assholes instead. "Besides, Leila's always been quiet and drama-free. That will work in our favor."

"Her father too," Creed adds, earning a growl from Brax. That's definitely up for debate, but we're not getting into that now.

"The only thing that matters right now is Raven listening to us." Brax's voice is as gruff as it was back at the dining hall, which means he's holding his ground.

"I feel like we should explain things to her a little more. She's not wrong about the fact that we're crowding her every move," Zane states, making my brows bunch in annoyance.

"Don't forget the overstepping, making an ass of yourselves, and attempting to dictate who I can and cannot speak to," Raven hollers, not even bothering to glance back over her shoulder at us. Is enhanced hearing related to her magic? Maybe I just need to ask her. The way Leila grins back at us, though, and Zane's neutral expression, tells me he was talking louder than necessary. So half of the campus probably heard him.

"I'm beginning to regret your idea." Brax swipes a hand down his face as we slow down enough to return to a private conversation.

"There's nothing to regret, man. You know it. Everything adds up. E.V.E.R.Y.T.H.I.N.G." I spell it out, trusting my gut as every letter slips from my lips. I only get a grunt in response, and when I glance to the side, I find Creed staring at me. He offers a simple nod, confirming he's in agreement with me.

Is this crazy as fuck? Yup. Is this entirely out of the norm for who we are and what we usually stand for? Yup. Are we still going to act like this going forward? Yup, I'm certain of it. I'm sure Brax and Raven will get over it... eventually.

A growl from in front of us snaps our attention away from our conversation and I turn to find the other Hendrix on campus. The one begging for me to kill him with my bare hands. I stomp two steps forward as I watch Sebastian loom over Raven, but before I can lunge at him, Zane has his arm banded around my shoulders, forcing me to stop.

My body tenses and my eyes squeeze shut as I calm the boiling rage welling up inside of me. As I blink my eyes back open, Zane relaxes his hold at the same time Sebastian steps around Raven and locks eyes with me.

"Rhodes, is it true?" He's pointing over his shoulder at Raven, who hasn't carried on walking like I expected. No. She's fully facing us now, seeing what unfolds.

Fuck.

"Is what true?"

I tuck my hands into my pockets, attempting to appear calm, despite my fury at him for his attack on Raven earlier.

"That you've been given the short straw and have my sister living with you. I've already spoken with my father and put in a request with the administration team to have that rectified."

"Is that so? And where are you trying to move her to?"

The sinister glint in Sebastian's eyes irritates the fuck out of me. "Well, I wanted her off campus altogether, but since that isn't possible, I'll settle with the pits instead of a house with a view and all of the luxurious things Silvercrest has to offer. She's from Shadowmoor, man. She doesn't deserve to sully all of this with her existence."

I look past him, locking eyes with Raven, who fails to

hide the pain his bite causes, but she doesn't quiver and hide like many others would. Especially someone who has already been hurt at his hands today. Instead, she steps toward him, hands fisted at her sides.

"Thanks for your concern, Seb, but we've already discussed it with the faculty and we're happy to proceed as we are. I'm sure she'll be able to refrain from *tainting* everything, especially since strength training will be starting for the first years in no time," Creed declares, speaking more words at once than I'm sure he ever has before.

Sebastian bares his teeth, not impressed with our stance, but I don't have the patience to stick around and listen to any more shit he might throw out. "Good looking out, man." I clap him on the shoulder, tightening my grip a little firmer than necessary before I breeze past him.

I don't slow near Raven and Leila either, keeping my pace as I hear footsteps following closely behind me. Every step irritates me, every fiber of my being begging me to turn around and smash my fist into his face again and again until crimson stains my knuckles and smears his skin. The graphic horror of me destroying him plays on repeat at the forefront of my mind as I head down the pathway to our house, keeping me so enraptured that I almost stumble into the person waiting on our front porch.

The soft giggle and swipe of a palm along my back,

attempting to slip under my blazer, is all too familiar and I internally berate myself for letting myself get so distracted.

"Eldon, baby, what are you doing tonight? I was hoping to…What the fuck is she doing here?" Genie's tone goes from sickly sweet to the rasp from the bottom of a barrel in two seconds flat and her eyes bug out of her head, lip lifting with a sneer as she looks through me.

Slowly following her line of sight, I turn to find Raven smushed between Creed, Zane, and Brax. Leila must have turned off toward her house. I'm sure it's around here somewhere.

"Well?" Genie hisses, wanting an explanation she doesn't deserve, but before I can part my lips and tell her just that, Raven is storming toward us.

"Eldon, baby," Raven starts, her tone mocking as she drapes herself over my side and shoves Genie back a step. "You promised me some fun. I didn't realize *this* is what you had in mind." A smile remains plastered on her face as she wags a finger in Genie's direction, and it's almost funny watching the horror take over her face.

I should say something to defend one of them, break up the tension before it escalates, but the feel of her gripping my arm and the press of her chest against my bicep has my dick springing to attention.

Fuck.

"Don't even play games with me, bitch. I've heard

all about you and your roots. How was Shadowmoor? As filthy as you?" If Genie was hoping to hit a sore spot with Raven, she didn't aim for the right target because it falls flat instantly.

Raven rises up on her tiptoes to press her lips against my cheek, stirring my cock even further, before she shoulders past our unwanted visitor and unlocks the front door. She sinks her teeth into her bottom lip, glancing from my best friends to me, before settling a glare on Genie.

"Are you coming, boys?" It's a purr. A fucking *purr* and I'm about to cream my pants like a fucking fool, but I'm beyond caring at this point. The kiss was enough to turn me into a raging inferno. The heated glimmer in her chocolate-brown eyes, framed by a few loose tendrils of pink hair, will be catastrophic for my sexual stamina if I don't get a handle on myself now.

Zane dips past me first, making sure not to brush against Genie, despite the small space, and I don't miss the grin on his lips as he keeps his head down, disappearing inside without a word. Creed and Brax are right behind him, too, more than eager to get away from the drama as I finally get a grip on my flaring dick's needs and join them.

The second my foot is through the doorway, Raven places her palm flat on my chest, looking up into my eyes with a heated gaze. "Eldon, say goodbye to our guest."

I swipe my tongue over my dry lips, fully aware of the

game she's playing, and keep my body angled and eyes fixated on Raven as I follow her order. "Bye, Genie."

I hear her lips pop, but whatever she's about to say goes unheard when Raven slams the door shut in her face. As soon as she's out of view, Raven puts herself out of arm's reach, and I'm quick to rectify that. I rush after her but can't grasp her arm until she's right at her bedroom door. Spinning her before she can go any further, her back hits the wall, making her grunt as I step into her personal space, leaving nothing but an inch between us from head to toe.

"Fuck off, Eldon."

I grin. "Little Bird, you get me hot as fuck. Please, keep talking dirty to me."

"Are you fucking with me or something?" She plants her hands on my chest again, only this time it's in an attempt to push me away. I don't budge.

"What?" My mind is reeling from the touches she just intoxicated me with while putting on a show for Genie and I have no idea what she's talking about.

"You're so hot and cold I don't know where my head is. You warned me about my brother, who I may not have seen for the last fourteen years, but I fucking know what he's like, only for you to be besties with his scroungy ass after he tried to fucking kill me this morning." I open my mouth to interrupt but she doesn't give me a chance. "You're clam jamming me without care, pissing me off and overstepping the mark, and not allowing me to set boundaries. I didn't come here to spend my life having someone else dictate it for me. If I could survive Shadowmoor alone, I can take on Silvercrest too."

Her chest heaves with every breath, her hands still wedged between us as I stare deep into her eyes. "Are you always this explosive?" I ask, unable to stop myself, and she huffs.

"Are you always this frustrating?"

I shrug. "This whole world is fucked, Raven. No matter what I think about many things, I must act indifferent out there. We have to choose our battles wisely and bide our time. That's how this place works." I don't know why I'm being honest and explaining that to her, but I can't seem to stop myself.

"Tell me something I don't know. I lived in a town drenched in death and darkness on purpose. *On purpose.* It's completely detached from the rest of the world, living in squalor to keep other realms at bay. Did I mention it's on purpose? Now I'm supposed to know how to walk and talk in a world with an abundance of knowledge and wealth. No one is hiding behind their magic here. I can't fucking tell how much of a threat anyone is to me, and on top of all that, you guys are running so hot and cold I don't know whether I'm going to get third-degree burns or frostbite."

She shoves at my chest again with her last word, but I still don't go anywhere. If anything, I lean in closer, the tip of my nose running along hers.

Our breaths mingle, wrapping around us in a cocoon for two. I'm sure Brax, Zane, and Creed are watching us with amusement right now, but fuck if I care. I'm caught in Raven's web and I'm more than ready to let her slay me. Whatever she wants.

"That's why we're here to protect you," I murmur, my lips hanging dangerously close to hers as she searches my eyes.

Kiss me. Kiss me, Raven, and let me show you how good it can be.

"You're not protecting me. You're controlling me. There's a difference."

My lips crash against hers, unable to stop myself from taking precisely what I want, and she melts into my touch. Her hands grip the lapels of my blazer as I press against her, my cock digging into her stomach without care as she sweeps her tongue along my bottom lip.

Fuck yeah.

Moving my hand from the side of her head to her exposed thigh, I hiss at the feel of her skin. Power storms in my veins, willing me to get even more lost in her, when a sharp sting runs through my bottom lip and I gasp.

I lean back in slow motion, noting a hint of blood

on Raven's lip as I lift my hand to my own. Did she just fucking bite me? Stunned, I blink at her, delirious as fuck, as she winks at me before slipping from her spot against the wall and ducking into her room without a backward glance.

Motherfucker.

Sweeping my tongue over my lip, the familiar taste of copper coating my senses, I slowly turn to find the others standing around watching the shit show that is my life.

Zane's eyes are wide in surprise, while Creed seems intrigued and impressed more than anything. Glancing at Brax, he drops down onto the cushions with a sigh, turning a dry smile my way as he nods.

"You were dead right, Eldon. This is all going to work out absolutely fine. Not a single issue is going to crop up. You've got it in the bag, big man."

Fuck him, and fuck whatever bullshit might rear its ugly head.

If I thought I was addicted before, I was wrong. That was before I got a taste of her.

Now…I'm captivated.

ELEVEN

Raven

Living with four hot guys who are overbearing, irritating, and constantly in my space is more challenging than I initially thought it would be. Avoiding them is practically impossible, not to mention stressful. I just have to get through today, then I can spend the weekend hiding in my room, earning myself some well-deserved peace and tranquility.

I've barely made eye contact with any of them since Eldon had me pinned against the wall, mouth fused to mine as he claimed a piece of me I didn't even know existed. Damn, I would have acted on the need clawing at my insides in any other moment, but I had a point to make.

Any attempt at a conversation has been stilted on my end, not from their lack of trying, and sometimes I feel shitty about it. Like when Zane sits beside me at the dining table explaining his love for some game, I don't engage, despite wanting to. They have a way of getting under my skin without even trying and it's driving me insane.

Creed still doesn't say much but the way his eyes caress my skin as he observes my every move is like the most deadly foreplay I've ever felt. On the other hand, Brax is a dick, a broad-shouldered asshole who inserts himself between me and anything he may deem a threat. Sometimes it's warranted, like how he hasn't let Sebastian get within ten feet of me for the past three days, while other times, it's to stop Finn from approaching.

I think my silence irritates Eldon the most. Or maybe he's just the one to show it, but he's the worst out of all of them. Leila was right, he's definitely their leader, and the fact that I'm not simply falling in line with them is pissing him off.

"Raven, let's go. Leila is here," Zane calls out, rapping his knuckles on my bedroom door.

Running my fingers through my hair one last time, I let the soft curls fall down my back and over my shoulders. I've been wearing it up and off my face, but today has me nervous and I need something to hide behind.

"Let's go." A louder knock against my door echoes around me, accompanied by Brax's gruff voice, making me roll my eyes.

Hiking my bag over my shoulder, I swing the bedroom

door open before they can knock again. Zane is standing an inch away from the door, a soft smile on his lips. One so enticing I almost look up to meet his gaze, but I manage to stop myself before it's too late. Brax is standing right behind him, his shoulders tense as always.

I wave my hand, encouraging them to move, and they take a small step back, still crowding me as I brush past them.

Fuck, now my body is tingling like a firework, ready to go off, fizzling and whizzing through the sky. I need to get laid or something because this is driving me crazy.

Creed and Eldon are by the main door but I don't stop beside them. Instead, I breeze past, linking my arm through Leila's as I have every other day, and head for the pathway.

"How's your avoidance technique going?" Leila asks with a chuckle, knowing just how little they seem to care about it.

"What matters is whether I'm going to be able to enjoy this party you've been going on about tonight or if they're going to fuck me over on that, too," I grumble, making her laugh a little louder. I'm sure she does it to get a reaction out of them, but it's slightly amusing, so I don't try to stop her.

"I will make it my mission to ensure you, Raven Hendrix, have the time of your life tonight. Okay?" The enthusiasm dancing in her eyes is infectious and I trust in her certainty.

We spend the rest of the walk in silence, basking in the early morning sun as the number of students around us grows, leaving me to get lost in my head over the first class of the day, power strengthening.

How the fuck am I supposed to strengthen a power that doesn't exist?

I'm screwed, and not in a good way.

I considered playing sick today but that would only delay the inevitable. Maybe once they learn I'm a Void, they might just kick me out. My gut twists at the thought. The excitement I first felt when I considered getting the hell out of here is waning. The past six days have been a whirlwind and I don't know how I feel about this place. I need a weekend locked away by myself to figure out the pros and cons before I do something reckless.

My lack of magical ability is still a closely-guarded secret. I haven't breathed a word to anyone, not even Leila, out of worry of how she may look at me. She took my Shadowmoor past effortlessly, but this feels different. More personal.

As we enter the academy building, the chatter around us increases from the mass of students darting through the halls. We don't get far before a bell rings out, just like it did the day I arrived, making me frown.

"Oh, damn. There's a gathering. Let's head outside."

Leila steers me toward the courtyard where I first met her. A quick glance over my shoulder reveals the guys are still hot on our heels, but Leila doesn't bother with any of that as she pulls us into the growing crowd of students, stopping dead center.

Looking around, I notice Finn and his friends to the far left. He's already staring my way and his smile grows when our eyes lock. Maybe I need to let off some steam tonight and, hopefully, I can get Finn not to quake in his boots as soon as the guys glare in his direction. I'm not looking for a forever kind of guy. I'm looking for someone to fuck my problems away. He winks and it does nothing for me, not even a flicker of excitement, but I drill that down to the fact that I'm stressed about today's class and turn my attention back to the front.

A projection flickers above everyone and a moment later, the headmaster appears. His suit is immaculate, his hair held perfectly in place as a wry smile takes over his face.

"Good morning, students."

"Good morning, Professor Burton," every student except me replies as one, sending an eery chill down my spine, just as it did the first time it happened.

"I have some exciting news for our first years," he starts, instantly creating a buzz through the students around me. "You may notice no third years are present today as they were surprised with a midnight visit to the warden's outpost in Pinebrook." The murmuring around us stops as everyone gives Burton their full attention. "The trip was successful, the threat a false alarm, and since no one has been harmed, we thought this would be an exceptional opportunity for our newest students to experience it."

"Holy shit, this is so freaking awesome," Leila whispers, bouncing on the balls of her feet.

Does this mean I get to avoid— "You will attend your first class then transportation will arrive for you to spend the rest of the day at Pinebrook. Have a fantastic day. Follow the sun, destroy the shadows, and survive another dawn."

He disappears before my very eyes, swiping away the hope of avoiding today's power strengthening class. Everyone starts to disperse around us and I, once again, let Leila lead us through the masses toward my impending doom. I didn't miss the fact that he mentioned the third years aren't present, though. Which means I don't have to have my guard up waiting for Sebastian to appear for the rest of the morning.

Genie, however, is still a threat. A shitty one, but she's on my radar nonetheless, especially since she hasn't done anything in retaliation for my little stunt the other day.

All too soon, Leila is pulling me through a large door, but instead of the ample open space I expected, there are rows and rows of tables and chairs, just like in the other classes.

"I thought this was power strengthening class," I murmur, taking the seat beside her as the telltale sound of chairs dragging along the floor rings out behind me. I don't need to look to confirm two of my housemates will be sitting directly behind me with the other two to the right, just as they have in every other class.

"Oh, we haven't started the practical side of it yet. I think we have one or two more lessons on this stuff before we head out," Leila explains, and I exhale heavily as a weight leaves my shoulders.

"Good morning." A rich, raspy voice swirls in the air as a man dressed head to toe in black approaches the front of the room. He oozes a presence I can't quite describe, like he's carrying the weight of the world on his shoulders while simultaneously slaying the enemy. He turns to face the room, eyes almost white as he scans over each student. There's a scar running down his cheek, three to be precise, which only seems to show what this man has been through.

"I can't decide if I'm in awe of this man's strength or scared," I whisper, and Leila hums.

"Definitely not the latter. He's not scary at all."

"Are you sure? He looks like he could break me in the palm of his hand with little to no effort," I insist, and she snickers.

"I keep forgetting you don't know stuff." I turn to face her, confused about why that matters. She nods toward the professor. "Professor Gunnar Fitch is my papa."

My eyes widen, surprise getting the better of me as I gape from her to the man up front a few times.

"Your father looks cool as fuck," I admit, making her shake her head.

"Most people despise me because of him," she whispers, avoiding my gaze, and I frown.

"Why?"

"Because they're intimidated by him. Not in the 'he looks a little scary' kind of way, more the 'I refuse to admit he's better than me' kind instead."

I sigh. "That's bullshit."

"That's life."

Before I can offer her some kind of philosophical empowering speech, Fitch's voice booms around us. "It seems we have a new student among us. Can anyone catch her up to speed on the lessons missed so far?" He's staring at me, intrigue in his eyes, but his mask of indifference slips ever so slightly when he glances to my right and smiles at his daughter.

Wow.

I can't even explain what I would do for someone to look at me lovingly like that. Unconditionally, without reservation and no expectations.

I half expect Leila to raise her hand but, to my surprise, he points to someone behind me. Excellent.

"There are seven main categories of magic that will help determine the groups you work in while strengthening your powers. Nature-based, divination, conjuring, psychic, medics, shifters, and the one subject not encouraged at Silvercrest, necromancy," Creed explains, all factual and to the point as I would expect. "Your magical ability will determine where you are categorized. Those of us with more than one gift will be placed in our strongest category while also training our other skills where possible."

More than one magical ability? I didn't even realize that was possible. And did he say...those of us? Is he talking about himself?

I can't stop myself from looking back at him, only to find his eyes already on me, but I don't turn away for the first time in days. I'm too intrigued, hoping he'll randomly disclose that information right now, but Professor Fitch continues to speak instead.

"Thank you, Creed. Since you're heading out to the Pinebrook post today, I thought organizing you into your groups would be a good idea. I've placed some signs around the room with each magical sub-group written on them. Discuss with your friends and find the one best suited to you."

Everybody rushes to their feet, excitement swirling

in the air as I remain frozen in my seat. My gaze slowly travels around the room, reading each sign like one will magically tell me what to do.

"I'm over in the nature-based category, but I'm just going to speak to my papa first," Leila murmurs, and I nod numbly as she walks away.

She's barely taken two steps when I feel a presence at my back. "Where will you be placed, Raven?"

Eldon.

Clearing my throat, I stand, turning to avoid his gaze. Not because I don't want to speak to him, but out of embarrassment. Dammit.

"That's none of your business."

"You still haven't read the handbook, have you?" Zane murmurs, a hint of humor in his voice, and I shrug.

"Maybe if we go first, she might be more forthcoming," Creed states, but I don't lift my gaze from the spot on Eldon's tie that I'm locked onto.

"I'll be focusing on nature-based, Brax will be with the shifters, Creed with the psychics, and Zane in divination," Eldon reels off, offering me an insight without telling me their abilities.

I quickly realize that I could say whichever I want, but lying isn't my strong suit. It's also what triggers my poor little mind and makes me anxious.

"And you…" Zane musters, hopeful that I'll divulge,

but I shrug.

Brax scoffs from my right, pulling my attention in his direction, but I still manage to avoid his gaze. "You know I can pull the information from you, right? All I have to do is place my hand on your head, and I'll have everything I need."

I gasp in horror, glaring at him for a split second before quickly looking away.

"You wouldn't," I spit, my heart galloping in my chest as worry starts to consume me.

"Try me," he snarks back, stepping toward me, and my spine stiffens.

"Go ahead. You do that. You take away my trust and prove you're no better than Sebastian."

Silence hangs over us, seeping into my body and clawing at my veins, ready to cut me open and offer me on a platter to these assholes.

"Whatever. Take care of yourself, then. See if we care."

TWELVE

Raven

Groups gather outside in the open field as a few Professors arrange everybody into organized lines. "Find your symbol and join your group," someone orders, pointing up to the sky. I follow their finger and notice six glowing symbols, each with a magical category etched beneath it, thankfully offering me the extra guidance to figure out where I will assign myself.

"Miss Hendrix, I'm going to assume you'll be joining the nature-based group I'm leading, just like your brother." I freeze at the mention of Sebastian as I turn to see a professor I haven't met yet. Despite my instant need to snarl at him, I put a forced smile on my lips instead.

"Thank you, but I'm nothing like my brother." Before he can respond, I spin in the opposite direction and settle in the line forming for the medics. I can't change my mind now, so I just keep my head down and wait.

"Raven?" I glance over my shoulder at the sound of my name to find Finn. "Hey, fancy seeing you here."

I'm acutely aware that someone is watching us, and I know it's one, if not all, of the Bishops, scrutinizing our every move right now.

"Hey, it's a small world, huh?" He smiles wide at me, inching closer.

This isn't going to end well. I can already sense it. He gazes around us as if feeling tension before looking back at me with a gulp. Yup. The Bishops are definitely watching.

It's irritating as fuck. I shouldn't be worrying about their reaction. I should be able to talk to whoever I want. They don't control me.

Looking up at him, I stare into his wide eyes, taking in his blond curls and considering my thoughts from earlier. He's handsome, sure, but not as hot as the Bishops. That's also a fact. Well, in *my* opinion, at least. Would trying to have a good time with him be more hassle than it's worth?

"Students, we're ready to roll out. Stay with your groups at all times and do not try to be with your friends. All off-campus visits come with safety precautions. Stay in your magical categories or find yourself taken off the next outpost visit," Professor Fitch states, and I turn to face the front, very aware of Finn's presence behind me.

"Nice, we're using gateways," he murmurs, almost

to himself, but I'm too intrigued not to peek around the person in front of me to see what he means.

The air swirls at the front of our line, morphing before my very eyes until a translucent oval appears. It shines in the morning light, a pale iridescent purple dancing in the wind as the person at the front steps through it.

Wow.

I don't recall hearing about or seeing a gateway in Shadowmoor. Your immediate mode of transport was on foot, or if you were gifted with the ability to teleport, you could do that. Although, if you had money, which nobody did, you likely owned a vehicle.

There's so much I don't know, so much that people around me are familiar with, leaving me at a disadvantage. Maybe I need to add this to the list of things I need Leila to teach me, but I don't want to put everything on her shoulders.

As the line starts to move, student after student stepping through the gateway, my body thrums with a mixture of excitement and uncertainty. I twist my hands together for a beat before turning back to Finn.

"Have you been through a gateway before?"

He smiles down at me with a nod. "Yes. Only once, but it was cool as fuck." I can't decide whether to push for more details or ask how he usually travels around, but I'm forced to take a step back when a figure stands between us, blocking Finn from my view.

The rich smell of sandalwood swirls around me and I don't even need to glance up to know who it is.

Brax.

Tilting my head back, I glare at him, but he continues to stand there unfazed, with his arms folded over his chest. Seconds turn into minutes as we stare each other down and I can't decide whether I'm surprised or not that Finn doesn't even try to move around him. Just when I'm sure he's turned into a statue before me, Brax suddenly juts his chin forward, signaling me to move.

Reluctantly, I glance over my shoulder to find the line has dwindled to only three people ahead of me waiting to go through the gateway, and one of them is Finn. Shit, when did he move around us? I was so focused on Brax that I hadn't even realized he had moved past us.

Asshole.

With a huff, I turn away from him and rush to catch up to the back of my line. Despite the urge to glance back at the overbearing idiot, I don't take my eyes off the gateway as I step through it.

A shiver runs down my spine, a sensation I've never felt before consuming every inch of my body as I move through the air. It can only be described as stretchy and thick, completely disorienting until my breath hitches and the cobbled ground returns beneath my academy-issued shoes.

The wind whips around me, the sound of chatter and mumbling increasing as each student takes in their new surroundings. Blinking, I look up from the ground, and a gasp lodges in my throat. There's so much happening simultaneously to be in awe of. I don't know where to look first, my eyes roaming wild as I slowly spin.

Water laps below and far into the distance where white cliff faces and gray mountain peaks continue for miles. A thick layer of clouds rolls in overhead and not a single ray of light breaks through the thickness as I move to the turret-guarded wall in front of me. It's made of the same material as the path we're standing on, small cobbled rocks, stones, and boulders, all looking battered and worn.

When my hands press against the rough top, I peer over the edge, watching as the waves crash menacingly on the rocks below. I'm on a bridge. Glancing left and right, I find two towers on either side, secure on land, with the bridge beneath me connecting the two. Spinning again, I find it's not the only bridge. One after another, each building is connected to another and another, joining the smaller islands and the guarded outpost towers that take up most of the land.

"It's crazy beautiful, right?" Zane's voice startles me, but despite my avoidance campaign with the Bishops, I eagerly nod in response.

"It's so battered and worn it shouldn't be so stunning. Imagine what the walls could tell you if they were able to talk," I muse, appreciating his hum of agreement.

"I heard a story once that the Pinebrook outpost was attacked by an army of stragglers who were overpowering the guards at every turn. Until Fitch showed up with his spirited familiar and burned them all to Hell."

"Spirited familiar?" I ask, enraptured by his story.

He shrugs. "Yeah. It's rare, and I don't believe Professor Fitch has ever confirmed if he has one, but it's when someone of magical ability connects with a spirited force. It can be an animal of any shape or size or a spirit apparition." I'm sure my jaw hangs slack, but he doesn't mock me. "I'm guessing that's not something you're familiar with in Shadowmoor," he murmurs, nudging me with his arm as he looks out to sea.

"No. There are a lot of things it seems I'm not familiar with," I breathe, my stomach clenching at the admission.

"That's what I'm here for, then. If you have any questions or confusion, just say the word and I'll explain it to you or help you find the answer. Deal?"

Looking up into his hazel eyes, I nod before I can actually consider his offer. "Deal."

"Are you two in your assigned groups, or are we breaking the rules?" I freeze at the sound of Sebastian's voice, irritated instantly. I'm about to voice my agitation when Zane's hand wraps around my arm in warning as he discreetly forces me to take two steps behind him.

"I thought she was going to go for a swim and I didn't think that was such a good idea for our visit. So I cut through the crowd to prevent an accident," Zane murmurs, shrugging like it's no problem at all. "You can just call me Zane the Heroic now," he adds, beaming from ear to ear as he nods at Sebastian and turns away without further concern.

He forces me to stay ahead of him until I'm back with the medic group and his thumb strokes lazily over my forearm as he looks down at me. I'm sure there are words on the tip of his tongue, but he keeps his mouth shut and saunters off with a sharp nod.

Rubbing my lips together, I glance back at him, mesmerized by his every step until a professor claps their hands, garnering my attention.

"Medics, please follow me. For those who don't know me, I'm Professor Duran. I'll be guiding you through your tour of the outpost." She smiles politely, standing tall as she assesses each of us. When she's satisfied that we're all paying attention, she nods before waving for us to follow her.

Intrigued by my new surroundings, I eagerly keep close to her, listening to the stories and folklore this place holds. She doesn't mention the same venture Zane told me about, but she talks about the many attacks on our realm as a whole that we've been able to stave off from this post alone. She speaks of the honor of the men and women fighting to protect us without ever meeting us, giving their life and sword to keep us safe.

It all sounds so loyal, regal, and awe-inspiring, but I can't help but wonder if they did it out of choice or because they were enrolled in this madness just as I was, just as we all are. All too soon, we're right back where we started, richer with knowledge and achy from our steps. I needed to lie down after all that, but it was totally worth it.

"The third years are setting up the gateways home. If you would like to return to the building on our right, they will assist you," Professor Duran advises, dismissing us.

Taking off in that direction, I startle when someone falls into step beside me. A glance to my right confirms it's Finn. I was so caught up in the tour that I forgot he was in this group too.

"How boring was that?" he says with a snicker. "I thought I was going to pass out from lack of interest, but at least we weren't back at the academy doing classes," he adds, and I frown.

I thought that was awesome. I don't know whether it's because we were never taught any kind of history at Shadowmoor, but I loved it. My mind is wild with everything I'm learning and I won't take that for granted.

I consider telling him as much but catch sight of Sebastian up ahead in front of the gateways and think better of it. I don't need to argue about how we thought the past couple of hours went when I have bigger things to be concerned with.

Upping my pace, I try to veer toward the left to avoid my brother, but despite my best efforts, our group is lined up with him. I can't decide between sneering at him and dipping my head to avoid confrontation, so I settle on ignoring his presence as the students in front of me start to go through the gateway.

Thankfully, Finn doesn't attempt to say anything else to me as the line clears. I glance around to see if I can find Leila or any of the Bishops but come up empty. As it's my turn to disappear through the gateway, Sebastian shoulders into me, knocking me sideways as my arms flail, making him grin.

"This one is for you, bitch. Good luck getting home."

The slightest squeak parts my lips as the world moves in slow motion and I fall through a different gateway. The iridescent sheen of the transporter clings to my skin as I pass through it, making it almost hard to breathe until my back hits the hard ground with a thud.

Uncertainty and confusion cloud my brain as the remnants of the gateway disappear before me. Pushing up onto my elbows, I shake my head, trying and failing to clear the fog consuming my mind.

"Where the fuck am I?" I blurt out loud, hoping someone will hear me, but as I slowly clamber to my feet, I'm more than sure that will not happen.

There's no one around me. There's *nothing* around me. It's just me and the orange and cream shades of sandstone under my feet that go on as far as the eye can see.

THIRTEEN

Raven

S econds drift into minutes which fade into hours. I keep walking, putting one foot in front of the other, despite having no fucking clue where I'm actually going or even if I'm even heading in the right direction.

The sandstone beneath my feet hasn't changed, going on for miles and miles as I wonder if I'm stuck in a time loop or something. The only sign that the world is moving around me is that the sun is slowly setting. It's falling to my right, my only indication that I'm moving south. It's a risky move, but after considering how doom and gloom Shadowmoor and Ashdale are described, I would assume that this is the complete opposite. I am betting all my chances on the fact that I'm still north of Silvercrest. If I ever find a town or a sign, then I can reassess.

It serves as a reminder that I was supposed to be

getting ready for the party now and I wonder if anyone has realized I'm not there. The Bishops are likely enjoying some peace and quiet, and Leila probably won't notice until she's ready to leave.

I'm going to die out here.

Perfect.

What a way to go, and at the hand of Sebastian too. That's what pisses me off the most.

Is this where my life starts to flash before my eyes? The world tilting on its axis to remind me of all the mistakes I've made and all the things I never got to experience?

Sighing, I roll my neck, trying to ease the tension that has caused my muscles to bunch together.

I need to stop being so dramatic and keep pushing. Something will eventually appear on the horizon; a glimmer of hope, somewhere to take shelter, or even somewhere to find a drink. At this stage, I'd take a mirage, anything, just something more than the orange and cream rock formations surrounding me.

Hiking my backpack up my shoulders, I kick at the stones as I walk. As if seeing the sandstone in every direction I turn isn't enough, I'm covered in it too. It clings to my uniform and skin with a vengeance I wish to harness for myself.

"Raven."

I freeze, a chill running down my spine as I glance

around. Where the fuck did my name just come from? When nothing appears, I'm sure it's a figment of my imagination and I continue walking. I've only taken a handful of steps when I hear it again.

"Raven."

It's like my name is floating on the wind, cocooning around me as the rest of the scenery remains the same.

"Raven."

Wetting my parched lips, I spin on the spot. "Hello?" My voice is meeker than I would prefer, but my spine is ramrod straight with anticipation.

All I can hear is my breath, surrounded by silence, which confirms it's all in my head.

Fuck.

Placing the sun to my right again, I take two more steps before I'm stopped dead in my tracks by a hard chest. I gasp, startled by the obstruction, and look up to find Creed staring down at me with a frown firmly locked in place.

"Creed?" I'm sure he's the mirage I've been waiting for, but when I lift my hand to his chest, testing his actual presence, he doesn't disappear. "Creed?"

"Where the fuck have you been?"

My head rears back, my eyebrows pinching at his tone as I wave my hand around. "Where does it look like I've been?"

Shaking his head, Creed squeezes my shoulders before

taking a step back. "Don't go anywhere."

It's on the tip of my tongue to ask him where the hell he thinks I'm going to go, but it's too late. He's already disappeared. Glancing from left to right, I blink, confused as hell over what's just happened, when a rift rips through the air in front of me. One by one, the Bishops step through the anomaly, their frowns getting darker as each one lays eyes on me.

I've been pleading for help, a savior to spite the depressive wasteland I'm stuck in, but by the looks on their faces, I'd rather face this mess alone.

"Where have you been?" Brax grunts while Zane and Eldon glance around at the bleak surroundings.

"Don't ask—"

I wave my hand, cutting Creed's response off as my nostrils flare. Avoiding Brax's glare, I stare at his chest. "Does this look like somewhere I would choose to come to? I have no fucking clue how I got here, I just arrived here from the transport. I've been walking for hours, miles, and nothing has changed around me. So, I really don't need you showing up and yelling at me. If you're here to be helpful, I might find it in me to use my manners and say thank you, but your surly attitude isn't making it likely."

"Raven, we've been looking for you for hours," Eldon explains, swiping a hand down his face.

They have?

"Why?" I fold my arms over my chest, putting an invisible barrier between us as I still refuse to meet their gaze.

"What do you mean *why*? Why wouldn't we? You're a part of our house," Zane states, like that makes perfect sense. I'm almost sure he will bring up the damn housemate handbook again, but to my surprise, he doesn't.

"We were waiting for you at the gateways in Silvercrest, Raven. What happened?" Creed asks, his voice remaining calm, lulling me into a sense of security I instantly don't like but fall victim to anyway.

"Sebastian happened," I groan, squeezing my arms tighter together. "None of that matters now. Can you please just take me back?"

No one initially answers, reluctantly making me lift my eyes to meet Creed's for the briefest second. The moment I do, he nods. "I can do that, but this conversation isn't over."

"I didn't expect it to be."

He closes his eyes and I watch in awe as he lifts his hand above his head and slowly slices it down to his knees, opening a rift before my very eyes. So Creed created the rift? What the fuck?

I keep my lips locked tight as he nods for me to proceed. Despite my uncertainty, I reach my hand through first before stepping to the other side, surprised that no weird sensation runs through my veins as I cross over to find myself in our house.

Home.

Shit, I didn't think that was ever going to happen.

I don't glance back as I charge for my bedroom door, but before I can reach for the key in my pocket, I'm blocked off by a bulky frame.

Brax.

Sighing, I turn away from him and head for the kitchen. I can feel all of their eyes on me, watching my every move as I grab a bottle of water and guzzle it down in one breath. I can't imagine what I look like, but I don't care.

I'm aware that a conversation is going to need to be had before they'll let me leave. I'd rather get it over with sooner rather than later, so I take a seat on the coffee table, not wanting to sully the sofa with my dirt from the wastelands. I kick off my shoes and tuck my legs under me.

Hoping to deflect from myself for a moment, I turn to Creed, who takes the seat across from me. "You can do that?" I ask, and he nods, aware I'm referring to the rifts. "Is that why you're grouped with the psychics?" He nods again, still not engaging in a conversation, but there are things I would like to know here too. "Where was I?"

"You were in the surrounding wastelands of Ashdale," Zane explains, sitting beside me.

Dammit. I definitely should have been heading north instead of south.

"How did you guys find me?" I look down at my hands, not wanting them to see any sign of vulnerability in my expression.

"That would be me." My eyes widened in surprise at Creed. "I'm still training, so it took some time, and I had to call out your name in hopes of you responding, so thanks for that."

Is this guy seriously thanking me when it was him who found me?

"I think I should be thanking you." I hate to give in to them but, surprisingly, none of them make a big deal out of it.

"How did Sebastian get you out there, Raven?" Brax asks, cutting the conversation back to me.

I shrug. "I was stepping through the gateway after everyone else in my group, and he shoulder checked me into another rift."

"Fucker," Eldon grunts, mimicking my thoughts as I swipe a hand down my face.

"I shouldn't be surprised. Not after his last attack."

"You do know what the wastelands surrounding Ashdale are known for, right?" I can't help but spy Brax pacing back and forth in front of me, but I keep my head low.

"Nope."

"How? How can you not fucking know? Do you *want* to die? Is that it?" His words bite, raising my defenses even higher as my hands clench. Despite the annoyance and anger consuming me, I simply shrug, not offering him more. But it seems he isn't willing to accept that. "Don't brush me off, Raven."

He crouches in front of me and I force my gaze lower. I refuse to give him the satisfaction of seeing me genuinely vulnerable. I can play timid all day long. I can avoid their gaze, step back from their demands, and save all of my ruthlessness for when it's needed most.

I'm very aware that I'm outnumbered here, and at the academy as a whole. I can't talk a big game when I have zero magic to back it up, and knowing that Creed and Zane used their abilities to find me is only another reminder of that.

"What are you hiding from us, Raven?" Brax pushes. "Why is it such a hard fucking task to tell us why you don't know things like what the wastelands are known for? Why can't you share your magic abilities? For this to work, we must be on the same side." His words surprise me, but they don't make me relent. His hands suddenly land on my upper arms, shaking me a little. "Look at me, Raven! All you do is avoid my gaze, and it's driving me insane!"

My mouth pops open in shock as my gaze immediately

finds his. His eyes hold me captive—one brown, one green, both brewing a storm ready to rage before me. I frown when his hands clench tighter around my arms, and I look down to find his fingers a cold shade of gray. What the hell?

"You're hurting me," I mumble, not in any distress at all as I stare at the startling difference and he quickly releases me. Leaning back, he quickly removes his hands from view and when they return a moment later, they're tanned and calloused again.

Eldon did mention earlier that Brax was under the shifter category, but what is gray like that?

"Raven." I blink at Eldon over Brax's shoulder. "The wastelands. If you had been there in another hour or two, you would be dead. Why don't you know that?"

Leaning back in my seat, I make eye contact with all four of them and decide to relent on one fact at least. "I left Amber Glen when I was four. Until the day I arrived at the academy, I hadn't spent a moment outside of Shadowmoor."

"Not even one?" Zane blurts, brows touching his hairline as I nod.

"You aren't taught anything beyond the borders of Shadowmoor because you're never going to leave. You heard them in class the other day. They suppress the region and the people within it. Until now, there was no reason for me to know anything at all."

"Fuck," Eldon grunts, and I'm sure there's a glimpse of sympathy in his eyes, but I look away before I can confirm it.

"What else aren't you telling us, Raven?"

I gulp despite myself, feeling Brax's intense gaze as he waits for an answer.

"There's nothing more you need to know."

"Don't fuck with me, Raven."

"Stop thinking you deserve to know everything about me. I've survived this long on my own. I can continue," I bite back, my gut clenching with how he keeps saying my name. It stokes a fire in my heart and coils my veins simultaneously.

"What aren't you fucking telling us?"

I scoff this time, untucking my legs and planting them on the floor beside him, but he doesn't move as I loom above him. "Like I trust you."

"Show me your magic."

My eyes flash to his, my nose wrinkling as we both glare at each other.

"No."

"We're the only ones here looking out for you. If we weren't set on finding you, you'd be unknowingly getting ready to battle with fucking serpents right now. Show me your magic."

Serpents? No thanks. But despite my relief at being saved, I still don't have the guts to admit the truth. "No."

"You said you were a medic, right? Heal me." He extends a finger, and I watch in surprise as it turns gray again. His nail sharpens as he brings the pointed edge toward his arm and panic kicks in.

He wouldn't. He fucking wouldn't.

The tip pierces his skin and before I can stop myself, I stretch out and grab his wrist. "Don't."

"Heal me."

"No."

"Heal. Me," he repeats, digging a little deeper as a knock sounds on the front door.

"I can't," I admit when it's clear he's not interested in whoever is on the other side.

"Why?" I shake my head, but he presses harder and blood droplets trickle down his arm.

Fuck.

"Because I can't, okay? I'm a fucking Void."

FOURTEEN

Raven

The knocking at the door becomes incessant as I remain frozen in place, panting with every shallow breath I take. Brax stares at me, but there's no surprise in his eyes and Creed, Eldon, and Zane all watch me just as intently as the silence continues to extend around us.

Clearing my throat, I slowly reach for Brax's hand and guide his pointed nail away from his flesh. His skin feels like stone against mine but I keep my mouth shut about it as I push to my feet. I can't fucking breathe and the knocking is escalating the stress even further.

"I should answer that," I mumble, heading for the door.

"No, you shouldn't," Eldon argues, and I turn to face him.

"What time is it?" His brows furrow at my question, but he still checks for me.

"Seven o'clock."

Nodding, I swipe a hand down my blazer. "It's Leila. We're going to the party. She's not going to stop knocking until I answer." I turn for the door but don't take a step as Brax's voice washes over me.

"Do you seriously think you're still going to the party after dropping a bomb like that on us?"

Rolling my shoulders back, I take a deep breath as my spine stiffens at the tone of his voice. I look back over my shoulder at him. "You are aware that I'm my own person, right? I can make my own decisions." The scowl on his face makes it clear that he really couldn't give a shit.

"Not when it comes to your safety, it seems."

Shaking my head, I stride toward the door. I manage to grab the handle and open it an inch before it's slammed shut again. The woodsy scent that envelops me confirms who it is. His front is pressed to my back and his arm is stretched out over my shoulder with his hand plastered against the door.

Fuck.

My brain is already messy. I don't need to feel his body heat as well right now. I can't think straight.

Eldon.

"We haven't finished talking yet, Little Bird," he breathes against my ear, and I have to force back a shiver.

Blowing a heavy breath past my lips, I keep my gaze

fixed ahead as I answer him. "Today has been a fucking mess."

"That's putting it lightly," Brax interrupts.

"Finally," I holler, tilting my head around Eldon's frame to lock eyes with him. "Something we can agree on." Zane snickers, making me relax a little despite Eldon's close proximity. "But seriously, I need to unwind before I self-combust. So I'm going to this party."

"Are you forgetting the part where you just announced you're a Void? You can't go to a party where everyone else has magical abilities." I turn to face Eldon and lift my palm to his chest. His eyes heat before me, but darken the second I knock him back a step.

"I didn't just turn Void this second, Eldon. I've been Void since forever and I have been surrounded by magic every day. I can handle myself. Now, give me some space." I turn with a huff, grabbing the door handle again. This time, I manage to open the door wide enough to see Leila. Her eyebrows are pinched in confusion and I try to offer her a reassuring smile before the door slams shut again.

I'm about to beat a man so hard.

Frustration simmers in my veins as I spin to stare Eldon down but, to my surprise, Zane is hovering closest to the door now. Sighing, I drop my face into my hands as I try to rally what little composure I have left.

"Here's the deal. I'm going to the party. I don't care

where you guys are or what the fuck you're doing, but *I* am going to let my hair down for the night in hopes of letting the stress of today fizzle out." Zane opens his mouth to interrupt me but I lift my hand to halt him before a breath even escapes his lips. "Then tomorrow, if you so desire, we will discuss this further." My heart races, ready for the pushback I know will come.

"Discussing it now would be better," Creed explains, a surprisingly soft smile on his face when I turn to him.

"That would be better for *you*, and, selfishly, I'm making this about me, but I don't care." Taking another deep breath, I look each of them in the eye before giving my peace offering. "Tomorrow, I'm all yours. I'll do whatever you want, even read the damn handbook, but tonight? This is for me. The alternative is I go anyway, but I've had enough of my life dictated for me by others. I'm already at my limit. Sebastian's bullshit has left no room for anyone else taking my options away."

Eldon steps forward, raising his hand out toward me. "Deal." I don't miss a beat as I lace my fingers with his and shake on it. A smirk spreads across his face as he leans in so close I can feel his breath on my lips. "You should have been more specific when you said whatever I want, Little Bird." His eyes drop to my mouth, tongue peeking out to swipe over his bottom lip as my thighs clench together.

Leila's knocking on the door is as ferocious as the

beating of my heart now, and when Eldon's hand loosens on mine, I stumble back a step. Blindly searching for the door handle behind me, my cheeks heat under their intense stares before I whirl around to look at Leila.

"Hey."

"Are the Bishops living up to their asshole-ish nature?" she asks with a smirk, and I grin, tucking a pink curl behind my ear.

"Something like that."

"Why aren't you dressed yet?"

I look down at my dirty uniform and cringe. I was supposed to go to the shops on campus after classes today to get something, but Sebastian's little adventure meant that didn't happen.

"Today has been eventful and I don't have anything to wear," I admit, the pang of irritation coiling through my veins getting tighter.

"You can borrow something of mine," Leila says with a smile, waving her hand in front of me, and I choke on a gasp as the air shifts around me. The feel of butterfly wings kissing my skin from head to toe sweeps over me, watching in shock as my uniform disappears. A light breeze now touches my exposed legs and arms as a shimmering silver mini dress covers my torso. Matching heels adorn my feet, and my hair blows around my face and shoulders in soft pink waves.

Holy shit.

"There we go. I made sure to put your uniform on the chair behind you. Since I haven't seen your bedroom, I couldn't put it away for you."

"Thank you," I muster, trying to hide the surprise from my voice as I run my fingers over the sequined dress.

"No problem. We might be the same size, but you're definitely taller than me," she says with a grin, indicating the hem of the dress stopping higher up my thighs than the blue dress she's wearing.

"You can't wear that." I turn around with a pointed look to question Eldon, but Leila beats me to it.

"Says who?"

"My dick," he retorts instantly, and all the guys chuckle at him.

These fucking Bishops have me so screwed.

"Are you ready for a good time?" Leila asks, and I turn back to her and grin.

"Like you wouldn't believe."

I don't know what I expected when Finn mentioned that the party was at the Silvercrest Memorial, but it wasn't this. Mausoleums frame a large open space with a drink table set up, bartender and all, along the far right, a dance space cleared in the center, and seating scattered toward the left. Music swirls in the air and other students already fill the dance floor.

It doesn't give any creepy vibes like I thought there might be, but I've seen worse in Shadowmoor. Far worse. For starters, there are no pits set up for fighting like there would be back home. Everyone is dressed to impress, dancing and drinking to their heart's content.

Tonight is going to be more fun than I thought. Especially when the grass doesn't give way under my heels. *That's* the kind of magic I need in my life.

"What do you want to drink?" Leila asks as we slow to a stop by the bar. "I'm having two shots of moon root and a bottle of pearl shine. They're my favorites." She claps excitedly as the line dwindles, but uncertainty makes me cautious.

"I don't usually drink at parties. I need to remain alert," I admit, making her eyebrows gather in confusion.

"What do you need to stay alert for here? Everyone is having a good time. You should join in too." I nibble at my lip. I didn't mention my little trip, courtesy of Sebastian. Not that it's a secret, but I would really like to not have to deal with that stress right now.

When it's our turn to order, Leila takes over, ordering double and taking a tray with our drinks. Instead of going to one of the tables across the space, she finds a high-top table at the end of the line.

Joining her, I don't immediately take the drinks she's chosen, still unsure what to do when my eyes lock with Creed's. He's with Eldon, Zane, and Brax, the four of them making their way to the bar. They're all dressed in jeans and polo shirts. Creed's is black with a floral detailed collar and Eldon's is white with a pocket on his chest while Brax's is navy blue and fits like a second skin over his muscles. Zane's, however, is an array of colors swirling across the material and I've never seen anything more fitting for the craziness that is him.

"Yeah, you definitely have them under some kind of spell, Raven," Leila says with a chuckle, pulling my attention away from them for a moment.

"Why?"

"Because they never *ever* come to parties at the memorial. Which means they're only here for one reason, and that's you."

I gulp, desperate to correct her on her assessment, but I can't deny how much I like that idea. I glance at them once more and my eyes find Creed's at the same time Leila thrusts a shot glass into my hand.

He nods subtly and I glance down at my drink. It's like he can sense my uncertainty and that's his little signal to indicate that it's okay…he's got me.

Fuck, that's a rush all on its own.

"Let's go in three, two, one," Leila shouts, and I bring the rim of the glass to my lips, letting the moon root burst along my tongue before swallowing it down. There's a sharp zing of an aftertaste, like lemon and lime battling it out in my throat, but it's nice.

"Holy crap, Leila," I gasp, wiping my mouth with the back of my hand, and she grins.

"One more," she encourages, offering me another glass. I take it more willingly this time.

Lifting my gaze to search out Creed again, I still when I lock gazes with my brother instead. The shock on Sebastian's face is evident as his top lip rises with a snarl. Smiling sweetly at him, I clink my glass with Leila and down the shot, needing a bit of liquid courage to deal with that motherfucker.

When I feel the sharp zing again, I turn to Leila, effectively dismissing Sebastian. "What does the pearl shine taste like?"

"Like Heaven," she insists, taking a sip of hers before handing me my bottle.

It's fruity, all coconut, pineapple, and something else I can't quite grasp, but she's right. It's so good.

"I hope you're ready to carry me home later," I say with a grin, my muscles relaxing as I let the music swirl through my being, mixing with the liquor and making my hips sway.

"No way, that's what the Bishops are here for." I shake my head at her, refusing to acknowledge the hope clenching my chest.

They're assholes, huge dicks, but they fucking found me in the wastelands. Found. Me. When no one else was even looking. That says more about them than it does about how isolated and lonely I actually am.

"Want to dance?" Leila thankfully interrupts the mental hole I was falling into and I nod eagerly.

"Lead the way."

I down the rest of my pearl shine before she grabs my hand and pulls me toward the dance floor. The music picks up as we squeeze our way to the center of the crowd.

"Thanks for this, Raven. I usually come to parties and just hide on the outskirts. It feels good to have some fun," Leila says as she leans in to be heard over the music.

I want to ask why she feels disliked so much but now isn't the time to be bringing her down with all of that. Tonight is about having some fun. One song leads into another and another. My hips swing more, my hands rise above my head, and I dance like no one is watching. I feel eyes on me the entire time, but somehow it only makes my body thrum for more.

Time passes in myriad colors as the moon glows down on us while the sky is lit with different colored spotlights. When my feet start to ache, I consider trying to grab a table. That's when a hard body presses into my back. Their scent isn't instantly recognizable, but I see why when I glance over my shoulder.

Finn.

"You look stunning, Raven," he purrs in my ear, and instead of goosebumps spreading over my skin with excitement, the hairs on the back of my neck stand on end.

"Thanks," I murmur, turning away from him. I'm hoping that will be enough to dismiss him, but his hands find my waist in the next breath as his body starts to move with mine.

I slow, not wanting his paws all over me, and take a deep breath. "I'd rather dance alone," I shout over the music as I look back at him, but his smile widens and the press of his dick nestles between my ass cheeks.

"Nobody ever wants to dance alone. Besides, I'll give you a good time," he insists, annoying the hell out of me as I come to a complete stop. Leila shuffles around to meet my eyes, her eyebrows pinching together as she sees the tension radiating from me at Finn's touch.

Spinning around, I come face to face with Finn, who smoothes the palms of his hands over the globes of my ass before I get a chance to whack his arms away. Shoving at his chest, he stumbles back a step, thankfully not taking me with him.

"I said no," I shout over the music, and he shakes his head.

"No, you didn't," he retorts, running his hands down his shirt as he glares at me.

He's technically correct. I didn't say *no* specifically, but what I did say meant the same thing. Any chance of explaining that to him is gone when Eldon stalks toward us with murderous purpose in his stride. He's not looking at me, though, he's focused on Finn and I know he's about to cause a scene.

Before I can think better of it, I eliminate the distance between Eldon and me before he can reach the asshole with a death wish.

"Hey," I gush, throwing my arms around his neck, and he comes to a complete stop, frozen at my touch. "Dance with me?" I flutter my eyelashes at him, praying that the rage burning in his eyes will dissipate.

He glances slowly from Finn to me and back again. "Fuck off before I add you to one of the mausoleums for laying hands on my girl."

I don't turn to see Finn's reaction but the way Eldon relaxes against me tells me his words did the trick.

"I need to sit down," Leila murmurs in my ear, and I move to take a step back from Eldon but he holds me tight against him. It's the complete opposite feeling of what I felt moments ago with Finn. My body is alive in his hands.

"Zane will take you to our table, Leila," Eldon explains, and she murmurs her thanks before disappearing with Zane.

"What if I want to sit down too?" I ask when it's just the two of us, despite the sea of people around us.

"You promised me a dance, Little Bird."

His fingers spread out at the base of my spine, holding me closer as our bodies move together. When I try to lower my hands, he quickly secures them around his neck again. Dancing no longer eases the tension I felt earlier. Now it bubbles beneath the surface, warped, different, infused with desire and need.

"I think it's time to take you home," Eldon murmurs after a while, my breath hitching at his lips against my ear.

Fuck.

"I have so much tension in my body. I need to get rid of it," I blurt, my body wrung tight, and he chuckles.

"I can sense it. Let me take you home." His voice gets huskier with every word, the meaning behind them making my thighs rub together, but I want to play with him first.

"I can't remember if I packed my favorite toy or not. Does a shop on site around here sell them?" The pearl shine and moon root is coursing through me, but it's too much fun to stop.

"You don't need a toy," Eldon states, leaning back to meet my eyes, and I grin.

"I do. It's not the same with only these." I waggle my fingers at him and he grabs my hand, slowly pressing his lips to each of my fingertips as he keeps his eyes fixed on mine. My heartbeat detonates, going off the charts as I scramble to breathe.

"Let me take care of you, Raven." He glances down at his watch before a sultry grin takes over his face. "Besides, it's after midnight, and you said I could have *anything I wanted today,* and what I want is to fucking taste you."

FALLING SHADOWS

FIFTEEN

Eldon

Holy fucking shit.

I can't get the feeling of her pressed up against me out of my head. Even as she walks beside me, my arm slung around her shoulders and her soft skin beneath my fingertips as I stroke her arm.

She's addicting and I need my fix. Then I might calm down. But hell, I wasn't joking earlier when I first saw her in the outfit Leila chose. My cock was going to burst and my pleas for her not to go anywhere dressed like that were real. I haven't been able to take my eyes off her since and now that I've had my hands on her...there's no coming back from that. I know Brax, Creed, and Zane have tracked her every move as well, but they wouldn't all admit to it.

I think Zane would acknowledge it instantly, and Creed too, if I pushed at the protective angle he clearly has over her, but Brax would turn to stone with denial. He doesn't let anyone get close enough for that, Raven included. It doesn't mean I can't sense his attention is piqued, and it's not just because she revealed she's a Void.

None of that matters for now, though. Right now, she's all mine. I somehow managed to convince the others to escort Leila home, giving me a few moments alone with her.

Pulling her in a little tighter, I inhale her sweet citrusy scent. "Next time, we won't have this ridiculous walk inconveniencing us," I murmur into her hair, and she snickers.

"You think there's going to be a next time?" Tilting her head back, she looks up at me with the most carefree expression I've seen her wear so far. She's almost serene, offering me a glimpse of the woman beneath the layers of walls she's strategically placed around herself.

"Absolutely," I retort, not doubting the inevitable. Even if I do want to get her out of my system, it's clear this mysterious new girl that has stumbled into our lives has wormed her way under my skin.

"Are you always this sure of yourself?"

"Yup."

She grins, shaking her head at me, but we both know she's not surprised with how cocky I am by now. "You know I'm attracted to the others, too, right?"

My brows rise in surprise, but not at the fact itself, more so that she's admitting it so readily. "Obviously, Little Bird," I mutter with a wink. "You're not as discreet as you think you are when checking us out."

Even though all we have is moonlight and sporadic lighting along the path guiding our way home, I can still make out the blush tinging her cheeks. She's badass *and* adorable. Why is that so hot?

Following the path to the left, our steps slow a little, even though the house isn't far away now.

"So what's this about?" she asks.

"What's *what* about?"

She rolls her eyes at me like I should know what she means, but I'm at a loss.

"What has you walking me home and promising me a good time?"

"I want to taste you," I reiterate, but it's clearly not enough when she continues to stare me down. "Little Bird, I would have tasted you the other day after I had the pleasure of your lips on mine, but you ran. I *can* be patient." The memory of that moment, the taste of her lips, her back against the wall and the desire I felt all comes back in an instant. The vision makes the same feelings zap through my body every time.

"Is it because I'm a Void? Do you want to see if that somehow makes me taste different?" I balk at the absurdity of her question, speechless to answer her as we turn down our path. When we reach the door, I don't move to unlock it as I turn to face her.

"Did your head really go there?"

"Yeah," she admits with a sigh, ducking her gaze, but I reach for her chin, tilting her face back to mine.

"Pull your head back from wherever the fuck it went because that is the dumbest shit I've ever heard. Did I know you were a Void when I kissed you the other day?" Her mouth pops open but I push on before she can say a word. "Did I know you were a Void when I jacked off in the shower over you? Dreamt about your pretty pink folds? Imagined what it would feel like when your body spasms from the orgasm I wring from your limbs? Hmm?" I step closer, forcing her head back a little more as I loom over her. My body craves to reach out and take her here and now but I need to get through the walls surrounding her thoughts before this goes any further. "I can't hear you, Raven," I add when she just blinks up at me.

"No." A whoosh of air leaves her lungs as she shakes her head.

"Good. Before we step inside, are there any other crazy reasons why you're trying to stop this from happening?"

She leans back with a frown. "I'm not."

Bullshit.

Loosening my hold on her chin, I inch closer, making

her step back until she's pressed against the door, and cage her in with my arms.

"You've tried to scare me off with the fact that you like my best friends too. We're the Bishops for a reason, Little Bird. We're brothers through and through. If I lined them up here in front of you now, they would all claim the same about you. So that's never going to be an issue. Then you come at me with the fact that you're a Void and I really couldn't give a shit about anything other than desperately wanting to know how sweet you taste. Now, is there anything else we need to discuss?"

Her jaw grows slack and she opens and shuts her mouth a few times before managing a breath. "Nothing."

Thank fuck for that.

Reaching around her, I unlock the door, holding her to me so she doesn't fall backward. Her feet dangle off the floor as I move us inside and shut out the world around us. Without a word, I take up the exact same spot by her bedroom door where we were the last time she let me this close. With a grin, I press my palms against the wall on either side of her head.

"Now that's all cleared up, can I kiss you?" My pulse thunders in my ears, desperately waiting for her response.

"Eldon, I'm shocked you're even ask—"

I crush my lips against hers, effectively interrupting the snark. I'm already a raging inferno and her skin against mine only makes me hotter. The press of her palms against my chest, her tongue dancing with mine, fighting for dominance, and her scent leaves me hanging by a thread.

Cupping her face in my hands, I raise her head as I press closer to her. The swell of her breasts against my chest, even with the material between us, makes me hiss. I hold her face with one hand, lowering the other to graze over her thigh, blindly finding the hem of her dress.

"Do you want me to taste you right here, Little Bird, where they could walk in or—"

"Oh, we're already here now. There's no need to stop on our account." Zane's comment whips our gazes toward the front door where the three of them stand.

I feel the muscles in Raven's thigh clench as she takes them in, but when I look at her, it's not fear or embarrassment in her eyes. It's arousal.

"Do you like an audience, Raven?" I whisper against her ear, trailing my hand toward her inner thigh, slowly making my way to her core.

"I don't know what you're talking about," she whispers, breathless and peering at me from the corner of her eye, but it's at that exact moment I feel just how fucking wet she is and there's no denying it. She knows it, too, if the way she sucks in a breath is any indication.

Resting my forehead against her temple, I slip my fingers underneath her panties and tease her drenched folds. She stifles a groan, but it's still music to my ears as I circle her clit.

"Do you want me to stop, Raven? Or do you like your audience?"

"Don't you fucking dare," she snaps back, her hands lifting to my arms to hold me in place as her nails bite into my skin.

Hot. As. Fuck.

Closing my eyes, I channel the tiniest bit of magic. Starting at my center and weaving it through my very essence to my fingertips.

"Oh my— Eldon," she gasps, whipping her head around to face me, and I smirk knowingly.

"Too much?"

She shakes her head viciously in response before I even finish asking. "N-No. Holy shit."

Heat radiates between us, my fingertips warmed by the fire magic that burns through my body and makes me who I am. "Do you like that, Little Bird? A heated pussy and an audience to watch you fall apart?" She nods, her nails digging deeper into my flesh as she holds on for dear life. "You're full of surprises."

"So are you." Her eyes roll to the back of her head as I press my thumb against her clit and tease two fingers at her entrance. I wait until her eyes are locked back on mine before I thrust deep into her core. The heat from my fingers is hit with molten lava as her pussy clamps around me.

My cock presses against the waistband of my jeans, desperate to feel the burn too, but none of this is about me. It's all about her—my newly claimed little bird.

"Please," she begs, her eyes hooded as she grinds against my hand. I rub my thumb over her engorged clit three times before she's bursting at the seams and coming apart at my hands. A low, long moan parts her lips as her back arches and her juices coat my fingers and trail down my wrist as I force the heat from my hands again.

I don't stop my movements until she is completely spent, fully aware that my friends are still observing, but I'm too caught up in her to worry about anyone or anything else.

Stroking my thumb over her cheek, I lift my hand from her core and bring it to my lips. Her release glistens on my fingertips and she watches my every move as I bring them to my mouth. Ecstasy explodes along my tongue, almost taking me to another world as my dick threatens to spill my own release in my pants.

As if sensing the need in my cock, Raven reaches out her hand and feels my rigid length through my jeans. I see the decision in her eyes and watch as she starts to lower to her knees but I stop her before she can go any further.

"Not tonight, Little Bird. This is all about you," I breathe, my cock pulsing even harder at the delayed gratification.

The corner of her mouth tips up as she lifts an eyebrow at me. "If it were about me, you would give me what I want."

"Holy fuck," Zane grunts from his position by the front door, making her smile grow wider.

"When my cock parts your lips and pussy, Raven, there won't be an ounce of liquor in your system to make you second guess yourself."

Her eyes widen before a pout puckers her lips. "I'm not under any influence." She squeezes my cock through the denim separating us and I almost fucking weep.

"You're still tipsy. When I make you mine, that won't be the case."

"Who said anything about making me yours?"

A door slams in the distance and I know without looking that Brax is no longer there. Crowding Raven's space again, our noses brush as I stare her dead in the eyes.

"One taste won't ever be enough of you, Raven. Consider your taste on my tongue a show of *me* being *yours.*"

SIXTEEN

Raven

The cusp of my dream escapes me as I seep back into reality. Stretching out my limbs, I yawn. My muscles ache in the best possible way as the feeling of contentment welling in my gut extends throughout my body.

Memories of last night flood my mind, reminding me where the feeling of serene calmness is coming from.

Eldon. Audience. Orgasm…

Rejection?

Was it rejection? I don't know, but I do know I was desperate to taste his cock and he refused. Yet he declared that he was mine with my essence still on his tongue. I'm so confused. The calmness I was basking in moments ago is depleting as I spiral.

"I can literally hear your brain ticking from here."

I startle, rolling to face the direction of the voice, but it all happens so quickly that I'm tumbling from the bed with a squeak before I can catch myself.

"Ahh, shit," I hiss, rubbing my hip as Eldon peers down from the bed at me with a grin. His eyes rake over me from head to toe and I remember that I'm only wearing an oversized tee and panties. Which means my pebbled nipples are visible through the material and he's enjoying the view.

Crossing my arms over my chest, I glare at him. "Why are you in my room?"

He lies down on his front, offering me his hand as I continue to stare at him. "Because I didn't want you to wake up and decide to hide out in here for the rest of the day."

"I wouldn't."

"Tell me that's not what you were just thinking about when you woke up," he retorts, raising a brow at me, and I shrug. "You're that predictable, Raven."

"I am not." I bristle, still sitting on the floor like I'm not wishing to bury my head in my sheets and hide away from him.

"Maybe not to everyone else, but to me, it's like I already know you." He grins like it all makes perfect sense while I feel more confused than I did moments ago. Why would he say that? He barely knows me, just as I barely know any of them. "Come on, let's go discuss all of the things we have going on like grown-ups." He stands beside me, offering me his hand again. This time, I take it.

"I don't want to be a grown-up." I huff as I climb back to my feet. "What do we even have to discuss?"

He turns to face me, hands falling to my waist as he crowds my space, and I finally notice that he's in a pair of black shorts and nothing else. Sweat clings to his temple, his hair brushed back off his face, and the veins in his arms protrude as if he's just finished a workout.

Damn, that's hot. And distracting. *Very* distracting.

"Remember, Raven. Today is still our day. Which means I get whatever I want, just like you promised. But as much as I would like to dive beneath the sheets with you, you also promised the others, and *they* insist on learning more about this Void business."

Fuck, I forgot about that.

Sighing, I nod toward the door. "Fine, let's get this over with."

I move to step around him, but his grip on my waist tightens. "We're not going anywhere until you kiss me though. Show me last night was real."

My eyes widen. Who the hell is this guy? He went from zero to asshole to the man before me and I'm not sure if I'm struggling with whiplash or the swoon factor.

Clearing my throat, I subtly shake my head. "I told you, your friends are hot too."

"And I told you I don't care. Sharing is caring in these four walls, Raven. The quicker you learn that, the more fun we'll have." His gaze cuts to my mouth as I drag my tongue along my bottom lip.

Sharing is caring? Share me? Is that even a possibility? My thighs clench with excitement at the thought and I irritate myself with how easily distracted I am. A lot is happening around me and I'm more concerned about getting some dick.

"You're jumbling my thoughts." I press my fingers into my temples as a headache threatens to consume me.

Eldon places his finger under my chin and tips my head back slightly. "Stop overthinking everything and it will go away." His lips descend on mine in a soft caress and my hands drop to his chest. My heart lurches as I forget to breathe, my body warming from his touch. All too soon, he pulls back, leaving me chasing after his lips, and he smirks. "So fucking addicting," he mutters before grabbing my hand and pulling me toward the door.

I'm nowhere near ready to leave my room to see Zane, Creed, and Brax spread out on the sofas. I expect to see tainted looks after what transpired last night, but they're looking at me the same as usual. The issue is they're all shirtless like Eldon and I can't be trusted with all the hotness on display.

Zane leans forward, bracing his arms on his knees as

his gaze trails over me from head to toe. "Whose t-shirt is that?"

My eyebrows pinch in confusion as I glance down.

"Uh, it's one I brought with me."

"Has it always been yours?"

I look back at him, noting the frown taking over his face. Why does any of this even matter?

"Uhh, no. What are you getting at?"

Creed cocks a brow at me, waving his hand in my direction. "Who did it belong to?"

I feel the muscles in my face drop as I slowly start to understand where this is going. Lying isn't my thing, so I tell them the truth.

"I think I kept it from a guy I used to be friends with."

"Friends as in 'let's braid each other's hair,' or friends like 'let me stick my dick in you'?" Creed pushes, and I feel my cheeks heat. I can't actually remember who it belonged to, if I'm honest, but it was definitely option two. Something tells me they'd only wind up dead if I did remember.

"Change," Brax blurts, eyes fixed on mine. His tone is deadly, catching me off-guard as I shake my head.

"What? No."

Before another word is even spoken, Eldon twirls his fingers in front of me, repeating the same magic Leila used, and the t-shirt I'm wearing transforms before my eyes. "There, you can wear one of mine," Eldon states, like it's completely okay to just change my outfit.

I whirl around to face him head-on, finger aimed at him, when a breeze brushes over my skin again and the t-shirt morphs before my very eyes.

"What the actual fuck is going on right now?"

"You can wear one of *mine*," Zane announces with a shrug. "Just don't ever wear another man's clothes again."

Gaping at him, I'm at a total loss for words. I don't know who to yell at first. Tearing my hand from Eldon's, I step back and glare at each of them.

"No more changing my fucking clothes without my say-so, assholes."

Brax leans back in his seat like I'm boring him. "So, who else knows you're void of magic?"

That's it? Conversation dismissed?

I purse my lips, considering whether I should continue to push my original argument or accept the change in subject. The fact that he doesn't outright call me a Void has me swinging in his favor.

"My mama knows. And I yelled it at Abel when he showed up out of the blue, forcing me to come here, but he didn't seem to think that was possible. Otherwise, it's mostly the people in Shadowmoor that are aware. Voids are common there and it's clear when you don't start using powers as soon as you turn eighteen if you are one or not."

"This has to be because of the suppression," Creed states as I let Eldon lead me to a free spot on the sofa.

"What do you mean?"

"You heard the lesson the other day, right? They purposely keep Shadowmoor in the dire state that it's in as a false front to ward off other realms. A lot of that is done by using some kind of magic or potion to suppress the inhabitants and the surrounding environment," Creed explains, but as much as it's making sense, it doesn't at the same time.

"What does that mean, though?"

"It means that you might not be void of magic," Brax clarifies, and my body freezes.

"How?" I breathe, too nervous to speak any louder as I look at him. Hope threatens to blossom inside of me but I tamp it back down, refusing to let myself feel it.

"I don't know, but not being in Shadowmoor could definitely be a big help," Eldon murmurs, throwing his arm around my shoulders. "Have you ever had any inkling or momentary feeling in your gut that you couldn't explain?

I consider his question for a moment, digging deep into my soul, hoping for a moment I know doesn't exist. "No."

The thought of magic running through me is all I used to dream about. It consumed my every waking breath until my eighteenth birthday rolled around and nothing came to me. Nothing has pained me more than realizing there was no magic in me, nothing to help me escape the world I was trapped in.

"But if Eldon's vision was right, there *is* something within you," Zane says so casually that it almost doesn't register.

"Wait, what?"

"Fuck, Zane. We said to keep your mouth shut," Brax admonishes, and I'm almost pleased to see him be irritated with someone other than me.

Turning my attention to Eldon, I immediately see the guilt in his eyes.

"I thought your magic was heat related." My cheeks warm at the memory of last night, the inferno burning from his fingertips as he watched me explode. He holds his hand out between us and a ball of fire appears just above his skin. I can feel the heat instantly.

"Fire is my nature-based magic, but I also have sight."

"You have two magical abilities?" Fuck, here he is with two and I can't even manage one.

Creed wasn't joking the other day when he explained some people have more than one ability.

"I'm assuming your sight has something to do with a vision?"

The ball of fire goes out in his hand as he shrugs. "I get them sometimes, but they're hard to decipher. It could be nothing."

"No, you said—"

"Shut. Up. Zane," Brax shouts, interrupting whatever he was about to say, and it pisses me off that they're keeping something hidden from me.

Zane sucks his bottom lip into his mouth, head down as he looks anywhere but at me, and I'm not surprised to find Creed avoiding my gaze too. Brax glares at me like it's all my fault while Eldon intently stares at me.

"It was a raven."

"For fuck's sake, Eldon, we agreed we weren't going to bring it up," Brax growls, his scathing glare turning toward his friend. Ignoring him, I grab Eldon's chin, just as he has with mine numerous times over the past twenty-four hours, and I draw his attention to me.

"As in the bird?"

"Yeah."

"What does that have to do with me?" A raven is a raven. I'm not stupid, but seeing a bird isn't the same as seeing a vision of me.

"It had pink feathers," he explains, pointing to my hair, and my eyes widen.

"Apart from the hair, what else made you think it has something to do with me?"

He rakes his teeth over his bottom lip, considering whether to answer or not. "Eldon, please. I'm already completely out of my depth here. If you want me to trust you at all, that will mean no secrets."

"There was a map and the raven's claw was placed on Shadowmoor." That could just be another coincidence, but my heart gallops like a herd of horses running free.

"What else?"

"Nothing." I can see the denial in his eyes.

"What else, Eldon? What else did the raven have or do that could possibly make you think it was me?"

He glances at his friends the second my hand drops to my lap.

"I don't know. I just know that in my vision, a war was coming, a war across realms, threatening all of existence. And the raven...she saved us all."

SEVENTEEN

Raven

With my hair braided back off my face and my uniform on, I'm ready for the week ahead. I've spent enough of the past weekend hiding away in here and I can't deny that I'm starting to go crazy. Avoiding the Bishops as much as possible after Eldon's revelations hasn't been as complicated as I thought it might be. If anything, they've given me the space I've silently asked for.

I've sat and had every meal with them, the conversations light and the complete opposite of any pink-feathered raven ready to save the world. Save the world? I couldn't save myself from drowning in a damn puddle at this point.

Grabbing my bag, I open my bedroom door as quietly as possible. As respectful as they may have been, I'm still hoping to tiptoe past them and sneak off with Leila this morning. To my surprise, the open living space is empty as I rush for the front door.

I don't look back as I let it click closed behind me, only to find all four of the Bishops outside, staring at me expectantly, with Leila grinning behind them.

"I told you she would try and sneak out," Creed states, a ghost of a smirk on his lips as Eldon chuckles.

Assholes.

"I wasn't doing anything at all."

"Of course you weren't." Zane hums with amusement. Everyone falls into step and I startle when his hand finds mine, lacing our fingers together.

I stare, dumbfounded, at where our hands are joined, trying not to stumble over my feet before meeting his gaze. "What's going on?" I keep my voice low as the rest of the group chats around us.

"You really do need to read the handbook, Raven," he says with a smirk, squeezing my hand, and my body tingles.

"This handbook is driving me insane. Why don't you just explain things to me?" I cock an eyebrow at him, internally berating myself for not reading the stupid thing already.

He shrugs. "It's more fun if you read it."

"There's no fun in reading unless it's inked porn," I say with a scoff, acutely aware that he's still holding my hand while other students start to join us on the pathway.

"Inked porn? Color me intrigued."

"It's the good stuff. The holy grail. The raw existence of slipping away from reality and escaping into another world. Sexy stories written by women, for women. Hot guys who know how to make a woman find ecstasy and look good doing it, even with their asshole tendencies. You don't find that in real life." I was going for the shock factor, but the smirk on his lips makes him appear unfazed.

"Fuck that bullshit about not finding it in real life. You just described me." Eldon's voice is so loud I almost blush from embarrassment over a game I started. "And don't you try to tell me otherwise or I'll be forced to give you a reminder of Friday night." He winks, making my cheeks heat as Leila grins at me.

"Girl, you got some explaining to do," she whisper-shouts, and I shake my head at both of them. I'm too speechless to come up with an excellent snarky response and find myself leaning into Zane, who squeezes my hand again.

The academy building comes into view, and the sound of the bell chiming echoes around us. Wordlessly, everyone picks up speed, heading for the courtyard for another gathering. As we enter the bustling, waiting crowd, I try to pull my hand from Zane's but he only holds it tighter.

"I feel like you're doing yourself a disservice

associating yourself with me." I look up at him, noting the frown that marks his forehead. I've never really walked around holding someone's hand before and I kind of like it, but with all the bullshit that's following me around already, I don't want to pull him under with me.

"I feel like you need to hold yourself in higher regard," he states, lowering his head slightly to murmur against my ear. As he speaks, my eyes lock on Genie, who glares at me from the front of the courtyard. The scathing look on her face could slay a man but I keep my chin high and shoulders back, refusing to wither under her gaze.

"Everyone is watching us."

"Nah, it's just Genie…" Zane explains, running his thumb over my knuckles. "Oh, nope, you're right. That's a lot of eyes," he adds when more and more people seem to turn in our direction. The two of us were leading the way for our group, but in an instant, Creed and Brax move in front of us as we stop. I can hear Leila and Eldon talking behind us like the four of them are standing guard.

Zane's hand flexes tighter around mine as I glance around Creed to see Genie still giving me her best death stare.

"Why is she mad at me for holding your hand if she was chasing Eldon?"

Zane nudges me forward a step and releases my hand, plastering my back to his front as his hands find my hips. I can't breathe. My body is so aware of his that I feel like I will fracture into a million pieces from the tension running between us.

He leans down to whisper in my ear, his soft lips brushing against my skin. "Because we didn't accept her. If you had read the handbook, you would know that when one of us is claimed, we all are. So when Eldon declared you had claimed him…"

I had claimed them all.

Holy. Fucking. Shit.

I'm hot all over. I definitely need to read the damn handbook.

The projection flickers in the sky and a few moments later, Professor Burton appears in a crisp white shirt and tailored suit with black-rimmed glasses framing his face. I'm in no state right now to listen to what he has to say but he starts despite the fact.

"Good morning, students."

"Good morning, Professor Burton," I mutter in sync with everyone else.

"We've had some changes arise this week, which means your usual timetables will not apply." He spreads his arms out wide, a touch of a smile on his lips, but it doesn't seem pleasant. "This week, we will have each year rotating in the Monster Gauntlet."

Gasps echo around me. People murmur over him

speaking for the first time since I've arrived. I don't know how this place operates yet, but something tells me this isn't the norm.

"If you're not in the Gauntlet, you will be spectating. Then on Friday, we will hold a celebratory banquet with families and The Monarchy in attendance." My body stiffens at the mere mention of family more than the fear of some gauntlet.

Zane pulls me even tighter against his chest as Eldon steps into my right side. Creed shuffles back to my left, positioning Leila in front of him while Brax moves back so far he's almost pressed against me.

"What don't I know?" I ask any of them, and it's Creed who turns to glance at me.

"The Monster Gauntlet is life or death, Raven."

I gape, eyes widening as Professor Burton repeats the same fucking mantra he does every time.

"Follow the sun, destroy the shadows, and survive another dawn."

"This is fucked and it makes no sense at all," Brax growls, swiping a hand down his face as we head toward the locker rooms. "First years haven't had a single lesson on honing our abilities, yet they want us to charge into the Gauntlet and survive? Whose idea was this?"

No one has an answer for him. Leila and the rest of the Bishops are seething just as hard as he is, but I'm used to bullshit being thrown my way. What difference is this?

"Move...out of my way...Leila?" My friend spins at the sound of her name and relief washes over her face. I turn to see who was calling her to find Professor Fitch with fury burning in his eyes.

"Papa?"

"Leila. Come. I am short on time," he barks.

"But my friends..." Her eyes dart to me, concern swirling in her irises, but I quickly wave her off.

"Go. Don't worry, I'll find you later."

She pauses for an extra beat but Professor Fitch pulls on her arm and she falls into step with him. Eldon throws his arm around my shoulders and steers me toward the locker room with everyone else.

"I can't believe Fitch is her father. They don't look anything alike."

"He's the reason she usually gets a lot of shit from people," Creed explains, making my eyebrows pinch.

"I heard. Why do they do that?"

"He's a harsh professor. Rightfully so, but some people don't like it. They seem to think this should be easy, like we're not offering our lives in sacrifice. When they can't give him a piece of their mind, they turn it toward Leila."

I gape at Creed.

"That's the dumbest shit I've ever heard."

"Almost as dumb as first years taking on the Monster Gauntlet," Brax snarks, and my gut twists. If he's mad about it, maybe I should be more concerned.

Life or death, Zane said. I faced that every day in Shadowmoor. A Monster Gauntlet, though? What kind of monsters are we talking about?

We arrive at the locker rooms before I can ask any of them. I slip out from under Eldon's arm and follow the girls inside. I'm sure I hear him call out my name but I don't stop. Emotion wells inside me and he will only draw it out of me.

Once inside, I startle at how much bigger it is compared to the last time I was here, but I immediately realize it's because it's accommodating more of us. The first, second, and third years are here. I'm not sure about the fourth-year students. When I find a free coat hook, I'm very aware of how close I am to Genie, but I keep my back to her and press my thumb to the tip the same way Leila showed me last time.

Quickly changing, I listen to the conversations happening around me. The uncertainty I felt from Leila and the Bishops echoes around the room. The biggest concern I'm hearing repeatedly is that we don't know what order the years are going in.

Would I rather be first and face my fate quicker to get it over with? Or would I rather watch everybody else beforehand? I've seen enough brutality in Shadowmoor that it no longer registers as entertainment, so I would rather go first, but the murmurs around me would suggest the opposite.

The hairs on my neck stand on end and I turn to find Genie behind me.

"Can I help you?"

Her eyes narrow at my question as she folds her arms over her chest.

"You can help yourself and stay the fuck away from what's mine."

I had a feeling something like this would happen after the way she stared at me in the courtyard, but a part of me thought she might be a little more worried about our fates instead. Apparently, she's more obsessed with the Bishops than I thought. Unluckily for her, I'm a hardcore petty bitch.

"I'm going to cut to the chase and assume you mean the Bishops, right?" She sneers at me as I take a step toward her. "They were never yours. The quicker you realize that, the easier all of this will be on you." I smile sweetly before shouldering past her. I count in my head, and when I get to three, her retaliation comes in the form of a fist in my ponytail.

"Listen here, bitch," she hisses, yanking me back as the room quiets. I drop my body and spin, just like I've done many times before, and drive my shoulder into her gut, making her stumble back.

Genie's hold on me loosens as her back hits the floor and I grin like a mad woman as I hover over her. "What did you say, *bitch?*" Her nostrils flare as she looks up at me.

Rising to my full height, I step back to let her stand. The girls move around me, creating a makeshift circle, but as soon as Genie is on her feet, a professor I haven't seen before steps between us.

"I don't care what your issues are; save your energy for what actually matters. If you're not ready, the Gauntlet will claim you without even caring for your name."

EIGHTEEN

Raven

Still biting my tongue to not react to Genie, I heed the professor's warning and follow everyone else outside. The girls seem to give me an extra wide berth but I don't take offense to it. Once we're through the doors, we mingle with the guys leaving their locker room all heading in the same direction.

A hand on my shoulder startles me and I turn back to see it's Creed.

"Don't startle me like that. I almost hit you," I grumble, falling into step with him as the others emerge from the crowd.

"What took so long in there?"

I roll my eyes. "Genie happened."

"What did she do?"

"Nothing. I can take care of myself," I reply, shaking

my head dismissively. I do not need these guys thinking I need their protection every moment of the day. I'm prepared for some backlash but, to my surprise, he lets it drop. "Where are we going for the Gauntlet?" I ask as the crowd moves outside.

"The arena."

Since when has there been an arena? I really need to explore this place instead of just bouncing between my room and class. Only knowing what falls in my direct path isn't giving me the upper hand, especially in comparison to how it was back in Shadowmoor. I had learned every trail, every hiding spot, every loose bit of pathing. All of it. But here, I seem to be in some kind of imaginary security blanket where none of that stuff matters.

If I survive this test, I need to change that.

The sea of people thins out a little as the pathway widens. I feel fingers brush against mine, and my body instinctively reacts, taking the hand at my right that my gut knows belongs to Zane. A quick glance in his direction confirms it and a pleased smile is evident on his face.

I have no idea what I'm doing, this isn't me at all, but I'm enjoying it too much to stop.

Veering to the left, my steps slow as a vast stone building comes into view at the end of the walkway. I try to recall if I've been down here before or not, but either way, it's standing obnoxiously in the middle of the grounds regardless of my memory of it.

"When we're in there, I need you to stay as close to us as possible. I don't anticipate them splitting us into genders, more likely year groups, so we can keep you safe," Creed murmurs against my ear. His voice is raspy, the resounding ripple like electricity zapping across my skin. Maybe it feels more intense because he seems the quietest out of the four of them.

"Keep me safe from what? I should be fine spectating. It's *in* the Gauntlet I should be most concerned, right?"

"You say that like you don't have targets on your back from both Sebastian and Genie. One of those is because of us and we won't let anything happen to you."

My eyebrows pinch in confusion, a refusal on the tip of my tongue, but we approach the open archway into the stone arena and I'm completely distracted.

A black dome replaces the bright-blue sky as we enter the arena. Torches burn every few feet, illuminating the entire space, and row upon row of tiered seats overlook the middle pit. When I move my head slightly, I notice an iridescent glow over it—an invisible mini dome hovers above the center, separating the action from the spectators.

"First years to the right. Second years to the left, and third years make your way to the bottom, go around the dome and fill the middle block of seating." I have no idea

KC KEAN

where the instructions are coming from, but I follow their order.

Zane tightens his hold on my hand, leading the way as Creed remains closer to my back. I search the crowd, hoping to see Leila, but she's nowhere to be found. Worry forms in my gut but I cling to the fact that she was with her father. She'll be okay.

Coming to the end of a row, Zane takes the next available seat and I drop down beside him. Creed shuffles into my left side while Eldon leaps forward and takes a spot directly in front of me.

"Move." I turn at the grunt that falls from Brax to find him stepping up onto the higher row behind us. He shoves the guy to the side who was sitting behind me and takes his seat. He doesn't look at me, his scowl firmly in place as he looks down at the pit.

Rubbing my lips together, I decide not to question what's going on and focus on the pit too. Beneath the iridescent dome, there's a large rock formation, a sandy floor, and a small puddle in the left corner. There's no hint of what lurks inside, what we'll have to face, offering the first person up no chance to prepare.

"How are we supposed to survive this thing?" I ask, smoothing my hair back off my face with one hand since Zane won't let go of the other one.

"The whole point of the Monster Gauntlet is to give

students a chance to use their magic in different scenarios. One, to strengthen their connection with their abilities, and two, to weed out those that aren't going to protect the realm the way The Monarchy deems fit," Creed explains, and my heart stings with the reality.

This is to weed me out. Get rid of me. A Void is no use at all to The Monarchy. Why would my father force me to come here, despite my insistence on what I am? If he was just trying to off me, that would have happened in Shadowmoor eventually. He didn't have to go to these extremes.

As if sensing the stress swirling inside my head, Zane nudges me with his shoulder to gain my attention. "Nothing is going to happen to you. We've got time to come up with a plan."

It's on the tip of my tongue to debunk his hopes when a flicker appears above the pit and the entire space grows silent. A slamming sound echoes around the room and I turn to find the entrance sealed off. A feeling of dread instantly rises, especially from the first years surrounding us.

"Students, I hope you are excited for the week ahead." Professor Burton appears above the dome and I wonder if I'll ever actually see him in real life, or will he remain a projection forever? "Let's not waste any more time and get straight to it, shall we? We're going to begin the Gauntlet with the third years. Since they have experience in here, they can show our first and second years how it's done. Or not, in some cases." The smile that spreads across his face at the mention of people's failures makes my gut sink. "Good luck. Follow the sun, destroy the shadows, and survive another dawn."

"Follow the sun, destroy the shadows, and survive another dawn." When the students around me echo his words, I notice for the first time that Creed and Zane don't join them.

The eery silence that draws out around us is palpable, pulling my intent gaze from them as I hear a girl's name being called out.

"Taryn Bracken, please make your way down to the entrance of the pits."

Murmurs echo around me, everyone seeking out the first unfortunate soul to be summoned. When she wades her way through the crowd of third years and down the steps, a few of the third years clap for her, but most of them sit in silence, ready to observe either her triumph or demise.

She's not someone I recognize but still, concern wars inside of me.

I can't help but compare anything and everything to Shadowmoor in my head. Back home, I felt no sympathy or concern for anyone. It was a dog-eat-dog world and everyone was trying to survive. In comparison, this feels barbaric. We're getting ready to be slaughtered by the system.

Zane pulls my hand into his lap as warmth spreads across my left thigh where Creed's hand rests. "From what I've heard, the monster remains the same for everyone. It's only Taryn that has the surprise," Creed explains, and I nod, too caught up in where both of them touch me while also trying to give my full attention to the pit.

A professor murmurs in Taryn's ear for a moment and I can just about make out her nodding in response before she closes her eyes and steps through the barrier protecting the pit. My heart starts to race as I watch her every move. The torches dim, lowering the outer glow of the arena as the domed pit seems to brighten.

She takes a few steps across the sand before climbing some of the boulders. It's unbelievable how much you don't notice the actual size of the pit until someone is in it. It's almost like a small town. You could easily fit a few dozen houses the size of the one I lived in back at Shadowmoor in there, if not more. The boulders become small hills and rocky peaks as she starts to climb, occasionally stopping to glance around in hopes of catching a glimpse of what lurks inside.

It feels like an eternity passes and nothing happens, making my nerves draw tight as the anticipation rises inside of me. A tap on my shoulder is followed quickly by Brax's voice in my ear.

"The water."

My gaze flicks to where the puddle was earlier, only to find a rising tide.

Holy shit.

Taryn hasn't noticed it yet and if anyone else has, they don't call it out to her. My pulse rings in my ears as anticipation burns through me, yet nothing reveals itself. She reaches the top of the rock formation, crouching as she turns to get a good view of what lies below. As she turns toward the water, she freezes instantly, and a soft hum begins to fill the air.

Sitting taller in my seat, I shuffle forward so far my knees bump into Eldon, but he just leans back against me as I try to place the tune. I don't recall hearing it before, I'm sure, but it's enticing, alluring, and captivating nonetheless.

Hands clamp down on either side of my face, covering my ears, and my face is twisted to look at Zane. *"It's a siren,"* he mouths, the intriguing melody muffled as his eyes scrunch together.

It takes me a second to realize he's covering my ears to sacrifice his own and I quickly reach up to replace his hands with mine, but he refuses to budge. Glaring at him, it goes unnoticed as his eyes remain tightly shut, so I do the only other thing I can think of and cover his ears with my palms.

A few beats pass before he slowly blinks his eyes open. My heart is racing in my chest and I can't fully decipher if it's from everything happening around me or the fact that he just protected me over himself.

His gaze is locked on mine, his shoulders rising and falling rapidly with every breath he takes. I'm staring at his lips, mesmerized by how full they are, when a gasp echoes loudly around us, pulling us apart.

Protecting my ears with my hands, I turn to the pit to see the source of the sound swimming through the crystal clear waters that have risen close to where Taryn is standing.

For a monster, she sure looks beautiful. Long pink fins for legs, hip-length blonde hair cascading in curls in every direction as her bright red lips open wide for her melody to consume us.

She bursts through the water's surface, startling Taryn, who stumbles back, losing her footing on the boulder, but she manages to stop herself from tumbling off it completely.

I press my palms deeper into my skull, the tune getting louder, and watch in horror as Taryn slowly gathers herself to her feet. All of the tension and panic is gone as she walks toward the water's edge instead of trying to rush away from it.

"What is she doing?" I gasp, even though no one can hear me, and a hand clamps down on me from behind.

Whipping my gaze behind me, I frown when I notice Brax isn't covering his ears. They're a stone gray color, just like his hand was the other day. What is that about? I need to ask, but I focus on what he's saying instead.

"Don't look."

Why wouldn't I look? He raises his eyebrow, demanding I listen to him, but it's too hard to refrain from knowing what comes next.

I turn at the exact same time a gut-wrenching scream burns from Taryn's lips. The siren's beauty is gone, in its place are rows and rows of sharp teeth covering her face as it takes bite after bite out of Taryn's flesh.

Gaping in horror, I lean back, desperately wanting to escape the awful sight. I should have listened to Brax. Holy shit.

Taryn's body goes lax as the siren drags her around like a doll before plunging back into the depths of the water with her. The water level drops all at once until only a small pool remains in the left corner again. I take three breaths before I realize the melody has stopped and chaos breaks out around me.

"What the fuck, Raven? I told you not to look," Brax snarls, and I turn to him.

That's not...

I'm not...

"I'm going to die," I choke, fear coating every inch

of me.

I can hear everyone else gasping and screaming with shock around me, but my gaze remains locked on Brax's, praying for him to give me some kind of answer.

"You're not going to die, Little Bird," Eldon states. I hear his voice but it doesn't penetrate through the fog clouding my judgment.

I walked in here thinking I could take on the world, just like I had in Shadowmoor, but nothing like that existed there. How can I save myself in the pit with no magical abilities against a fucking siren?

"I'm going to die," I repeat, wondering how I ever thought I was a strong person to begin with.

A hand grips my chin, tilting my head until I face Creed. "You. Are. Not. Going. To. Die. We won't let that happen, Raven."

At a loss for words, I nod, despite not believing him one bit.

"Thank you, Taryn. Next up, we have Sebastian Hendrix."

My eyes widen at the mention of my brother's name and I spin to face the pit. Creed's hand drops from my face as I watch my smug sibling saunter down the steps where the third-years are seated.

"Don't worry, I'll show you all how it's done," he hollers, earning a few giggles from some of the third-year girls while the rest of us gape at him.

Is it wrong to want to watch him meet his demise so that he can eat his fucking words?

"I hate your brother," Zane mutters, and I nod.

"Same."

He barely speaks to the Professor waiting at the pit, entering immediately. Instead of climbing straight to the top of the peak like Taryn did, he keeps low, eyes fixed on the water level.

I hate how much you can tell he knows what he's doing. I hate that he's skilled at this. I hate that he's still the asshole he always has been instead of a caring and supportive brother who could guide me through this mess.

He's the enemy. That's not going to change.

I notice the water level rise instantly, but so does he. The water doesn't immediately rise high like it did when Taryn was in there, it stops about knee-deep, and he seems to take that as his cue to sneak closer. He's hiding behind a boulder when a flash of blonde hair peeks out above the water, revealing the siren, and her melody quickly floats through the air once more.

Before I can plant my hands over my ears, Brax does it for me. This time saying nothing as I watch everything unfold. Sebastian presses his back against the rock, holding his arms out before him. His palms are turned inward, aimed at each other, and a bolt dances from one hand to the other.

My heart lurches, my chest aching as I try to breathe.

He has Mama's magic. He has her magic, and I have nothing.

Another zap and a crackle buzzes between his palms as he glances around the rock at the searching siren, who is looking around in confusion for him. Before the monster can locate her prey, Sebastian spins from behind the rock and thrusts his hands in her direction. Thunder rumbles around the room as a zap of lightning hits the water, making the siren scream in pain before the bolt hits her directly.

The water disappears completely, the siren along with it, and the unmistakable rupture of applause consumes the room as Sebastian throws his hands up in the air in victory.

Motherfucker.

Brax removes his hands from my ears as my pulse throbs so prominently I'm sure my eardrums are going to burst.

Somehow, Sebastian manages to find me in the crowd and a smile spreads across his face as he makes a show of slicing his hand over his neck. I don't react. I just stare him down.

He's not wrong. Not one bit.

He's the winner and I'm about to sign my life away to a cause I don't even understand.

NINETEEN

Zane

Monday passed in a blur. Tuesday saw the third years finish and the second years take to the pits. They dwindled into Wednesday, rounding out the day with the final second-year student dying at the hands of the pit, and now it's Thursday, also known as first-year day.

With every passing moment, the anticipation among the first years has only grown. But today, sitting around the pit like we have every other day this week, it feels even more heavy and fearful.

"Janica Feron, Victor Walton, and Rufus Meadows." Professor Burton reads out the last of the students who didn't make it out of the pits yesterday.

This Gauntlet has cost more lives than I expected and the amateurs haven't even had a turn yet. Thirteen third years are dead. Just like that. And nineteen second years, bringing our death toll to thirty-two. I get the feeling it will be over fifty by the time we're done. The years prior to us have had far more training with their magic than we have and we're expected to compete at their level.

It's surreal.

Professor Burton rambles his usual shit before spouting the same line he ends with every time he talks. I won't repeat it. I never have. I don't really understand what he means by it and I sure as hell am not chanting random words for the sake of it.

His projection disappears and the professor at the pit starts to rattle off some details. The pool of water at the far left of the pit keeps capturing my attention as I try to imagine what it will feel like to be in there with a siren. Every time one has been destroyed, another is summoncd in its place—a deadly, never-ending cycle.

If I never see another scaled beauty in my life, it will still be too soon.

Raven's thigh brushes against mine, pulling me from my thoughts. She's murmuring about something with Leila, who sits on her other side. Brax is behind Raven again, Creed in front of her, and Eldon on the other side of Leila. It's weird suddenly spreading ourselves out like this to protect someone, but it's also the most natural thing I've ever done.

I can't explain the how or why; if I asked the others,

I'm sure they would be as confused as I am.

My hand instinctively moves to Raven's knee, my thumb brushing back and forth over her ridiculously soft skin. She peers up at me with a faint smile before returning her attention to her friend until the professor by the pits speaks.

"First years, the final two days of the Gauntlet are now for you, and we're going to begin with…" She looks down at the paper in her hands, trailing her finger over the sheet as everyone holds their breath. "Eldon Rhodes."

"What? No," Raven whispers with a gasp, her body stiffening as she turns to look at Eldon, just as everyone else in the arena does.

He stands, a smirk plastered on his face as it always is as he leans over Leila to grab Raven's chin, and then his lips are claiming hers. Lucky fucker. Raven is left gaping at him as he retreats and saunters down the steps like he doesn't have a care in the world.

Raven's hand falls to my lap and I place my hand on top of hers as her breaths come in short and shallow gasps.

"You've got this, Eldon. I love you."

I frown, as does Raven, until Leila points a few rows ahead of us. "It's Genie."

As expected, I find her making a spectacle of herself as she tries for Eldon's attention.

He doesn't even glance in her direction as he searches

out Raven again. With a quick wink, he points at her before heading around the domed pit to where the professor waits.

Peeking at Raven at my side, I find her cheeks rosy-pink and it makes me grin.

What I would do to keep a constant blush on her face.

Raven's nails dig into my thigh through my shorts as we all watch Eldon enter the pit. "I can't breathe," she whispers, fear swirling in her eyes.

"He's got this, Raven. Don't worry. I swear," I soothe.

"Asking me not to worry is like asking a bird not to fly or the sun not to shine."

I have nothing that will work as a response to that, so I clutch her hand and bring her knuckles to my lips instead. Brax's hand finds her shoulder and Creed reaches his hand behind him to find her leg, each of us touching her. I'm not sure if it's for her comfort or ours. Likely the latter.

Eldon remains on the sandy ground between the boulders and rocks, following the same idea that all of the survivors have. My leg starts to bounce with nerves as Eldon presses against a rock to check the water and, sure enough, as if sensing his glance, it starts to rise.

"Fuck. Fuck. Fuck," Raven chants, nails forever marking my flesh as she grips my thigh in fear.

The water level stops at Eldon's knees before the telltale melody drifts around us. Lifting my hands to my ears, Raven does the same, giving my leg some much-needed relief as a flash of red hair floats through the water.

Brax's hand remains on her shoulder and I instantly hate that he doesn't have to cover his ears like the rest of us. Asshole.

I spot the moment Eldon sees the flash of hair too, locating the siren as she starts to drift toward him. He flicks a fireball in his hands, once, twice, and on the third time, his whole body turns red. The water starts to bubble around him, his body heat quickly increasing the water temperature, and an almighty cry reverberates from the siren as she leaps from the water.

Rows and rows of teeth contort her face, attack mode activated, and as she launches through the air at Eldon, he aims the fireball in her direction. In one clean throw, she's a roaring inferno of flames as they lick across her skin and draw pain from her soul.

The siren evaporates into nothing as the water level lowers once more and Eldon throws his hands up in triumph.

"Ah, shit," Raven gripes, wiping a hand down her face. "I was so worried about his safety. I didn't actually consider how much of an obnoxious winner he would be."

Students cheer around the colosseum, celebrating the first first-year to successfully make it through the gauntlet. I either succeed too and have to listen to his rambling about how awesome he is, or I let the siren take me instead.

I can't decide which might be worse. But the fact that there's hope for us all is the only thing that matters.

Student after student steps into the pit as it continues to claim lives. Sixteen people have entered since Eldon succeeded, or "slayed that bitch" if we're using his words, and five didn't make it out. I do not like those odds, especially when the woman sitting beside me, who has officially captured every inch of my attention, has no magical abilities to protect her.

Many of those who aren't making it out have psychic or divination magic, which puts Raven at bad odds, and it messes with my head.

Genie surprised us all with her nature-based telekinesis abilities, though. It did take a few attempts but, much to my dismay, she managed to dislodge a boulder and successfully aim it at the siren.

Lunch passed far too quickly and now we're reseated as the professor runs her pointed nails over the script of names again.

"Next up will be Leila Fitch."

She squeezes Raven's hand as she stands. Her nerves are so shot that I can practically feel it in the air. The worry from Raven increases again and she nibbles on her bottom lip as she watches her friend head down the stairs.

Professor Fitch meets her at the bottom, draping his arm around her shoulders as he walks her to the waiting professor. She wrings her hands out as she nods at whatever they're saying to her and, just like that, she steps through the protective barrier.

Eldon shuffles closer to Raven and I offer her my hand. The four of us silently try to give her the support she needs.

It feels like time moves in slow motion as I will the siren to appear and get this shit show over with. This time, her hair is brown when she appears in the rising water, and Leila stiffens in her spot in the sand.

Gaping in horror with her mouth wide, she doesn't move, losing the opportunity to react quickly and catch the siren off guard.

"Move, Leila. Fucking move," Raven hisses under her breath, but, as expected, it does nothing and the siren's melody dances through the air. Once again, my hands lift to my ears, but the tune becomes stilted as the water rises to Leila's knees.

The tune gets quieter and quieter until it stops altogether. "What's happening?" Brax murmurs from behind, and I shrug, just as bewildered as he is.

"Look at the water," Creed points out, briefly glancing back at us before returning his attention to the pit.

It takes a second for me to understand what he means

but, ever so slowly, the water begins to cloud. "She's freezing it," I murmur. "The siren along with it."

I'm not entirely sure Leila realizes what she's doing, but it seems her frozen state is aided by her ability to... freeze?

"Shatter it, Leila," Professor Fitch growls from the outskirts of the pit, and his voice seems to break whatever trance she's under. Her hands clench at her sides, speeding up the freezing process, and the water turns to solid ice except for where she stands.

Leila lifts her hands in the air, spreading them wide before clapping. The boom that echoes from the motion is astounding as the ice splinters into millions of shards and explodes around her. The pit becomes a snow-dome before our eyes and Fitch heaves a sigh of relief I didn't realize we were all holding.

Raven claps as Leila rushes back up the stairs with a dazed look on her face. She's barely sat down when the professor calls the next student.

"Zane Denver."

Well, shit.

Turning to Raven, I smile, despite the panic flashing in her wide eyes. If I fuck this up, I want her to be the last thing I see. Lifting my hand, I cup her cheek. My body stiffens when she leans into my touch and lust floods my brain as I move toward her, delicately pressing my lips against hers.

She responds instantly, prompting my dick to come to life, and now really isn't the time for that. I pull away, despite my reluctance, and stand.

Adrenaline pumps through my system as I make my way down the steps. I can feel all eyes on me as I come to a stop beside the organizing professor.

"Mr. Denver. Be safe," she says with a tight smile and waves toward the pit. Excellent, like those are the last words I want to hear. There are no words of wisdom or hint of encouragement before I'm sent into the pits of Hell. I don't know how I keep my lips locked tight and snark to myself, but I turn and step into the pit.

A weird sensation ripples through my body as I pass through the barrier.

I let my instincts take over as the sand sinks slightly beneath my feet. The water teases me from my right, like it's not hiding a monster intent on devouring me. As Eldon did, I keep on the ground, my fingers flexing at my sides as I test the connection to my magic. I'm blessed with two abilities. Divination is my primary skill, which should work in my favor, so my secondary skill may not be needed.

Taking cautious steps, I'm acutely aware of the crowd watching me and I hate that they get a glimpse at my magic. It's private, personal, yet they're making us put on a show for everyone to see.

I instantly hear the trickling of water as I round a boulder, stunned by how fucking big it is. Glancing around the edge, I check the water levels before I rush to the next formation. By the time I'm in my calculated position, the water is past my ankles and the sound of the siren's song starts to flood my senses. I don't have long to act if I don't want her music to capture me, but I can't press my hands to my ears while trying to defend myself.

Curling my fingers, I focus on the larger rocks, testing the weight of them against my magic. Too heavy. Fuck. Genie risked it with a smaller one, and I don't like those odds.

My brows furrow as the music gets more challenging to fight off and I catch a glimmer of purple hair before it breaks through the water's surface. She's attacking quicker than the others did. I don't have much time.

Her big blue eyes and full pink lips don't hold their form for long and I watch in horror as her face transforms before me.

Move, Zane.

Curling my hands tight, the boulder nudges but doesn't dislodge at my attempt. Fuck. Shaking my hands out, I try again, my brain ready to splinter in two to give in to the tempting siren's tune and it's all too much.

Pain rips from my arm down to my fingertips and

across my chest, searing deep into my veins as the Siren gets her teeth into me.

The gasp from the crowd echoes in my ears as I close my eyes and focus on my secondary ability. My arm throbs, but the grip on my limb softens before I fall to the floor in a heap. The melody around me stutters as I glance down at myself. A second round of gasps bounce around the arena and I hate that I've revealed myself. Well, my magic, anyway.

My *self* is a different story.

I'm not there. I don't exist. Only my mind and thoughts as my body becomes invisible to the naked eye. I don't know how long I have before she realizes I'm still here, still a threat to her, and I need to act quickly.

Agony ripples down my arm as I poise my hands in front of me, biting back a grunt as I focus on the rocks once again. It moves a little easier this time but it still takes three attempts to get it completely dislodged. I'm using so much force now that it goes hurtling through the air, crashing into the siren without any further effort.

I stand frozen in place, waiting for the telltale sign that the siren is gone—when the water disappears. My breath is lodged firmly in my throat until the water level slowly drops.

Zane.

Creed's voice in my mind has me releasing the

secondary magic clinging to me and my body reappears before the crowd. My gaze instantly lands on Raven's, her pink hair like a beacon in the mass of people.

Cheers erupt but I don't feel like a winner as I head for the outer ring of the pit. I'm injured, sure. I can get over that. But people knowing I can turn invisible, better than I can use telekinesis to move shit, feels like a loss to me.

TWENTY

Raven

I can't breathe. My body is coiled so tight with tension I think I'm going to pass out. I might be the first to die from just *watching* the Gauntlet. I'm sure of it. Sweat beads at my temple as I watch Zane enter the pit, taking a piece of me with him.

One minute he's trying to channel his magic; the next, the siren is sinking her heinous teeth into his shoulder. I choke on my breath, my hands dropping from my ears as horror consumes me. And then he's gone.

Just…gone.

Invisible. He went in-fucking-visible.

I'm almost one hundred percent sure that I've imagined the whole thing until the boulder sweeps through the air and claims the siren's life. Time stands still, my world spinning as the pit starts to reset itself. The water slowly recedes, the siren defeated, and just as quickly as he disappeared, Zane reappears before everyone.

A roar of shock, surprise, and triumph echoes through the crowd. The tense look on Zane's face as he looks at the spectators tells me he's not happy and I get the feeling it has nothing to do with the gaping wound on his arm. Blood trails down his body, his t-shirt torn at the sleeve and crimson droplets dripping from his fingertips.

His eyes lock on mine and I finally manage a short, sharp breath. I'm out of my seat and taking the steps down to the pit two at a time before I can consider my actions. Not that I care. My only priority is getting to him.

I clamber down the steps in a flurry, the rest of the world a blur around Zane as I near him. He steps through the iridescent barrier and I stop just short of launching myself at him.

"Are you okay?" he asks, concern flitting in his hazel eyes as he reaches out with his good arm to grab mine.

"Fuck that. Are *you* okay?" My gaze drifts to his bleeding arm. Instinctively, I reach out to touch it before quickly dropping my hand. *Fuck.*

"We need to take care of this," Creed announces, moving to my side, and a quick glance over my shoulder reveals both Eldon and Brax aren't far behind.

"*Not* the medical center," Zane states with a wince.

"Why not?"

Eldon rolls his eyes. "Because he's adamant the medical center staff can't be trusted."

Frowning, I glance between the five of them, expecting to see humor, but he's not joking.

"It's a pity our housemate, who claimed to be a healer, doesn't actually have the ability," Brax muses, quietly, and I glare at him.

What an asshole.

Before I can snap at him, Creed steps between us. I'm sure we're causing a scene right now but Zane is the first person to be attacked by the siren and make it out alive.

"Thank you, students. The final day of the Gauntlet will commence tomorrow. Then there will be celebrations aplenty. Follow the sun, destroy the shadows, and survive another dawn." Relief washes over me at the professor's announcement and I lean into Zane.

Banding my arm around his back, I encourage him to drape his arm over my shoulder and we take the steps one at a time. I'm almost certain he smells my hair as we ascend the arena but when I turn to look at him, he's looking off into the distance.

When we make it to the exit, the late afternoon sun cascades over us and I'm relieved to still be standing for another day. Tomorrow could be entirely different but that's not a problem for right now.

"Let's get him out of here." Eldon takes charge, walking

to Zane's other side without touching the injured area.

"Where to?" I ask, still confused with where we can get him help.

"Back to the house," Zane states, and the others nod in agreement.

Instead of following the crowd down the usual pathway, Eldon steers us all behind the arena where it's completely dead, only stopping when we're hidden behind a tree line. Zane leans heavier against me as the others do a triple glance around us. Before I can ask what they're doing, Brax presses his palm into the bark of the closest tree.

"Let's go," he grunts, nodding toward the gaping black hole that now fills the space.

Creed steps through without a backward glance but none of the others move, waiting for me to follow after him. Pursing my lips, I consider my options but decide they wouldn't do anything to put Zane at risk right now, so I approach the abyss.

Zane remains with me, his body getting heavier with every step we take. Worry consumes me but when I give myself over to the swirling darkness, I startle when I realize the other side of the abyss leads us straight home.

"What the…" Creed is already searching through the drawers in the kitchen as Brax and Eldon step through behind us. "Is that your ability?" I ask, glancing at Brax, but I don't get to hear his response as Zane slumps in my hold. He's a dead weight at my side and the others have to help me guide him down onto the sofa.

The second his back is against the cushions, he shakes his head. "No. No. I want Raven," he slurs, each word elongated more than necessary. My eyebrows pinch as I glance at Eldon and he shrugs his shoulders.

"Is he okay?" I ask, crouching beside the sofa as I instinctively run my fingers through his hair.

"Side-effects of a siren's bite. If you live to tell the tale, that is," Creed explains, approaching with a hot mug in one hand and a rag in the other.

He soaks the fabric in the water and presses it against Zane's wound, making him hiss in pain.

"Imagine if you were actually a healer right now. That would be really useful," Brax grunts *again*, and my nostrils flare in anger. Instead of arguing back, I glower in his direction.

There's only one thing I can offer. It's not the same, but it might be worth *something*.

Fucker.

Wordlessly, I rise to my feet and march to my room. Zane calls after me, his slurred words worrying me more and more, but I'm rushing back to him the second I have what I'm looking for.

"What's that?" Eldon asks as I open my small bag on the floor next to where Zane lies.

"They're healing herbs and potions," I murmur, not lifting my gaze as I search for everything I need. The small vials clatter as I dig for what I want. It's been a while since my last class at Shadowmoor, but I think I recall what I need.

"Where did you get them from?" Creed asks.

I don't reply until I have all of the needed ingredients lined up. "I brought them with me from Shadowmoor."

"What is it you're trying to make?"

"A healing elixir. We were taught how to do it back at school but I've never felt like my injuries or wounds warranted such a grand effort, so I've never made it before. It's worth a try, though, especially since I'm not *actually* a healer."

If Brax hears my snark, he doesn't take me on. Creed drops to his knees beside me, eyeing the ingredients.

"Why have I never heard of any of these ingredients before?"

I glance at the quiet and observant man beside me and get lost in his onyx eyes for a moment before I clear my throat. "Because it all grows in Shadowmoor." I grab the small bowl from my bag, adding a little of everything before taking a little of Creed's water.

"Is that concoction even safe to use on him?" Brax barks, raising my hackles further.

"Your comments are starting to piss me off. You don't

like that I'm not a healer, so I find an alternative and that's not good enough either. So, unless you've got something *useful* to add…" I bite back, cheeks heating. His eyes draw me in. One brown, one green. Disgust tinges both of them, nonetheless.

"I'm just speaking the truth, Shadow."

The bowl clatters on the floor as I scramble to my feet, wagging my finger in his direction, ready to give him a piece of my mind, but a hand on my leg stops me in my tracks. Distracted, I look to see Zane touching my knee. Following his hand to his arm and trailing up to his face, I find him smiling softly.

"Do whatever you're thinking, Raven. I trust you." He's slurring heavier than before and that doesn't leave me filled with confidence. I exhale sharply and do as he asks, but not before giving Brax a deathly glare.

Thankfully, nobody speaks as I create the paste needed. When I'm happy with it, I move my attention to cleaning his wound the best I can.

Bile burns the back of my throat as his flesh hangs loose in jagged patches, torn loose by the siren's teeth. When I'm sure I can't get it any cleaner than it is, I slowly spread the paste over the affected area as gently as possible.

It smells disgusting but no one complains. Satisfied with the coverage, I reach for the bandages I usually use to wrap my knuckles. Swathing his shoulder, I repeat the process until the wound is completely protected.

"Thank you," Zane breathes, his voice a little more sated and his face not quite as pale as it was earlier.

"What now?" Eldon asks, offering me a hand to rise to my feet. I take it.

"Now, we wait. It should take about eight to twelve hours, so he should be good by morning."

"And if not?" Brax interjects. I shrug.

"Then you can complain about my lack of powers all over again?" I retort with an eye roll.

"No, he won't," Zane murmurs, lifting his good arm slightly to point in Brax's direction, but the execution isn't quite there. "What are your plans for the evening, Raven?"

Putting the small vials back into my bag, I shrug. "I was going to find that damn handbook in my room and see what the hell you keep referring to."

A smile breaks across his face and I want to be mad at him, but I let him off the hook since he's in bad shape.

"Maybe you could keep me company?"

"Sure. I can read it while I sit with you," I offer, and he nods meekly.

"I'm going to train for a bit. Then we'll figure food out," Creed suggests, and everyone hums their agreement. He takes the bowl from my hand and I murmur my thanks as he takes it to the kitchen.

"Maybe after we've eaten, you and Eldon could give

me all the hot tips for surviving tomorrow."

"Of course." Eldon leans in to kiss my cheek sweetly before he takes off toward the glass doors with Creed.

"I'll give you whatever you need, Raven, but you'll be fine. I just know it." I smile down at Zane. It's not lost on me that he's giving me such a carefree pep-talk when he's injured from the same thing that I will be facing tomorrow. He has magical powers and he still got hurt.

I'm screwed.

Zipping up the bag, I rush back to my room to switch it out for the thick handbook Zane gave me on my first day. Deciding my pajamas would be more comfortable, I quickly realize I'm still wearing my exercise clothes and my uniform is back in the locker rooms.

Hopefully that's not something I will get into trouble for. I'll mention it to Leila in the morning. She missed the afternoon sessions after her father called her away.

Slipping into a pair of shorts and an oversized white tee that *definitely* didn't belong to anyone else before me, I grab the handbook and make my way back out to the lounge area to find Zane quietly snoring.

I smile at his calmness and the serene aura that always seems to grace him. Sleeping or not, I'd rather be by his side, so I move to sit at the opposite end of the sofa.

"It's for the best." I startle at Brax's words as he looms in the doorway of the room behind me.

Despite not wanting to get involved with him right now, I sigh and push for him to elaborate. "What is?"

"That he's asleep."

"Oh, yeah?" The sweet smile on my face is so forced that I'm sure I'm going to snap my jaw. But, in spite of Brax's need to hit me with the constant hot and cold treatment, I don't want him to see the emotions he makes me feel ripple down my spine.

"Yeah. Because when you die tomorrow, he might not be quite as attached to you as he could have been."

I gape at his retreating form as he heads for the back deck with the others.

What a motherfucker. How fucking dare he?

"You're an asshole. You know that?"

"I do," he grunts before letting the glass door slam shut behind him.

I want to scream. My lungs burn to feel a roar rip from my lips but I can't give him the satisfaction. Not when I know a sob lurks so close to the surface right alongside it. Flopping back onto the sofa, I panic that I might jostle Zane, but he doesn't budge.

Clutching the handbook to my chest, I try to take a calming breath but it's futile at this point. Brax's words stir something so deeply inside of me because they're true. They're factual, and there's nothing I can do about it.

All I can control is this moment.

With that in mind, I inhale long and hard through my nose before exhaling just as slowly from my mouth. I repeat the process four more times before I can finally focus on the front cover of the housemate handbook.

Opening the folder to the first page, the surprise I find raises my eyebrows. Tentatively flicking to the second plastic wallet, I snicker. Running my fingers from the first page to the last, I gape as disbelief washes over me.

That sly motherfucker has been playing me hard. And I'm not even mad about it.

It's a pity it's a done verdict that I won't make it past tomorrow. Otherwise, this would have been far more fun.

TWENTY ONE

Raven

Fingers stroking through my hair rouse me from my sleep. The grogginess clings to me like a second skin, but evaporates as soon as I blink my eyes open to find Zane looking down at me. A smile spreads across his face as he continues to wake me and, despite my immediate tiredness and usual cranky morning vibes, I smile back.

It takes a moment for me to remember where I am. We all left Zane to sleep last night once Creed put together some food, but the second I was done, I curled up on the sofa at Zane's feet again and I must have fallen asleep. There certainly wasn't a blanket covering me, though. Someone must have draped it over me once I passed out.

"How are you feeling?" I ask, sluggishly pushing to sit up and face him.

"I feel amazing. I just need to remove the bandages and

see what it looks like underneath. Want to help?"

"If it's still gruesome and the fabric tries to stick to your skin, then definitely not." I cringe at the thought, making Zane snicker at me.

Tentatively reaching for the end of the bandage, I slowly start to unwind it, my movements getting more cautious as I get closer to his wound. Much to my relief, other than the remnants of the ointment still clinging to the fabric, I find nothing else.

Letting the material flutter to the floor, I mindlessly run my hand over the healed skin in complete shock. I did it. I actually healed him.

"Thank you," he rasps, placing his hand on mine, and I look up to meet his gaze.

"You're welcome."

With his gaze locked on mine, he gently grabs my hand from his chest and lifts it to his mouth. His lips pepper over my fingers and knuckles, sending a promising shiver down my spine, and I gasp at the contact.

"Are you ready for today?" Zane's words cut through the desire coursing in my veins, reminding me of exactly what lies ahead.

I gulp, unable to hold back the nerves as I gently shake my head. "Not even a little bit."

His brows crease and I get the sense that he wants to comfort me and guarantee a path out of the Gauntlet, but it's impossible. I'm not going to stand out for showing no powers or abilities. Many have entered with only psychic power and I'll look no different than them. The only issue is a lot of them have died. It bewilders me why they would even do this because I imagine a lot of the psychic abilities are powerful, just not physical, which a lot of this task demands.

"Where are the others?" I ask, hoping to change the subject as I slip my hand from his hold and sweep my hair back off my face.

"Probably outside training."

I turn to glance out of the full glass doors to find all three of them doing some kind of cardio or lifting weights.

"Do you guys do that every day?"

"Pretty much." He continues to smile at me, his gaze roaming over me appreciatively, and I feel a blush coming on.

"Why am I getting the feeling I'll be roped into that if I survive today?"

"You *will* survive today." His nostrils flare as he bites the words out. Not angrily, but in a show of determination. I try to cling to that level of surety, but it's harder than I want to admit. "Besides, the handbook explains everything, even morning exercise," he says with a pointed look, and I laugh.

"I've read your damn handbook, mister."

He swipes a hand over his mouth, trying to hide his grin, but it's pointless. "You have?"

"I have." Mischief flickers in his eyes as I point to the actual thing on the table.

"And what do you think?"

My tongue sweeps out over my bottom lip, excitement rushing through my body as I shake my head at him. "I think you're a menace."

I barely finish my last word before my back is flush against the sofa again and Zane is hovering over me. Only, this time it's not a gentle smile on his face. It's a heated gaze filled with desire and want.

"Once today is over with, the party included, you, me, and that handbook, are going to be well acquainted with one another. Agreed?"

My thighs clench as I nod. "Agreed."

I just hope he's right about today. Because despite my growing fears and wavering strength, I can't bring myself to ask for help.

Not even from them.

Now with two sets of uniforms piled high in the locker room and a fresh set of shorts and a t-shirt on, I exhale. Nothing I do is going to alleviate the nerves consuming me. This is so far from anything I've had to handle before, even in Shadowmoor, reminding me that I'm nothing but a Void masquerading as one of the powerful.

I may have faced dangers back home, but never sirens or whatever else might exist here. I'm out of my element and I'm not embarrassed to admit that, but the sinking feeling that I'm simply waiting for my execution is all I can think about.

Leila links her arm through mine as we head out of the locker room. The space is quieter and less busy than it was on Monday, and that reality seems to be weighing heavy on everyone's shoulders.

"Are you okay?" she asks, eyes filled with concern, and I offer her a tight smile in response, unable to piece together the right words.

She accepts my silence as the Bishops come into view, waiting for us as they have every day. Brax, Creed, and I are the final ones waiting to face the Gauntlet, but the impassive looks on their faces would make you think they weren't about to do something crazy.

They take their usual formation around us, Eldon up front, Brax behind, Zane at my right, and Creed on the other side of Leila. They stay like that until we enter the arena, just like every other day, except Eldon and Brax switch places when we take our seats. There's no need to shuffle anyone out of their spots, though. With the casualties we've faced, there's more space than there was.

A projection flickers above the dome and Professor Barton appears like clockwork. "Good morning, Silvercrest. I hope you are all basking in your victory or prepared to face the Gauntlet today. For all those who prove triumphant, the gala will commence this evening. This is a regal event, so if you haven't paid a visit to the on-site seamstress, I highly recommend that you do so after today's events. I look forward to seeing my Gauntlet champions then. Follow the sun, destroy the shadows, and survive another dawn."

"Follow the sun, destroy the shadows, and survive another dawn."

A regal event? Shit, I'm almost glad I'm dying today. Although, the Bishops dressed in suits is a sight I'll regret not seeing.

Before I can get sucked too far into my thoughts, the professor pulls out her scroll and calls the next name. Thankfully, I'm not first, but it doesn't end well for the girl who starts. I recognize her as one of Genie's friends, and that fact is confirmed when she dies at the hands of her siren and Genie starts to sob uncontrollably.

I can't decide if she's genuinely hurt or vying for attention, but I refrain from judging since I made a spectacle of running to Zane yesterday.

The announcing professor glances down at her sheets

and my breath catches in my lungs. "Creed Wylder."

Fuck.

I turn to my left, watching him rise to his feet. He rolls his shoulders back and glances in my direction, nodding slightly in acknowledgment before he trudges down the steps.

Did I want him to kiss me like the others did? Am I disappointed? I'm not sure, but worry for his safety claws at me. Maybe I should have gone before all of them so I didn't have to deal with this crippling anxiety.

Zane laces his fingers with mine and draws my hand into his lap, but I don't pull my gaze from Creed as he speaks with the professor before stepping into the pit.

I know when we went on the trip to the outpost, Creed joined the psychic group, which doesn't help my stress, but he enters the siren's lair with unwavering confidence.

My heart hammers in my chest, waiting for the siren's song to begin, and the second it does, I clamp my hands to my ears, too scared to blink as I watch Creed climb the boulders.

"What the fuck is he doing?" I mutter to no one, panic taking over as he does what everyone else who has failed before him did.

He's climbing the furthest boulders from where the pool sits but, surely, that won't make a difference. The higher ground has worked for no one.

The water starts to rise and, to my surprise, Creed is almost to the top. The moment he reaches the highest point, he turns back to look at the water, his eyes scanning for the siren. My eyes narrow as I do the same and it takes a moment for me to see her.

Blue hair, blue tail. She's blending in with the water, which is making her harder to locate. Alarm rattles through me but I spot the moment he sees her. Creed crouches down as the water level rises, faster this time, like it's seeking him out. All at once, the siren's melody stops and the water halts its ascent.

I'm on the edge of my seat, hands falling from my ears to my mouth as I wait with bated breath for what may follow. Waves start to form in the water, lapping at the barrier separating the pit from the observers, and it quickly becomes apparent that it's because the siren is thrashing around beneath the surface. An almighty scream crackles through the air as the siren rises from the water, her face contorted with teeth protruding, ready to attack.

The second she's out of the water, it evaporates into a small pool again as she starts snapping at her own tail. My gaze flicks between the siren and Creed. He looks deep in thought, his hands twisting slightly as the siren repeatedly attacks herself, and the spectators gasp as blood splatters against the iridescent wall.

"That's sadistic as fuck," Eldon states as the lifeless

siren flops to the sand in a heap of blood and gore.

"It can be whatever he wants if it means he survives," I murmur, still in shock as Creed climbs down from the boulder. Claps and cheers erupt and I join in, rising to my feet even though I'm still confused by what the fuck just happened.

Creed pays no mind to anyone as he takes the steps two at a time to rejoin us. Blood coats his bare arms and legs and people try to give him a wide berth as he passes. Leila jumps from her seat before he can sit down, clambering over Zane and me to sit on his other side, leaving the spot free beside me.

"Hey." He drops into the seat and, before I think about it, I launch myself at him.

"I'm so glad you're okay," I breathe, wrapping my arms around his neck, and he slowly squeezes my waist in response.

"She likes them unhinged. Noted," Eldon jokes from behind me as I lean back out of Creed's hold. He shrugs, not responding to Eldon's statement as he turns to look at the pit. His thigh brushes against mine and I smile.

Unhinged…

Sadistic…

Whatever we're calling it, he's right. I like it.

I just need to survive the damn thing myself to enjoy more of it. With exactly zero ideas of how I can achieve such a task.

Apprehension continues to rattle my bones as the list of remaining first years to take on the Gauntlet dwindles. Each name being called out is like a missed arrow aimed at my heart, including the next name.

"Brax Carlsen."

He stands and heads toward the pit without a backward glance at his friends or me. I don't know how or why I'm becoming so goddamn attached to these men, but as much as he's an asshole, and despite the shitty stuff he said last night, I still worry for his safety.

I can't figure out how they got under my skin like this. Once again, bile burns my throat as I watch him enter the pit. His ears turn to stone first as he walks across the sand. He doesn't climb, like Creed, or even consider hiding as the others have. Instead, he stands dead center in the open space facing the pool of water.

"He's crazy," Leila states, and I nod in agreement.

"Did you expect anything less from him?" There's no humor in Zane's voice like there usually would be. I guess I'm not the only one filled with trepidation.

The siren's song starts, inciting fear in us all as my hands clamp down on my ears again. The water levels rise, quickly traveling toward Brax, but before it laps at his ankles, he turns completely to stone.

What the fuck?

His entire body is an array of grays covering him from head to toe, but I only get a moment to appreciate him before the water engulfs him. It rises to the top of the highest boulder before continuing to touch the top of the dome covering the pit.

Gasps ring out, my own mingled in with them, as the entire Gauntlet is flooded with water. As the white-foamed top calms, the water clears into a stunning turquoise, revealing the siren. Pink hair floats through the water as lime green scales sparkle, shimmering in the light, and the siren dances around Brax's stone statue.

She swims past him once, twice, three times, and it quickly becomes apparent that she doesn't recognize the stone statue at the bottom of the pit as her target.

I turn to Creed, tapping his arm with my bent elbow to get his attention. When his eyes meet mine, I speak. "What's he going to do?"

The shrug he offers in response doesn't fill me with confidence, it seems he could use the reassurance too. As if sensing my question, I watch as the stone statue starts to move, unbeknownst to the siren, whose attention is now on the watching crowd.

Her melody gets louder, trying to lure us closer, leaving her completely open and exposed to Brax, who remains in his stone form as he grows taller and taller until a shadow forms over the Siren as she waves sweetly at the second years.

She doesn't stand a chance as his immense hands grab and crush her with no effort at all. It's like someone pops the dome and the water drains from the pit once more. Brax tosses the lifeless body over his shoulder without a backward glance. Relief washes over me as I watch with rapt attention as Brax shrinks back to his usual height and turns back into flesh and blood. His cheer is deafening and I clap along with everyone as I turn to Zane.

"What is he?" I ask, still confused, and he grins at me before leaning in to press his lips against my ear.

"Brax is a gargoyle."

Wow. That's mind-blowing. I didn't even know they existed, never mind ever seeing one before.

I stand with everyone else as he steps out of the pit, but my heart turns to ice as the professor calls out the next name.

"Raven Hendrix."

My pulse thumps so hard it feels like my head has its own heartbeat, and Brax's words from last night replay in my mind. "*Because when you die tomorrow, he might not be quite as attached to you as he could have been.*" I can't shake the thought as I head toward the steps, deciding it would be better if I don't glance back.

"Raven," Eldon calls out, but I can't look. I can't stare into the eyes of the people I'm suddenly enthralled with. I can't see the hope and excitement for a life, a future, when none of it matters now anyway.

My eyes lock with Brax's as he slowly walks up the steps, ascending to victory as I descend to my doom. It's fitting, really. I can look into his eyes and recall the anger he stokes inside of me.

I expect him to step past me without a backward glance but, to my surprise, he grabs my arm at the last second, pulling me into his side without looking down at me. "Moss in your ears. Left boulder stack."

I frown at his words, but before I can question him, he's gone. Focusing on one step in front of the other, I force myself not to worry my bottom lip, attempting to put on a strong front.

"Everybody say goodbye to the Hendrix family's black sheep." My spine stiffens at the sound of Sebastian's voice and the round of laughter that echoes around me, pissing me off even more.

It takes everything in me not to react to his attempt at showing dominance at my expense as I stop in front of the professor. "Good luck, Miss Hendrix," she breathes, barely looking up from her scroll, and I take that as my cue to move.

Approaching the iridescent barrier, I reach my hand out first before I step through fully. I can't describe the sensation and I have no time to delve further into the thought as the atmosphere around me changes.

Being *in* the pit is nothing like seeing it. I feel like an ant under a microscope for everyone to look at and assess. The boulders are twice as tall as I assumed and the smell reminds me of the fish market at Shadowmoor, but scarier. A thing I didn't think was possible.

My gaze darts straight to the water and every single thought and consideration I've had about how I'm going to handle this thing evaporates from my mind. I don't have long before the siren's song is going to start. I need to move quickly.

Dashing to my left, away from the source of the water, I stumble a little when I step off the sand and onto the lower boulders. The surface is slicker than I expected and my arms fly out at my sides to keep my balance. With my eyes wide, I freeze in position, attempting to catch my breath as I look down at where I nearly face-planted and spot a flash of green.

Moss.

What did Brax say?

Moss in your ears. Was he trying to help me?

I reach for the small splattering of moss, plucking it from the ground and feeling the spongy texture in my palm. A melody begins, enveloping me, and my eyes clench closed at the assault on my senses. Holy fuck, it's ten times louder in here.

Prying my eyes open, I glance toward the pool, noting the slow rise, and I don't have time to think, only act. Tearing the moss in half, I plunge it into both of my ears, and the world becomes muted. I can still hear the tune coming from the siren, but it's not overpowering, more like a hum in the background.

Thank you, Brax.

Water ripples around my sneakers, and I remember there's a time limit on my life right now. Rushing further into the center of the pit, I pass the first boulder and the water is at my knees by the time I'm halfway toward the second set.

I think I'm going to be sick.

My pace lags with the water restricting my movements and a flash of blond draws my attention, swimming effortlessly through the shallow water on the opposite end of the pit.

Fuck.

Time's up.

Splashing my way to the second set of boulders, I press my back against the jagged, damp surface, my heart pounding. I try to take a deep breath and imagine that I'm facing some asshole from Shadowmoor, but my gaze snags on the spectators and it becomes a lot more difficult.

I spy Sebastian with a smug look on his face and my teeth clench. Refusing to waste my last seconds on him, I whip my head to the right and find the Bishops. The fear on Zane's face is as real as the tightness in my chest. Creed's brows pull together and Eldon clenches his hands, leaning so far forward in his seat that I'm sure he's going to tumble over the seat in front of him.

I should have said goodbye. I shouldn't have been a coward. But it's too late for all of that now.

Spying Brax, I'm at a loss for how to feel. The annoyance on his face is clear, the tightness of his jaw close to cutting glass as he nods sharply at me. I don't know what he's trying to convey to me until he shakes his head in irritation and mouths one word at me.

Push.

Scowling, I turn away from him and lean further into the boulder. My foot gives out under me again, but this time it's not because of the damp surface. It's a cluster of small rocks. I look down at my feet with the same confused expression. There's debris floating under the water.

I turn to look at the boulder and my eyes widen with shock. There's a gaping dent in it. It's only noticeable since I'm close-up. From a distance, it would just look like another jagged edge. The gray marks scratched across the charcoal boulders stand out too. I don't see them anywhere but here.

'Moss in your ears. Left boulder stack.'

My gaze flicks back to Brax. Did he do this…for me?

The look on his face tells me no. His anger is bubbling at the surface, but something tells me it's aimed *at* me, not *because* of me.

Holy fuck.

Adrenaline zaps faster through my veins as the water hits my waist and I search for the blond hair floating in the water. Testing my weight against the boulder, I push and it budges a little. If I can get the siren in the right spot...I could survive this.

Rubbing my lips together, I take a deep breath and drag myself to the other side of the formation. I feel like I can't breathe as the siren spots me and quickly starts swimming in my direction.

Shit.

Darting around the boulder as fast as possible, I plant my hands firmly against the smashed remains and push with everything I have. My arms burn, my palms cutting against the ragged edges, but it starts to move. I need to be quicker for this to work, though.

I'm going to need to throw all of my weight at it. Now.

Dropping my arms, I tilt to my side, slam my eyes shut, and throw my shoulder into the boulder with all of my strength. I grunt at the initial contact, the pain crippling, but I don't stumble backward. I continue moving as the boulders crumble.

Solace consumes me, but it's short-lived as the rumbling

comes to a stop and the boulders settle. If it worked, the water will start to drain. If it didn't, I'm up on a silver platter, ready for the siren to claim.

Disoriented, I can't fight any longer. I curl up on the boulder I landed on, water lapping at my body as pain takes over, and await my fate. Shallow breaths are all I can manage.

One... two... three...

Nothing. She's coming for me.

Four... five... six...

At least I can say I tried.

Seven... eight... nine...

I went down fighting.

Ten... eleven...

The water retreats, forcing me to push up with my good hand. Too scared to get my hopes up, I remain locked in place until only a pool remains at the far end again. Swallowing feels like nails slicing at my throat, it's that raw.

I try to stand, but I really did throw all of myself at the damn thing. *All* of my strength, and now I'm feeling the repercussions of that. Cradling my weak arm, I manage to get down from the boulder and make my way to the edge of the pit closest to the first years. I can see people clapping and a gentle hum of cheers, but the moss in my ears dulls it all.

My eyes lock on the three Bishops, who race down the steps to greet me with Leila hot on their heels and, as much as I'm appreciative of their presence, my eyes are fixed on a lone Bishop.

Brax.

I survived the Gauntlet. I'm still breathing, still here, and undefeated as a Void.

I made it.

And it's all because of the guy who hates me the most.

TWENTY TWO

Raven

I'm swamped with pain, but I refuse to leave, insisting on watching the final first years face the dread and terror of the pit. Zane gently rubs small, comforting circles at the base of my spine, Creed's hand doing the same on my knee as I focus all my attention on not throwing up.

I feel clammy and, even after the final first year survives the Gauntlet, I can't bring myself to rise to my feet and clap along with everyone. Brax remains seated in front of me but he doesn't turn around. He hasn't glanced at me once or responded to my tap on his shoulder.

Of course I owe my thanks to the most complex person I have ever had to deal with. I'm sure, deep down, he's loving that he can hang this over me.

I wince with pain again, unable to hear the professor who draws the entire mess to a close, and everyone starts to filter out. I decide it's better to stay seated until everyone else leaves. Leila and the Bishops don't try to encourage me to my feet or coax me back to the changing rooms, which is a telling sign that I'm not hiding my pain and discomfort as well as I had hoped.

Eldon braces his hand on my shoulder when the masses have almost gone. "I'm going to go and grab someone real quick. Meet you back at the locker room, okay? Take your time."

He doesn't wait for a response, disappearing through the exit as Zane offers me his hand. Taking a deep breath, I lace my fingers with his and take his assistance as I manage to stand. My weak arm is tucked in tight against my body and he instinctively stands protectively at that side.

Creed leads the way to the end of the row, waiting on the stairs as I take slow, measured steps. Everything hurts so fucking much, I just want to pass out, but that's not an option for me right now when I have to act unfazed.

My legs get shaky as I ascend the steps, and I must be walking too slowly because Brax eventually stomps past me, taking the remaining stairs four at a time to leave. Guilt melds with annoyance in my gut, but I push it to the back of my mind as I reach the exit.

Stepping outside into the mid-afternoon sun, I exhale softly at the feel of the gentle breeze floating around us. "Do you want to link me?" Leila asks, coming to my left side. I'm about to take her up on her offer when my response is interrupted.

"Leila, come," Professor Fitch murmurs, waiting impatiently to the left of the open entryway.

Disappointment flashes in Leila's eyes as she turns to look at me. I can sense her conflict so I quickly wave her off.

"You're good. I'll see you later."

"Hell yeah, you will. I can't wait to see your gown," she replies before bouncing off with her father.

"My gown?" I question, looking at Zane, and he shakes his head at me.

"Let's worry about one thing at a time, shall we?"

That sounds like a plan.

I'm sandwiched between Creed and Zane as we head toward the locker rooms. When we get close, Creed tucks his arm around my waist and guides me toward the guys' room instead of the girls'.

"What are you doing?" I ask, but don't stop walking as they lead me inside.

"Cover your tiny penises, fuckers, there's a lady present," Zane hollers, and I chuckle at his choice of words.

I hear a few guys call bullshit but I'm not in any shape to confirm or deny it, especially when Creed lifts his free hand to try and shield my eyes.

Fools.

They walk me through to the bathroom and showers at the back of the room where we find Brax and Eldon waiting.

"What's going on?" I ask, hopeful I'll get more of an answer this time. Eldon nods for me to step into the large, curtained shower area. Creed keeps his hold on my waist as I try to peer behind the curtain and find Finn standing in his uniform with a frown on his face.

The second he sees me, his eyes light up. I'm definitely missing something here.

"Okay, last time I'm asking. What is going on?" The bite is evident in my tone this time and even Finn flicks his gaze between me and Eldon. Brax grunts, moving to stand between us, his finger poised and aimed toward me.

"Heal her." The order comes from Eldon and it's aimed at Finn.

Finn runs his fingers over his lips as he assesses me, a smile tracing his lips before he glances back at Eldon. "What's in it for me?"

"The fact that I don't snap every bone in your body for even looking in her direction is gift enough," he grunts in response, and Finn rolls his eyes.

"Fine, but only because she's cute," he murmurs, stepping toward me. Creed intercepts him before he gets too close.

"She's not fucking cute to you. Do you understand?

Heal her before I scramble your damn brain."

Finn also rolls his eyes at Creed, their threats rolling off his back without concern. "Are you going to let me get close enough to heal her or not?"

A moment passes, followed by another, before Creed relents and steps back. He still crowds my space, though, as Finn moves closer. "Are you okay?"

"I've been better," I admit, forcing a smile.

"Let me take care of you," he breathes, making more than one Bishop growl in response, but I don't turn to confirm exactly who it comes from as Finn reaches out his hand.

I brace for impact against my shoulder, but he hovers just above my skin, sending a warm tingle from his palm to my wound. I don't know what to expect, but the temperature rises to an almost unbearable level before he drops the connection.

"And your head." He lifts his hand to my face, his fingertips at my temple as he cups my cheek, and I feel the heat again. His eyes are trying to search mine, but I can sense he's either using me to play with the Bishops or trying to have a moment with me. I don't fucking know. I'm too tired to care and I opt to stare at the top button of his shirt instead.

"You've got to be done by now," Zane states, pushing at Finn's shoulder and knocking his hand from my face.

"Fuck off."

"Don't I get a thanks?"

I finally lift my gaze to his, rolling my shoulders back as relief floods my limbs. The pain has subsided almost completely. "Thank you."

"Not from you, but I'll take it," he says with a wink before breezing past Zane without a backward glance.

Eldon seems to check that the coast is clear before turning back to me. "How do you feel now?"

I take a second to feel every bone, muscle, and limb before answering. "So much better, thank you." He may not have been the one to actually heal me, but I get the sense that this is what he rushed off to do and I appreciate it.

"Good. Let's grab our things and head back. We've got tonight to prepare for." His nose scrunches in distaste and I finally remember the gala we're supposed to attend.

Fuck my life. Do they not think I've been through enough today? Making me be social on top of a near-death experience is too much, but I already know I don't have a say in the matter.

"Okay, I'll get my things in a minute. Can I speak with Brax for a second first?" I ask, hoping he can't avoid me if I ask him in front of the others, but he's already shaking his head.

"No."

There's no explanation, no reasoning, nothing. Just two letters forming the most frustrating word I could have asked for. My mistake was clearly letting him have a choice in the matter, but before I can try and rectify that, he's storming past the curtain and out of the showers.

Dammit.

"What am I missing here?" Eldon asks, and I shake my head in response. I don't want to talk about it in such a public place. I don't know if either of us could get into trouble or not.

"It's nothing. I'll speak to him later. Let me go change and I'll meet you outside." My pain might be gone but the exhaustion is still real, so I don't wait for any of them to approve.

Thankfully, the guys' locker room is empty when I step out and the girls' is the exact same when I enter. I'm relieved when I find my belongings exactly where I left them. I run on autopilot as I switch out my clothes for my uniform, forgoing the tie before I make my way back outside.

I find Creed waiting for me and, when I lock eyes with him, I can already tell I'm not going to like what he's about to say. For someone who remains so quiet and observant, I can read his gaze today; for the first time.

"Are you ready to go shopping?"

My eyebrows pinch. "No."

"I didn't think so, but I'm also guessing you need a dress for tonight."

Shit.

He's right.

"Did you draw the short straw to come with me?"

"If I get to watch you change from one dress to another, I wouldn't call that the short straw. Would you?"

I feel better about being in the shopping district with a sugary coffee in one hand and a pastry in the other. I'm bone-numbingly tired, but the coffee will help with that, for now. When I set out my demands for heading over here, Creed accepted without batting an eye. Not that it's his fault we're here; it's mine. Mine for surviving, mine for not being prepared for doing said surviving. He's here, helping me despite my crankiness, and I will say thank you eventually.

"Are you ready?" Creed asks, slowing outside *Silhouette's*. Various floor-length ballgowns frame the delicately decorated window fronts and I gulp. I've never worn a long, elegant dress before.

"As I'll ever be," I murmur, stuffing the final bite of pastry into my mouth before we enter.

Creed holds the door for me and a powdery floral scent

immediately hits my senses.

"Good afternoon. My name is Louisa. I'm assuming you're here to prepare for tonight's event?" I turn to find a brunette with a broad smile and bright green eyes walking toward us.

"We are. We'll browse the racks if you wouldn't mind setting up a dressing room for us." She flutters her eyelashes at Creed's request, nodding eagerly.

"Sounds perfect. Congratulations on your success this week. I'm sure you're proud to be attending tonight," she says before giving us some space. If only she knew how I would rather claw my eyeballs out than deal with tonight. I bet that would make me sound ungrateful, despite the fact that I had to risk my life to be in attendance.

"Thank you," I breathe as soon as it's just myself and Creed in the room.

He turns to face me with his eyebrows raised. "What for?"

"For helping with…all this," I state, waving my hand around at the room's grandeur.

"Don't worry about it." His words from earlier replay in my mind as he places his hand on the small of my back and guides me to the first rack of dresses.

If I get to watch you change…

Fuck.

I grip my coffee cup tight with one hand and run my

fingers over the material of the dresses with the other. There's an overwhelming array of choices and I have no idea where to begin.

"So, what is tonight supposed to be about?" I ask, trying to distract myself from the overwhelming task I now face.

"I'm not entirely sure, It's the first one of the school year, but I believe it will be all about connecting families, giving our parents a chance to see us alive, and letting The Monarchy see what talent is coming through the ranks."

"I don't like the sound of any of that," I admit, pausing at a silky option for a moment before continuing down the line.

"Me either, but we're the byproducts of our surroundings, Raven. Until we're stronger, they say jump and we ask how high. It's all about biding our time and surviving the mess they throw at us."

I hate *that* even more.

"Have you found anything you like?" Louisa asks, appearing out of nowhere.

"Uhm…"

"She'll try these, please." Creed walks back down the line and points out six options that I lingered on when passing. "Are you happy with them?" His gaze turns to me and I smile, nodding in agreement before we're waltzed toward the back of the store.

Curtains section off the space into five different areas

and Louisa leads us into the first one on the left. The pale pink drapes offer a secluded area with ample space to try the dresses on in private. The options Creed selected are hanging on a rail to the right, the far wall is lined with floor-length mirrors, and there's an oversized chair to the left against the far wall.

"I can see there are a few options here that will require lacing up. It's always better to have an assistant do this instead of magic. I will just go and see who we have available."

"That won't be necessary, but thank you." Creed's words wash over me like a heavy dose of ecstasy. It will just be the two of us in here while I try each dress on. How am I supposed to survive that? Louisa's gaze momentarily skims between us as if she's trying to find a reason to decline, but before she can, Creed continues, "We'll call you back when she's decided on one."

He moves toward the curtain behind us and she follows him. "Of course," she says with a nod, but Creed is already closing the drapes, sealing us off from the rest of the world.

"Where do you want to start?" Creed asks, taking the coffee cup from my hand before getting comfortable in the oversized chair.

I nibble on my bottom lip nervously. He's serious about watching me and it's turning me on to no end. Needing a moment to think before he offers to help with the lace, I opt for the most effortless dress first.

Shaking off my blazer, I drape it over the small stool by the clothes and glance back at him. "You're just going to sit and watch?"

"Until you need my help, yeah."

My heart rate kicks up a notch, a slight tremble in my fingers as I try to shake off my nervousness under his intense gaze.

Removing the rest of my uniform, I'm in just my black bra and panties when I reach for the black dress. The chiffon material clings to me like a second skin as I turn in front of the mirror. It's cute, but the draped sleeves aren't really my style.

I catch a glimpse of Creed in the mirror. He doesn't say a word. His eyes are transfixed on me as I undo the zipper and move on to the forest-green option. I don't get as far as stepping into it, though, because when I hold it up against me, the green clashes with my pink hair.

The yellow one is too puffy, the white one too... ceremonial, which leaves me with the pink and lilac dresses, both of which need to be laced up. I'm sure there's a hot flush all over my skin from being acutely aware of Creed's gaze, but I try my best to act unfazed. Reaching for the pink one, I turn to ask for his help, only to find him standing in front of me.

"Come," he mutters, standing in the center of the white

rug. He takes the dress from my hands and pools it on the floor before holding his hand out for me to take.

Warmth ripples through my fingertips and up my arm from the contact as he helps me step into the bundled material. His calloused fingers skim over my heated skin, hitching my breath as our eyes latch onto one another in the mirror.

I slip my arms into the dainty sleeves before he laces up the corset. Every pull hits me straight in the core, my breaths coming in short, sharp bursts as I watch him fixate on every last detail. Once he's done, his hands fall to my waist, squeezing slightly as he finds me in the mirror again.

Without a word, he pulls the hair tie from my bun, letting the messy pink curls fall around my shoulders. He sweeps the locks back off my shoulder, exposing my collarbone and neck, and his eyes simmer with fire.

"You look stunning."

"I think I like this one," I manage, running my hand over the material. A fuller, lacier skirt compliments the bodice top and the pale, dusty pink makes my hair stand out even more.

"Do you want to try the last one or not?" His hands are still on my hips. The thought of moving anywhere right now seems impossible.

"No, this is the one."

Creed nods but doesn't say a word as he slowly unties

the corset, one link at a time, until the material slips over my skin and pools at my feet. He's standing so close, his body heat radiates against my back. His hands return to my hips, scalding my bare skin with his searing touch as he continues to watch me in the mirror.

I already feel like I can't breathe, today has been a whirlwind of emotions, but I still know how desperately I hated that he didn't kiss me before he entered the pit. It's selfish of me, I know, but I'm drawn to the Bishops like a moth to a flame. There's no denying it, no escaping it, and among all of the madness I now face, it's the only thing that makes sense.

As if sensing my thoughts, he bends slightly to press a kiss to my shoulder blade while his eyes remain locked on mine through the mirror. I gasp, my back instantly arching, and he grins as he steps back.

Motherfucker.

"You're a tease," I pout, breathless, and he shrugs.

"Maybe."

All I can do is gape at him, my body tense with need. "Eldon was right. You are sadistic."

He cocks a brow at me.

"Do you actually want the first time I touch you to be in a dressing area at a store where anyone could walk in?"

I huff in frustration, planting my hands on my hips and giving him a pointed look. "It would definitely be memorable."

The distance he had placed between us quickly vanishes and he stands before me again, hand under my chin as he tips my head back.

"Oh, Raven. When I get my hands on you, you're never going to forget."

TWENTY THREE

Raven

Apparently, the event isn't starting until after dark, which means I managed to sneak a little nap in. I feel more refreshed but not rejuvenated. It's going to take sleeping for a solid week to achieve that and that's not in the cards for me. Refreshed will have to do.

The sleep came surprisingly easy to me, despite Creed's heated words remaining on my mind and infiltrating my dreams. My slumber was laced with desire, drenched in ecstasy, and consumed with every touch and caress.

Now, with my nude eyes and blushed cheeks, my makeup is set. Half of my hair is pinned back off my face and braided, while the rest falls around my shoulders in waves. Louisa insisted I match the dress with a pair of nude heels with glitter soles and a small purse. I decorate my fingers with my favorite rings and choose a pair of dangly earrings.

I have everything on but the dress, a task Creed made me promise was still his. It sits pooled and ready at the foot of my bed, I just need to get it on. As if sensing I'm ready, a knock comes from the door. I peek my head through a small gap, shielding my body, and Creed comes into view.

Nervously, I step back and let him in, feeling his eyes on every inch of my bare skin. The dress is designed to not wear a bra, so I'm standing before him in my panties, heels, and jewels.

"Fuck, Raven."

I could say the same to him. He's dressed head to toe in black. A fitted black dress shirt with a black silk tie and a tailored black suit that fits him to perfection. The polished black shoes finish the look and his black hair is swept back off his face with a loose lock flicking over his eyebrow.

"Where do you want me?" I breathe, my throat drying with need as he smirks at me.

"Patience is a virtue," he murmurs back, making me laugh.

I step into the dress and bend down to grab the straps and sense him approaching. I gasp when I feel warm lips press a delicate kiss to the globe of my ass. My thighs clench, my pussy already dripping for him, but he doesn't do anything else as he grabs the straps from my hands and lifts the fabric up to dress me.

"I think I might hate you." I stand tall, slipping my arms into the straps as he gets to work on the laced corset.

"No, you don't."

"You don't know that," I tease, and he lifts his gaze, aiming a pointed stare over my shoulder into the floor-length mirror in my room. I glare back at him, but falter, glancing down at my feet in an attempt to calm myself.

Asshole.

Once again, his hands fall to my hips when he's done. Looking at our reflection, awe rises inside me. It should be criminal for us to look this put together and sophisticated. His hand splays across my stomach, pulling me back into him, and I feel the outline of his cock at my ass. Instinctively, I place my palm against his hand and he presses another sweet kiss to my temple.

Who knew it would be Creed that was the biggest fucking tease?

Clearing his throat, he takes a second to hold me close before taking a step back. "We should go. The others are waiting."

I nod, my pulse thrumming in my ears as he takes my hand, grabs my purse from the bed, and guides me to the door.

Tingles run up and down my spine, the chemistry between us palpable, and when he opens the door to reveal the rest of the Bishops, I'm almost positive I died in the

Gauntlet because this is surely what Heaven looks like.

Eldon is wearing a white shirt, a deep-navy suit, and a matching tie. His hair looks like he spent hours raking his hands through the ends, but it's the sultry shimmer in his eyes that has my lips parting. Zane is dressed in all black like Creed, only his tie is silver, making his hazel eyes gleam. The corner of his mouth is tipped up as he rakes his eyes over me from head to toe and I'm sure I'm going to combust from his look alone.

Brax stands a step back from the other two, not looking directly at me, but I spot him glancing out of the corner of his eye a time or two. The gray suit fits him like a second skin, reminding me of his ability, and it befits him perfectly.

It's on the tip of my tongue to try and talk to him again about the Gauntlet, but Eldon steps closer to me, interrupting my thoughts. "You look radiant, Little Bird." He places his hand under my chin before peppering small kisses at the corner of my mouth.

"Stop hogging her," Zane grumbles, shoulder-barging Eldon to the side so he can stand in front of me. "We got you this, beautiful." He holds up a white rose corsage decorated with pearls and silver and my heart lurches.

Everything is so overwhelmingly gorgeous that I have no words. I hold my hand out and he slips it onto my wrist.

"Thank you," I manage, and he smirks down at me.

"It was Brax's idea," he replies with a wink, making

my eyes widen in surprise. The man in question just grunts and stomps toward the door as I gape after him.

Creed is the secret tease, Eldon the declarer of being claimed, Zane the handbook king, and Brax is the one that runs so hot and cold that it leaves my head spinning.

"Are we ready?" Brax grunts from the door, swinging it open with a glare, and I smile despite his animosity.

Tonight suddenly feels more exciting than it did before, and I'm more than ready for the distraction. Following him outside, I gasp at the carriage that sits idle at the end of our path.

"What's this?" I ask, turning to Zane at my side.

"They're old school when it comes to events like this, so they use traditional carriages to escort each house to the ballroom."

I turn back to the grand mode of transport, noting the jingling of chains as I get closer. They hang up front as if attached to an animal, but there's nothing there…not that I can see, at least.

Brax climbs in without a backward glance and I shuffle in after him, sitting right beside him instead of taking the spot facing him like Creed and Zane do. Eldon slips into the seat to my right, his hand instantly finding my thigh, and I place my hand on top of his but focus my attention on the broody asshole on my other side as the carriage starts to move.

"Brax…"

"Don't."

Taking a deep breath, I try to not let his gruffness get to me, as my usual response is to be an asshole back, and that's exactly what I'm trying *not* to do right now.

"In the Gauntlet—"

"I. Said. Don't," he bites, swinging his deathly glare in my direction, but I match it with one of my own.

"You're an asshole."

"You've already told me that," he grunts, rolling his eyes at me before turning his attention back to the window.

God, I would love to kick him in the dick and listen to him squeal like a pig but, despite the excitement at the thought, I bite back my anger, remembering that the only reason I'm sitting here is because of him.

"Thank you."

His gaze slowly swings back to mine, the glare still intact, but he offers a subtle nod, accepting my gratitude while simultaneously drawing the conversation to an end. The darkness outside the window claims his attention once again and I let him distance himself this time.

If the other Bishops are intrigued or confused by my thanks, they don't say anything. Not even Zane and *he* usually has an opinion on everything.

We ride in comfortable silence, Eldon's thumb gently running back and forth over my knuckles until we approach our destination. Carriage after carriage is lined up and a porter opens the door for us once we come to a full stop.

"Please, follow me."

Eldon steps out first, immediately offering me his hand, which I take, letting him escort me down from the carriage. The second Zane is out, he's trying to push Eldon off me to take me for himself while Creed watches with his deep onyx eyes, never saying a word. Brax, however, climbs down and stomps toward the entryway without a backward glance.

"Am I causing issues between you guys?" I ask before I can think better of it.

"No. Brax is just...Brax," Eldon explains. There's no irritation in his tone, no anger or anything that would indicate he's worried, so I take his word for it.

Focusing on my surroundings, I notice we're back at the academy building, the large circular double doors I first saw when I arrived standing before me. It feels like an eternity ago, yet very little time has actually passed. I'm still not much wiser about the world around me, no stronger than I was back at Shadowmoor, yet my life feels like it's...superior.

"Raven."

I turn toward Leila's voice, watching her rush toward me in a red dress. Her blonde hair is braided back into a bun, and her smoky eye makeup accentuates her blue eyes.

"You look amazing," I say as she gives me a hug. She's practically buzzing with excitement. I can feel it and it's contagious.

"So do you. Are you ready for an evening with your brother?" I frown at her question, glancing back at the Bishops who look just as confused as I do.

"What do you mean?"

"Oh, we have to sit with our families in there."

My gut clenches and my heart instantly aches. "I thought we would be able to sit where we wanted, or in our houses at least," I mutter like it's going to change the circumstances, and Leila grimaces.

"Sorry to be the bearer of bad news. We can mingle once the meal is over, though," she adds, and I cling to that fact as we head inside.

The crowd is directed to the left and I startle at the room we're led into. Candles float across the ceiling in an array of sizes, lighting the entire space and creating a cozy atmosphere. White, gold, and cream drapes decorate the walls, matching the flowers placed as centerpieces on each table.

"Family name, please." I turn to the man, who looks at me with a warm smile, and realize I'm worrying my bottom lip.

"Hendrix," I murmur, already hating the taste of that word on my tongue.

"Follow me."

I glance back at the Bishops, offering them a wary smile as he leads me further into the room. They look about as happy as I do, but as much as that fills me with reassurance, it doesn't save me from the dinner I'm going to have to endure.

A chair is pulled out for me far too quickly and I attempt to turn my grimace into a smile, but the glimmer in his eyes tells me I'm failing miserably. "Thank you," I murmur, not sitting down straight away as I build up the strength to see who is here.

Exhaling, I bite the bullet and turn to see Sebastian, Papa, and Mama to my left. While another family fills the other half of the table. Not just any family, though. It's Finn's. Great, this just got even more awkward.

"Hey, Raven. You look exceptional," Finn says from the seat beside me, and I offer him a tight smile, opting to focus on my mama across from me instead.

I don't bother taking my seat as I rush around the table to greet her. She cuts the distance, meeting me halfway as she holds me in a tight embrace. I feel heavier and lighter all at once. She's always been my home, my safe place, despite how far apart we may have grown. Right up until the last time I saw her. It was back at the old family house, where she stayed inside and let Papa ship me off. I don't understand the politics behind anything that happened, but the way she holds me now, pouring all of her emotions into our hug, none of it matters.

"I've missed you so much, my sweet girl," she whispers against my ear, and I hold her tighter.

"I've missed you too."

"I'm so sorry, Raven. I thought I could stop the inevitable, but I was stupid, naïve, and hopeful for a better life for you. It was silly of me to think one existed. It's hard here, I know that from experience, but I hope you'll turn it into a beautiful journey, just as you do with everything else."

Overwhelmed, I lean back to meet her gaze. "You came here too?"

"Of course she did. We all did. It's the Hendrix way," Papa interjects, irritating me, and I take that as my cue to find my seat.

I get comfortable without looking at Sebastian, hating that I'm sandwiched between him and Finn. Not that Finn has technically done anything to me. Shit, he healed me earlier, but I know it's going to piss the Bishops off and something tells me he'll enjoy doing it.

Water is poured into a glass for me and I instantly wish it was something stronger. Glancing around the room, I try to spot where Creed, Brax, Eldon, and Zane are sitting but there are too many people for me to catch a glimpse of their faces. I can't spot Leila among the crowd, either.

I've spent the past fourteen years being a lone ranger and now I can't even handle sitting at a table with my so-called family without my one friend and the Bishops' presence.

I need to get a handle on myself.

"So, how are classes going, Raven? Sebastian tells me you survived today's Gauntlet by the skin of your teeth." Papa cocks a brow at me and if I didn't want to leave before, I certainly do now.

"You wouldn't believe it now, but she was pretty banged up. It took a little healing, but I hope you're feeling much better now, Raven," Finn interjects. Turning to face him, I can't decide if he's defending me or tooting his own horn for his ability to heal me.

"I am, thank you," I murmur to him before turning my attention back to Papa. "They're going as well as they can be. Random mishaps that land me in the wastelands of Ashdale make it a little difficult, though. Wouldn't you agree, Sebastian?" I finally turn to him, hating the smug grin on his face.

There I was, thinking tonight was going to be a good ending to a shitty week.

Fuck was I wrong.

"Ashdale? What were you doing there?" Mama asks, and I smile sweetly at her and Papa.

"Why don't you ask your son?"

I can't decide if it's a blessing or a curse that the food starts to arrive, halting our conversation. I can sense Finn watching me from the corner of my eye but I can't handle him on top of the mess I'm already sinking in, so I eat in silence.

Seven courses of small portions come and go and I still feel hungry. From fish to poultry, finished with a selection of cheeses and a chocolate cake. Wiping the corners of my mouth with my napkin, I notice others start to mingle around us and I'm ready to join them. I've barely scraped my chair back an inch when the room goes silent.

"I'd like to start off by thanking the parents and families for attending tonight. The victory of our children, of our future, should be celebrated." Professor Barton's voice booms throughout the room and I glance around to see where his projection is, only to find the man himself standing on a stage to my right. Instead of wearing a suit like most of the men here, he's draped in a red velvet cape with leather armor underneath. "I'd also like to thank The Monarchy for attending tonight's celebrations. Seeing the future guardians of our realm before us is a wonderful thing." He waves his hand to the left but I can't see who he's referring to over the heads in the way. "I don't really want to say much more, but enjoy the rest of the night, and I'm excited to watch you continue your journey here at Silvercrest Academy. Follow the sun, destroy the shadows, and survive another dawn."

My parents mouth the final words, as do Sebastian, Finn, and his parents too.

I'm ready to make a break for it but, as if sensing my eagerness to leave, Papa halts me with his gaze. "Raven, we must discuss more about how you're adjusting here."

I'd rather wash my face with a cheese grater. My hands clench in my lap, my desperate need to put some distance between us tightening my chest.

"Actually, Mr. Hendrix, I was hoping Raven would dance with me," Finn interrupts, catching me by surprise.

What is his angle now?

"I—"

"Of course, Finn. Raven couldn't refuse such an offer now, could she?"

I mean...I definitely fucking could, but the excuse to get the hell away from him wins out.

"Lead the way."

Finn offers me his hand but I don't take it. He takes the hint and waves for me to step ahead. His hand instantly goes to the small of my back but I glare at him over my shoulder and he swiftly moves it.

"I'm doing you a favor, Raven. Calm down."

"What's in it for you?" I ask, glancing over the crowd in search of Leila and the Bishops while heading toward the dance floor, which is already filling with couples. I don't catch sight of anyone I need at first, but I do see Barton talking with a group of people by the stage he'd stood atop moments ago.

"Please, I've been dying to snap your neck." The snarl comes from a furious Eldon, who appears out of nowhere from the other side of Finn. The relief I feel at finally finding one of them is quickly lost when I'm sure he's literally going to commit murder with his bare hands.

"You were fine for me to heal her. Besides, I'm doing her a favor, aren't I, Raven?" he replies, draping his arm around my shoulder and instantly making the situation ten times worse.

I'm ready to hand him over to his maker, but he's right, he is doing me a favor. Before I can say a word either way, Eldon has him by the collar, his eyes darkening as a fireball forms in his free hand.

Fuck.

"He's right, Eldon. He got me away from Sebastian and Papa. I owe him one." Eldon's eyes don't lighten at my words or my touch on his arm.

"Did you hear that? She owes me."

"And I'm paying you back now by saving your fucking life," I snark, hating the whole power trip unraveling before me. "Tonight's absolutely fucked, Eldon. Can you get me out of here? I'm done."

My words seem to sink through his anger and concern

flickers in this gaze. "Get the fuck out of here before I change my mind." He shoves Finn back a step, who stands still for a moment, shaking out his suit jacket, and I'm sure he's going to keep pushing.

"A pleasure as always, Raven," he murmurs before disappearing into the sea of people now joining the dance floor.

Eldon grabs my waist and pulls me in close, resting his forehead against mine. "I'm sorry I wasn't there to help you, but if you want to leave, I can make that happen. We just have to go and say goodbye to my mother."

The thought of meeting his mother makes me want to be sick, but I really want to leave, so it's the lesser of two evils I guess. "Sure, where to?" I ask.

I spy the grimace before he can hide it.

"She's talking with Zane's father at The Monarchy's table."

TWENTY FOUR

Eldon

Fuck obligations and everything else this shit show stands for. It's been driving me insane being apart from her. She scanned the room for us over and over again, but little did she know I was staring at her the entire time.

Seeing her stuck between Sebastian and Finn had my mother noticing the rage in me. It didn't take her long to find what was holding my attention and the smile on her face grew. That still didn't allow me to break protocol, but the second we could "mingle," I was on my way to her, but Finn beat me to it.

Fucker.

Now, with Raven in my grasp, I just needed to say goodbye to my mother so we can get the fuck out of here.

"I'm trying to remember the details Leila gave me about you guys," Raven murmurs, not hiding the fact that she did some digging on us. "So, Zane's father is a member of The Monarchy?" She sticks close to my side as we weave through the crowd.

"Yeah. He's actually The Monarchy's liason on the board. His sister is part of the Monarchy council too."

She nervously nibbles on her bottom lip as she glances out of the corner of her eye at me. "If what she said about Brax and Creed's parents is correct too, where are they sitting if their...family isn't here?"

A sad smile touches my lips as my stomach clenches. "Brax is at my table over there," I state, pointing to where I've spent the evening, but I don't stop moving us toward my mother. "Creed's mother is still here but my mother always makes sure to have her seated at the same table as us. Maybe going forward, I'll make her do the same for yours."

Her nose wrinkles in distaste. "Nobody wants to be seated at a table with my father. Even Finn's family didn't utter a word to him."

"That's because your father is known for being an asshole," I admit, and she hums in agreement.

Approaching the main table, Zane spots us first, quickly rising to his feet when he sees who I have with me. Since his father is a member of The Monarchy, he's even more restricted at these kinds of events than we are.

"Are we getting the fuck out of here?" he asks, eyes

wide and pleading.

"I just need to speak with my mother, then we're leaving." His shoulders sag in relief. "Get Brax and Creed so we can head straight out," I add, and concern flickers in his pupils as he glances at his father.

He must sense his son's gaze because he pauses his conversation with my mother to look at him. Mr. Denver momentarily glances down at his watch before smirking at his son. "I'm going to let you sneak off early but *only* because I want to schedule a meet-up with you in a few weeks, check in on you properly. Agreed?"

"Thanks, Pops." He throws himself at his father in a quick hug before rushing off to my table. Raven turns to me with a quirked brow.

"Did he just call him Pops?"

"I'm quite sure he's the only child of a High Monarch who can get away with it," I reply with a nod.

Zane's father isn't what you would generally expect from a Monarch. They're usually uptight, pretentious, and self-righteous in both their professional and private lives. Mr. Denver, however, loves his children very much. He almost gives my mother a run for her money.

"Are you leaving too, Son?"

I move around the table to my mother, lacing my fingers with Raven to keep her at my side. "Yeah. We're going to head out but I wanted to say goodbye first." Everyone says

I'm the double of my Mama. Same smile, same mischievous eyes, and the same brown hair.

As I expect, she plants her hands on either side of my face like I'm still a small boy and smiles at me lovingly. "Okay, but can I also schedule one of these meet-ups with you too? Hopefully your father will be home by then. It feels like forever and the Gauntlet was a complete surprise to everyone so I want to make the most of seeing you in the flesh." She gives me her best pout and puppy dog eyes and I nod. It was never even a question. "I would love it if the boys came too. Raven, you as well."

My mother's gaze turns to Raven, who stiffens at my side. Her jaw goes slack as she stares helplessly at my mother. "I-I…uhm…"

"I insist. Once I'm done speaking to this old fool, I'm going to hunt Evangeline down. It's been forever since I've seen you both. Gosh, you were such a sweet little girl and now a beautiful young woman."

Raven's eyes widen, unsure how to handle all of the compliments being directed toward her, and I grin.

"Mama, don't overwhelm her." I clutch Raven's hand tighter, stroking her fingers with my thumb.

"Thank you," she finally breathes, and my mother takes that as a cue to hug her.

I still keep hold of her hand as my mother embraces her. She doesn't overdo it, thankfully, and quickly releases her.

"I'll see you soon, but make sure you send those boys over to me to say goodbye as well." She gives me a pointed look and I salute her, which earns me an eye roll.

"Evangeline...Raven...As in Raven Hendrix?" Zane's father chimes in as we're just about to leave, halting us.

"Yes, Sir," Raven replies, standing taller, as if preparing for some kind of attack.

His eyes crinkle as he takes her in. I can't read his facial expression as he does so, but I don't get a chance anyway before my eyes slam shut.

Pink-feathered raven.

Black and white chess set.

A storm.

Everything shakes with the chaos, but only one piece falls.

A bishop.

The raven slowly moves toward it, rolling it around with its claw a few times before it finally manages to get a good grasp on it and stands it up again. The moment the base of the bishop reconnects the chessboard, the raven's feathers turn black.

Blinking my eyes open, I squint at the overwhelming noise. My disoriented gaze instantly lands on Raven, but it's my mother I can hear talking.

"Eldon...Eldon, are you okay?"

I can't respond right away, I'm too locked onto the

worry in Raven's eyes combined with the vision that just consumed me.

Raven's hand lifts to my arm, squeezing gently, and it seems to pull me from oblivion. "Sorry, I'm good," I breathe, the noise around me no longer as amplified as it was.

"Are you sure?" my mother asks, and I nod.

"I'm fine. Just a…"

"Vision," she finishes, keeping her voice low as she leans in to press a kiss against my cheek. "If you have any concerns, you know how to reach me, alright?"

I nod and take a step back just as Creed, Brax, and Zane appear. I let them say their goodbyes as I turn for the door with Raven still at my side. She doesn't pepper me with questions as we head out, which I'm beyond grateful for.

The second we step out into the fresh air, I sigh with relief. Reluctantly, I let go of her hand to dig into my pants pocket, retrieving my small pad and pen that I carry everywhere with me. I jot down the entire vision. Even though I can see them in my mind all of the time, it can be therapeutic to handwrite them. It can sometimes help me piece it together too.

Once it's secured in my pocket again, I turn my attention back to Raven. "Sorry about that."

"Why are you apologizing? I just want to make sure

you're okay."

Cupping her cheek, I eliminate the small distance between us until our noses brush. "Thank you. It was a vision, that's all. I don't get a say as to when they come through and I don't *really* have a handle on the way that it consumes me so completely when it does. But with practice, I'll eventually have more control over them."

"That's hot," she murmurs.

"What is?"

"That you can admit that you're learning. The amount of swagger you have, I sometimes expect you to think you're mightier than thou."

"I am," I reply with a snort, and she snickers at me. "I guess we're both full of surprises," I muse, and her eyebrows pinch together.

"What surprises have I had?"

"Where do I even begin with you?"

She pouts, but I kiss her before she can say a single word. It's slow, deliberate, and consuming. Her lips melt against mine, parting to reveal her tongue as she entices me further, awakening my cock.

Resting my forehead against hers, I look deep into her eyes, but before I can speak, I feel a slap on my back. Creed, Zane, and Brax circle around us, the latter wearing a frown as he has all evening while the other two smirk.

"What now? Our pretty Raven looks far too delectable

to call it an early night," Zane says with a wag of his eyebrows as he pulls Raven from my grasp.

Asshole.

"I'm ready to get out of this dress. It feels fake as fuck, just like the evening I've had," Raven grumbles, pointing back at the venue. "But my brain is too wired to sleep, too, so past getting out of this dress and heels, count me in."

TWENTY FIVE

Raven

I'm one thousand percent positive that today has been the longest day in existence. It may be close to three o'clock in the morning by now, but it still counts. I don't think I've ever been through so much and felt so many conflicting emotions in such a short space of time.

I witnessed Creed and Brax in the pit and faced the Gauntlet myself, only surviving with the aid of one surly gargoyle; had the joy of getting healed by Finn; went shopping with Creed, who enjoyed teasing the fuck out of me; then got all dressed up in a beautiful gown only to have to suffer through a meal with my brother and father.

What I want to do right now is numb my brain, switch it off so I'm actually able to get some sleep.

Hopeful that there's some kind of liquor in the fridge, I wrangle myself out of my dress, kick off my heels, and scoop my hair into a bun. Removing my jewelry and washing off my makeup, I opt for a pair of shorts and a tank top before stepping out into the lounge.

I'm not surprised to find the four of them filling the sofas, but it does startle me when they all turn their attention my way. It's unnerving and alluring all at once. They're all out of their suits. Brax and Creed are wearing black fitted tees and black shorts. Zane has a loose-fitted white tee and a pair of gray shorts on, while Eldon has forgone a top all together, opting for just a pair of black shorts.

Fuck.

Enjoying the attention, I shut my door behind me. "Do we have anything good to drink?"

"Already on it, Little Bird," Eldon says with a smirk, pointing to the discreet decanters on the coffee table.

"Perfect. What is it?" I ask, not really caring as I take a small glass and pour some of the pale liquor into it.

"Moon root and soda," Zane explains, and I hum in approval before downing half of the glass.

It was tasty as a shot but even more delicious as a cocktail.

Brax is sitting on the sofa beside Creed to my right, while Eldon and Zane have a space open between them to my left. Deciding not to push Brax again tonight after forcing him to accept my appreciation, I take the spot between Eldon and Zane.

Eldon instantly tries to wrap his arm around my shoulders but his arm disappears when Zane grabs my thighs, draping my legs over his and turning me sideways. Eldon doesn't miss a beat, though, as he twists in his spot, nestling me between his thighs as I take another sip of my drink.

I'm already hot and bothered by every glance in their direction, the pent-up tension that continues to bubble beneath the surface making it hard for me to breathe without any of them even touching me.

I glance across to the other sofa and find Creed staring at me intently. What would it feel like to have him caressing my skin too? It's already intoxicating, but I'm a greedy bitch who always seems to want more.

My gaze flicks to Brax at that thought, but he's staring down at the glass in his hands. I'm also a delusional bitch for seemingly wanting what I can't have.

Zane runs his palm down my leg, distracting me from my thoughts. "What can we do, Dove?"

I frown at him. "Dove?"

"Yeah, it suits you. You might be a big bad raven to the rest of the world, but in these four walls, you're softer, calmer, more pure. Like a dove." I'm speechless and my heart is hammering in my chest as I peer up at him. How do they all have a way of getting under my skin? "So, *Dove*, want to play a drinking game?"

I'm not sure how I feel about this nickname. His explanation is heart-warming, but it also leaves me feeling exposed, vulnerable, and uneasy. Three emotions I don't do well with. A drinking game is definitely needed to wash it all away.

"What did you have in mind?" I ask, my voice huskier than I expected.

His face lights up with mischief as Eldon runs his fingers down my arm, making me shiver. "Hmm, we can do truth or dare, a stripping card game, or spin the bottle," he offers, and Creed scoffs.

"If we play spin the bottle, it will only be Raven spinning because I sure as shit am not touching any of you fuckers," Creed grumbles, and a chuckle slips past my lips.

"So it would basically be Raven spins the bottle and we escalate what the prize is after each spin? Sounds like fun to me," Eldon murmurs against my ear, but it's loud enough for everyone to hear.

"I like the sound of that," Zane adds, winking at me.

"Are you trying to use a drinking game to segway into sex?" I ask with a quirk of my brow and Eldon gasps from behind me.

"We would never."

Liar.

Smirking, I down the rest of my drink and place the empty glass on the table. "If I don't want the prize that's laid out, we take a shot instead. Fair?"

"Fuck, you'll play?" Zane startles, awe flashing in his eyes as excitement radiates from him.

"You better be quick before I change my mind," I murmur, and he slips from beneath me a moment later, racing to the kitchen for an empty bottle.

I glance at the others, worried this isn't something they're interested in, but Creed and Eldon are looking at me with heat consuming their pupils and Brax hasn't left the room, even if he hasn't lifted his gaze. I'll count that as a win.

"Spin number one... you kiss the winner on the cheek."

It sounds light and simple, but I get the feeling it's a telling sign that he's easing me into it before things get deeper.

Nodding, I stand at the end of the coffee table, teeth sinking into my bottom lip as I focus on the bottle and not the guys. I'm a walking ball of need at this stage and it looks like I'm willing to go to whatever extremes are necessary to get myself closer to the edge of climax.

I spin the green bottle, my body clenching as the sound echoes around the room until the bottle comes to a rest pointing at Creed. He leans forward in his seat without a word, making me smile as I move closer. He taps his finger expectantly on his cheek and I give him a fake glare before pressing my lips gently against his skin. I linger an extra second longer than necessary before pulling back.

Bouncing back to the table, I meet his gaze for a split second, seeing the hunger that I'm sure radiates from me, too, before turning to Zane. "What's next?"

"Next spin gets a five-second, closed-lipped kiss."

I grin, nodding as I spin the bottle again. Panic flickers through me when the bottle lands on Brax. When he sits forward in his seat, I expect him to reach for the glasses to take a shot but, to my surprise, he braces his arms on his knees.

Holy fuck.

Rubbing my lips together, I move around the table and slowly drop to my knees in front of him. I don't know why I do that instead of waiting for him to tilt his head back, but it's too late to stand now.

I don't want to force myself on him, though, so I wait until his eyes meet mine. I'm hoping to catch a glimpse of what he's feeling, but he's a closed book, leaving me to stare dreamily at the cover. "Are you ready for the worst five seconds of your life?" I ask, hoping to lighten the mood, and it earns me an eye roll. I take that as my cue, tentatively placing my hand on his thigh as I inch closer.

My skin tingles, anticipation consuming me as we get closer and closer until our lips touch. I gasp, my eyes fluttering closed as the world drifts away. We're not moving, there's no passionate embrace or fired-up urgency, yet it sets me on fire.

His lips are so soft, his touch gentle, and his body warm.

I want to get lost in him, I want him to part my lips and claim more of me, but all too quickly, Eldon calls time. It takes everything I have to lean back, breaking the contact, but I'm acutely aware that it's me that does so and not him.

Blinking my eyes open, I'm met with his fierce stare but he doesn't say a word as he leans back in his seat. I drop my hand from his thigh and rush to my feet, tucking a loose tendril of hair behind my ear as I scurry back to the bottle.

I need a cold drink, something to take the edge off. I feel like I'm going to combust and we all still have our clothes on.

"Next?" I ask, refusing to look up.

"Next, the prize is a sweet thirty-second passionate kiss."

I nod, clenching my hands to try and stop the tremble from showing before I let the sound of the spinning bottle consume me. It feels like it whirls forever until it lands on Brax again.

"How the fuck am I getting shafted at my own game?" Zane grumbles, swiping a hand down his face as Eldon laughs.

Brax remains laid back against the cushion, but he

spreads his legs slightly. Nervously moving back toward him, my core clenches with desire. "How do you want me?" I breathe, and before I've even finished asking, he pulls me down onto his lap, my knees landing on either side of his thighs.

I place my hands on his shoulders as he moves one hand to my waist and the other finds my neck. His grip is firm as I lean into him, pressing my mouth against his, and this time, he instantly pries at the seam of my mouth with his tongue. I let him in, groaning at the contact as his fingers flex along my skin.

The outline of his cock is nestled between my thighs and it's impossible to stop myself from grinding against him as yearning takes over me. My fingers dig into his shoulders, my nails dragging along his top as I crave to feel his bare skin, when Creed calls time.

Our lips part but neither of us move an inch, our breaths mingling between us as we pant. His brown and green eyes stare deep into my soul, leaving me speechless, until he suddenly rises and deposits me in his spot on the sofa before he disappears.

Scrambling to my feet, I watch as he keeps his back to everyone, waving over his shoulder. "I'm out." His bedroom door slams behind him, leaving nothing else up for question as I turn to gape at the others.

"It's okay, Dove, he needs a minute. He'll be fine."

"Are you sure?" It all happened so suddenly, I really don't think he's fine.

"We swear it, Raven. Brax is…"

"Brax," I finish with a sigh, recalling the exact words that were said earlier. It might make sense to them but it leaves me with a niggling feeling in my gut that I just fucked up somehow and I don't know how to fix it. I don't even know why I'm eager *to* fix it, either, but it's the truth.

I can feel my mood souring, but Zane quickly comes to stand beside me. He cups my cheek, tilting my head back so I can look at him. "Do you want to stop? Or do you want to continue the distraction?"

"Distraction from what?"

He gives me a pointed look, and I sigh. Of course he can see right through me. Glancing toward Brax's bedroom door, it's clear he's not going to suddenly reappear and, as much as I want him here, I can't force him or bring this whole thing to a complete halt because of it too.

"Can we carry on?"

"Definitely, but I swear to God I'm spinning it this time because this is bullshit," he replies with a wink, calming the worry inside me. "What's the next prize?"

"We get to feast on her tits," Eldon blurts, sending heat to my core as I nod in acceptance.

Zane lifts the bottle, whispering to it before kissing the glass and placing it back on the table. He's so dramatic and

I love it.

The room is silent apart from the glass whirling on the table, until it settles on Eldon.

"Fuck yeah," he murmurs as Zane curses. "Show me those babies, Little Bird," he adds, cutting the distance between us in one step. His hands grab the back of my thighs, hoisting me in the air so my chest is level with his face. "Top off, Raven."

I reach for the hem of my tank top without argument, pulling it over my head unceremoniously, letting my breasts bounce in his face. A salacious grin spreads across his lips as he looks into my eyes and captures my left nipple with his teeth.

"Fuck."

My fingers find their way into his hair as I cling to him. My legs tighten around his waist as he swirls his tongue around the tight pebble before switching to my right breast. I want more, I *need* more, and I want it all now.

"Time," Zane grunts, breaking through my brain fog, but Eldon doesn't stop or release me.

"Spin again, add another prize to the mix," Eldon barks, barely breaking away from my chest.

"Raven?" Creed asks, and I nod vigorously, loving the sound of Eldon's demand.

"Next prize is to finger-fuck our little dove," Zane declares, and the sound of the bottle spinning follows after.

"What is this bullshit?" he exclaims as Creed snickers.

"Lay her down, Eldon," Creed mutters, and I'm unsure if he's going to listen or not. But, to my surprise, he lowers me to the sofa. The cool leather presses against my bare back and I shiver.

Eldon releases my breast from his mouth, reaching his arm behind the back of the sofa, and in the next breath the back goes flat, creating a bed. My eyes widen in surprise but he just grins. "I knew these sofas would be good for something," he states before capturing my nipples again.

I gasp at the same time hands find their way under the waistband of my shorts and I lift my butt up to help with the process. The cool air on my core excites me more as I anticipate what's to come.

"Are you ready, Raven?" Creed asks, and I nod.

"Please," I beg, writhing beneath them as Eldon licks, sucks, and bites at my breasts.

Rough fingers stroke through my folds, instantly circling my core, and I shudder. This is going to be my undoing, I can already sense it.

"You're so fucking wet, Raven," Creed grunts, slowly pushing two fingers deep into my pussy, and my back arches up off the sofa.

"Make me wetter," I plead, awe-struck by the fact that they're both touching me.

He swirls his fingers inside of me, making my walls

clench around him and tingles instantly flutter over my skin, my need to come already making itself known.

"The next prize is mine," Zane orders, and I nod, unsure if he can tell with the way I'm thrashing between Eldon and Creed.

"The next prize comes once she's climaxed on my fingers." Creed's dark tone makes me clench around him even tighter. When I reach down to stroke my clit in time with his thrusts, he bats my hand away, pressing his thumb against the needy nub as my back arches.

"Oh my…" There's no further warning as the ecstasy travels through every inch of my body, wave after wave of pleasure claiming me as I go limp beneath them.

"That was hot as fuck," Zane states, looking down at me, and I feel my cheeks heat. "Next prize is making her come with your tongue."

My teeth sink into my lip as my eyes widen. Looking down the length of me, I spy Creed licking my release from his fingertips as he trades places with Zane, who splays his hands on my thighs, parting them further as he dips his head and traces my folds with his tongue.

"Fuck," I hiss as Eldon relents on my breasts for a moment to look. His pupils are blown as he looks up at me, likely matching my own.

"Is that good, Little Bird?"

My jaw falls slack as Zane's tongue laps at my clit. My

head falls back, succumbing to the pleasure that consumes me, unable to find an answer to Eldon's question.

"Next prize is to—"

"Fuck my mouth," I blurt, interrupting whatever Creed was going to say, and the three of them curse in sync. "Please," I add. Needy as fuck, but I don't care.

Zane starts to ravish my core, feasting on me like he needs it to breathe, and my hands latch on to his hair since I have nothing else to hold on to. Eldon holds up the green bottle, aiming it at himself as he drops his shorts.

"I win."

His cock glistens, long, thick, and begging for me to taste, and he doesn't disappoint as he steps toward me, resting the weight of it against my tongue. It makes me hotter, needier, and I push up onto my elbows so I have a better angle to take more of him into my mouth.

"So fucking sinful," Creed murmurs, making me preen under his stare as he drops his shorts just enough to reveal his cock. He engulfs his length with his hand, tugging hard and rough as he watches me.

Eldon thrusts deeper into my mouth and my eyes water, making me groan as Zane rakes his teeth over my clit, and I detonate like a bomb once again. I moan around Eldon's cock, my body overcome by my pleasure reaching another peak at their hands.

"You taste so sweet, Dove." I exhale heavily, unable to

speak as my body aches in the most delicious way possible. "Tell me the final prize is to fuck you because I'm going to explode," Zane pleads, and I blink at him through the sexual haze gripping me as Eldon slips his cock from my mouth.

"Please." I don't know how I can be asking for more, but as spent as my body is, my essence needs everything they have to offer.

Zane grabs my waist, effortlessly flipping me onto my front, and it takes me a second to get up on my hands and knees as I hear the crinkle of him grabbing protection behind me.

"If Zane gets to fill your cunt, and Eldon gets your sweet mouth, I get to paint your back," Creed states, his onyx eyes melting me as I nod.

His hand works faster on his dick at my agreement and Eldon brings his cock to my lips again. I open willingly for him as I feel the tip of Zane's length at my core.

Holy fuck.

What did I do to earn this?

Despite how wet I am and the two orgasms that have rippled through my body, I still feel the stretch of Zane's cock. His fingers dig into my hips for leverage, grounding me as he starts to thrust his cock deeper with every pass.

As he retreats, Eldon dips to the back of my throat. Between them, they find a rhythm, keeping me filled at every moment, winding me up tight as I desperately anticipate the feel of Creed's cum touching my skin.

My body is a raging inferno, ready to collapse between them as I use them and they use me to find the euphoria waiting for us.

"Fuck," Creed grunts first, and a second later I feel his release coating my back, cool against my heated skin, and it makes my core tighten around Zane's cock.

"Damn, Dove," he grinds out, thrusting harder and deeper into me at a brutal pace, falling out of sync with Eldon so they're both filling me at the same time and I can't take anymore.

A frenzy consumes my body like I've never felt before, my body in the throes of the most intense orgasm I've ever experienced, and it's my complete undoing when Eldon grips my hair and paints the back of my throat with his release. I feel like I'm floating, my muscles spasming over and over as Zane slams into me with a finality that has him reaching his climax too.

My brain is foggy, my vision blurred, my body spent, and I've never felt better.

TWENTY SIX

Brax

Eat. Sleep. Workout. Repeat. Eat. Sleep. Workout. Jack off. Repeat.

That's been my mantra for the weekend while I hide away from the rest of the house. I'm a fucking basket case, but that's not new information. Classes might start again in a few hours but that just means I add them to the cycle as opposed to stopping what's currently helping me.

Although, *helping* feels like a big stretch of the word since nothing has kept *her* off my mind. It's fucking annoying as hell and embarrassing as shit, but that's where I'm at.

I haven't made eye contact with the devil herself since she was in my lap, claiming my mouth. The feeling hasn't gone away, the tingle on my lips and tongue still present, and it only makes me more frustrated with her. I don't act like this. I'm not weak like this. But she seems to have a way of bringing it out in me.

Fuck.

Dipping down into another press up, I do two more and finish my set before pushing up to my feet with a sigh. Sweat clings to me as the early morning sun peeks over the mountain range in the distance. The view from this house is my favorite thing about it. It's calming and breathtaking, offering a hint of serenity to this crazy life and the overwhelming emotions that continue to plague me.

I take a deep breath, exhaling hard as I step through the grass toward the low fence that lines the perimeter of our garden. Birds chirp in the distance, the waves crash below and the clouds float through the sky like my world hasn't been flipped upside down. I still breathe it all in, letting my mind pretend everything is actually calm, but I know I'm lying to myself.

The unmistakable sound of the patio door sliding open pulls me from the moment and I slowly turn around to see Eldon. Uncertainty wars in his eyes, just like they have since I stormed out on Friday night, but I get the sense I can't avoid him this time.

Maybe that's a good thing.

"I had a feeling you would be out here early," he says, moving toward the weights we have set up, and I make my way over to him.

"Well good for you," I grumble, swiping a hand down my face, and he snickers.

"You're a snarky bastard sometimes, you know that?"

"I'm aware." I reach for my water bottle on the table beside him and feel his eyes on me the entire time I take a drink. Once the cap is back in place, he plants his hands on his hips and cocks a brow at me.

"Is there anything you want to talk about?"

"After all these years, you suddenly think I'm a talker?" I laugh, shaking my head at him in disbelief.

"No, but you *are* my brother and I can sense something going on inside of you."

"I don't need you analyzing me," I grunt, grabbing my towel and wiping it over the back of my neck.

"I never said you did, but if you're hurting, I want to understand and help, Brax."

It's moments like this where the self-doubt worms its way in again and I'm left questioning if we're standing here today as friends, as brothers, or because I'm a project for him. Despite his swagger and charm, he wears his heart on his sleeve and I can read him like a book. Which is why I also have to remember that he fucking loves so easily once he lets you in and, as bizarre as it may seem, that includes me too.

My parents were friends with his when I was small,

both warriors in their own right, both lost to the shadows. I was five when the news came in and the confusion I felt over why my mama and papa weren't coming home still haunts me to this day.

Eldon's mother didn't bat an eye at taking me in, she demanded it. My mama had a sister, my aunt Faron, but she refused to allow me to go anywhere but with her. The solace I find in her, her husband, and Eldon stems from her unwavering love.

My head space right now weirdly feels more fucked up than it did back then. I've never felt this level of confusion before, but I can sense why it has a hold on me and that's exactly why I don't like it.

Am I hurting? No. Do I wish it was as simple as that? Yes.

His eyes continue to search my face and it's pointless for me to try and hide my true feelings from him because he always fucking knows.

"I don't know what you want me to say to you," I finally murmur, meeting his stare. I can't deny that I'm obviously lost in my head, but I'm definitely not understanding my own feelings and emotions enough to blurt them all out to him.

"I'm not asking you to say anything, I'm just telling you I'm here when you're ready," he responds, clapping me on the shoulder, and the tension that was starting to rush up my spine eases.

The second he gives me an out, all of the words that have been spiraling in my mind all weekend threaten to explode from my lips but I lock them shut. His hand drops from my shoulder and I clear my throat.

"Are we done here?"

"No," he snorts. "We've got loads more reps to do before breakfast and you know it."

Without another word, he grabs the weights and signals for me to join him. It takes two whole seconds for me to drop my bravado and do just that.

This is exactly why he's my brother. Because, just like that, he understands the mental space I need, drops the questions, yet remains present enough to be my pillar of support.

Walking to the academy building, I keep one step ahead of the others. The hairs on the back of my neck stand on end every time a certain someone looks at me, and it gets so overwhelming that I channel a drop of my magic and turn my neck to stone to stop it from happening. But, although the sensation may have disappeared, the sense and knowing that she is looking remains.

I know I'm going to have to address her at some point

but there's no way in hell it's happening now. So I settle on listening to her and Leila gossiping about whatever random shit Leila always seems to know.

Entering the academy halls, there's no congratulations, no excessive introduction back into school life. Just... nothing. It's as if last week never happened, but the number of students tells a different story. There's a somber feeling around us until I hear Genie and her friends cackling and everything is back to normal again.

I slip inside the guys' locker room without a backward glance. Finn and his friends are already here, joking around in the corner, while others focus on getting changed, and it blows my mind that no one else seems to feel the underlying tension from when we were last here.

It sounds harsh, cruel, and ridiculous, but would it not be better to lose students in battle? Like dying for an actual cause rather than some test that benefits nobody? Instead of staining every inch of the academy with their blood, why not on a battlefield? It's all completely fucked, but what do I know?

If Eldon told the others about our stilted chat this morning, none of them mention it. They're used to my silent phases by now and today's no different.

Switching out my uniform for my athletic shorts and tee, I'm ready for ordnance class. It feels like the likeliness of them finally pulling out some weapons is getting further and further away at this point. As much as I agree that our bodies are our number one weapon, give me something to play with.

I silently wait for the others to be ready before we head outside. Surprisingly, Raven is already waiting with Leila and I make the mistake of meeting her gaze. Uncertainty wars in her brown eyes, her teeth nervously sinking into her bottom lip, and my cock instantly swells at the sight of her.

Clenching my hands at my sides, I storm past her and head for the field without a backward glance. I'm never going to survive living with her, especially if I can't even look at her without my body responding.

Professor Figgins is wearing a grave expression as I near her and it's unnerving. Not that she's usually very smiley, but the tightness of her jaw and the pinch between her eyebrows is not the reception we usually receive.

I join the already-forming group surrounding her, my friends right behind me. Eldon stops at my right, Creed on my left, while Zane edges in front of us with Raven secured under his arm. I startle when Leila comes to a stop beside the she-devil, her gaze fixed on me with an inquisitive glint in her eyes.

She rubs her lips together before leaning closer to Raven to whisper in her ear. I know she's talking about me, I can feel it, but what am I going to do about it?

Nothing.

"If everyone can join us as quickly as possible, that would be appreciated," Professor Figgins hollers, silencing the group already here as the final stragglers arrive. She waits a moment to be sure she has everyone's attention before she releases a heavy sigh. "While we've spent the weekend recovering from the Gauntlet, two of our outposts were attacked. The first was at Pinebrook, which was completely neutralized within minutes." Damn. We were just there too. "However, the second attack on one of Ashdale's outposts wasn't so seamless," she admits, her shoulders sagging slightly.

"What happened?" Raven asks, her voice etched with concern as she folds her arms tightly over her chest and Zane's hold at her waist tightens.

"The attackers managed to get past the first wall, resulting in four fatal casualties…all fourth years."

Shit.

Murmurs dance in the air around us as the news washes over everyone. My gut clenches, reminding me of my earlier thought of dying in battle instead of a fucking academy-based Gauntlet. Death is death in the end, we're all heading to the same place, and those who died here and those at the outpost all deserve the same grace. Yet we're feeling more remorse now than we did all of last week.

"What attacked them?"

Everyone's attention shifts back to Raven and Figgins shrugs. "Those details haven't been confirmed yet. I'm hoping we'll learn more when the remaining fourth years from that station return this evening."

It must be serious if they're returning. But who is going to protect the barrier without them?

"I'm assuming alternative defense measures have been organized for the outpost for that to happen," Raven states. There's no disheartened approach to those coming home, just a simple observation.

Like mine.

Fuck. She needs to stop weaving her web. She's the black widow and I'm the embarrassing insect, eager to fall into her clutches despite knowing it's no good for me.

"That information is above our pay grade, Miss Hendrix, but good questions. Let's hope you'll survive this place to use them in the right circumstances." With that, Figgins steps back, dismissing the conversation.

The dangers are getting more frequent and closer to home, but from whom? And why? They don't give us much information and we deserve some answers.

Figgins whips her arms out at her sides and rack after rack of swords appear. "It's time we start upping our training. Take a walk through the racks, you'll know which sword belongs to you."

My eyebrows rise at her vague-as-fuck instructions,

but she's the professor so we all start to move without questioning it. I hold back, needing a little distance from everyone as my mind whirls. Assessing the racks, I consider where to start. Despite Raven being at the stand to my right, my body is drawn in that direction too.

"Each row of swords is made with a different metal and blessed with a different engraving. Whichever one you select is yours to keep. I'll provide sheaths at the end of the lesson, but once assigned, they are yours until you die."

Optimistic. Excellent.

Raven hasn't moved along by the time I get there and, as much as I try to keep my distance, I get a tingling feeling down my arm, drawing me closer to the sword on the other side of Raven. Avoiding any connection, I slip past her. Before I can stop myself, I reach for the blade at the exact same time she grabs the one behind it. Our eyes connect, surprise flickering in her gaze.

We both hiss at the same time we make contact with our chosen swords, the edges cutting into our palms, and droplets of blood quickly trail down the silver blades before pooling on the ground. A round of hisses ricochet around us from the rest of the students as they too seem to go through the same weird ritual of selecting a sword.

"Why does it feel like the sword chose me? Not the other way around?" Raven murmurs, searching my gaze for an answer. But I don't have one. I felt it too. The fact that they just drew blood feels like an omen or something. I don't know how to feel about this; the swords, the same selection as Raven, Raven in general…all of it.

I get the feeling the brutality we're going to face at the hands of the academy is only going to worsen with the news of the outpost.

"Excellent. If you've all selected, let's begin, shall we? The swords are going to be a new limb for each of us, a weapon when our magic isn't enough."

Raven gulps and my heart clenches.

Eventually I'm going to have to accept how fucked I am. And I get the feeling it's not going to be on my terms.

TWENTY SEVEN

Raven

The news of the fourth years is unsettling. It plays on my mind even after class is over and the day is almost done with. Ordnance class was a blur, from the swords to the news, my head was awash. I hate that there are always ten more questions for each answer you get and a whole heap of deflection that follows.

I spent the weekend walking on cloud nine after Friday night's revelations, yet one minute into classes and I've plummeted back to the ground again. I'm still unsure what everything means between the guys and I but, in comparison to the deaths that keep on coming, it's not the first priority.

Nothing has happened between us since the drinking game, just some small touches here and there, but nothing more. All I know is I'm hands down ready to do that again. Sooner rather than later, even if it's for distraction purposes.

I just need to get through the next class, then I can get out of here. Everyone's swords were transported to their rooms and I'm eager to learn more about mine.

We're back in the main building this afternoon, rows and rows of desks lined up for us, and I take the same one I was encouraged into on my first day. That puts Brax behind me, much to his discomfort, I'm sure. He's driving me insane with his closed-off exterior and gruff approach, making it impossible for me to even attempt to speak to him without starting in a fit of rage.

It seems the Bishops have me twisted and there's nothing I can do about it.

My ass has barely hit the seat when the professor turns to me with a tight smile. "Miss Hendrix, I believe a third year is coming to collect you. You've been called for a meeting."

What?

"A meeting for what?"

"I don't know. I'm sure the prefect can confirm more with you," she explains, waving her hand toward the door. I turn to look at the entrance and my stomach sinks when I find Sebastian standing there. The smirk on his face instantly pisses me off. He doesn't say a word and stands there waiting.

"You're not going with him," Eldon states from behind me, making Sebastian chuckle and my defenses continue to rise.

Not going would mean putting on a spectacle that he would likely enjoy, but there's some weight behind what Eldon's saying. Sebastian is never going to lead me anywhere good, I know it.

"Professor, who informed you of the meeting?" I ask, not yet rising from my seat.

"Sebastian did. Now, hurry along. The quicker you go, the quicker you're back." She claps her hands for me to get a move on but I'm still uncertain.

"Yeah, *Sis*, let's speed this up. I have shit to do too," Sebastian grunts from the door, making the professor gasp.

"Sebastian, language," she scolds, but he doesn't care.

Feeling eyes on me, I sigh, rising slowly as I throw my bag over my shoulder.

"It's a set up, Raven," Zane murmurs, irritation morphing his features as he slams his hands against the table and stands too. "Professor, I'll escort her," he starts, and she immediately shakes her head.

"You'll do no such thing," she retorts. "Take a seat, Mr. Denver." His nostrils flare, indecision warring within him.

"It's okay, I won't be long. I'm fine." I know my

reassurances fall flat and as I glance at the other Bishops, I can tell they're feeling the exact same way as Zane. Brax included.

Glancing at Leila, she nibbles nervously on her bottom lip and I can't handle the unnerving vibe stemming from Sebastian's presence. I'm sure he's loving it.

"I'll be fine," I reiterate once more before marching toward the door.

Sebastian takes off before I reach him, always trying to place himself one step ahead of me. I don't ask where we're going. It's not worth my breath and he either won't answer or will give me some bullshit response.

He leads the way down the long, marbled hall, through the main entryway, and along the west wing of the building. He doesn't slow until we're approaching the medical center and my eyebrows start to pinch in confusion.

"Why are we here?" I finally ask, relenting against my better judgment as he raps his knuckles on one of the blue doors.

"I'm just the messenger, Raven. Papa's here to take you away." The sinister smile that spreads across his face infuriates me.

"I call bullshit," I bite back. This might have been what I was asking for when I first got here, but hell, a lot has happened since then. Leaving isn't what I want. I know that instantly. Not when I'm learning so much. The Elivin

Realm is nothing like I thought it was. There is death lurking in all corners of this life. People are dying to protect the outposts while those suppressed in Shadowmoor are fighting just to survive. As much as I hate the latter, I would rather die for a cause than simple existence.

"You can call it what you want, Raven. He's here, Mama too. I hope you weren't getting attached to anything. Or anyone," he adds with a smirk, winking at me as he knocks harder against the door.

I shake my head, a sneer on my lips as I get ready to lay into him, but the door finally swings open and it's Mama standing on the other side. My heart sinks, horror at her presence slashing at my insides as Sebastian salutes her.

"Tell Papa I did his bidding. Next time, he can leave you at home," he grunts and my mother says nothing, just takes his wrath before he storms off.

I don't understand where his anger and hatred stems from. If it was new, a sudden shift because we left for fourteen years, then I might get it a bit more, but he was like this before we left.

Once he's out of sight, I twist my lips and turn to my mother. The pity in her eyes is instantly evident and it does nothing to calm the turmoil rising up my spine.

"What's going on?" I ask, shuffling my bag up my shoulder. She offers me a tight smile as she opens the door wider and steps back into the room but nothing more.

"Come in, Raven."

To anyone else she would sound soft and delicately spoken, but I can sense the unease in her tone, the cracks in her confidence.

"Not until you tell me why I'm here and what the medical department has to do with it," I demand, remaining frozen in place as her gaze drops.

"Because your mother asked you nicely. I can use the alternative route if you wish." My gaze whips to Abel, who stands behind my mother. His lips form a thin line, his eyes boring into mine as he waits for me to follow his command.

I'm not entirely sure what the alternative route is, but if the grimace that takes over my mother's face is anything to go by then I'm probably not going to like it. Exhaling, I glance down the corridor, confirming no one else is here to rescue me before I reluctantly step inside the room.

I remain by the door, taking in my surroundings as I try to figure out what the hell is actually going on. There's a medic bed against the far wall and the wall directly to my left is lined with cabinets filled with potion ingredients.

"Why are you here?" I ask, glancing between the pair of them as mama inches closer to the bed and papa rolls up the sleeves of his shirt.

"To see you," my mother murmurs, the tight smile not reaching her eyes as she twists her hands.

"I just saw you both on Friday. What the hell has happened since then?"

"Nothing. We were hoping to do this after you danced with Finn, but what a surprise it was when we learned you had already left."

I gulp, watching as my father knocks on the opposite door, all while keeping his eyes on me.

"I don't understand," I murmur, and he shakes his head.

"I know, but you will."

What does that mean? Glancing to Mama for more information, I find her gaze is tipped downward again. Where is the woman with a backbone who picked me up off that porch and got us the hell out of there? Where is she now when I need protection from this man who is supposed to be my father? I don't even know what's happening, but I already know it's not good.

Clearing my throat, I inch closer to the door behind me as I drop my backpack on the floor. If I have to run, the extra weight won't help. There's nothing important in there anyway.

"How about you explain it to me then?"

"Take a seat on the bed and I will," my father counters, making my gut clench. He's playing me, I fucking know it. "The door behind you is already locked, so running isn't an option. The quicker you follow my orders, the quicker this will all be over with."

"*What* will be over with?" I grunt, frustration coiling tight in my stomach at his lack of information.

"On the bed."

Grinding my teeth, I step back and test the door handle, confirming it is, indeed, locked, and my heart sinks. It's always the same with this man: submit or feel his wrath.

I don't want either.

I flex my hands as I go against my gut and move toward the bed. Mama plumps the pillows, still avoiding my gaze. Sitting at the foot of the bed, I hate that my feet dangle, not touching the floor, making me feel like a small child.

"Well…" I push, and my mother grabs my hand.

"When you and Sebastian were younger, your paternal grandparents gifted us with a seer who specialized in exploring a child's gifts before they came of age," she starts, looking deep into my eyes as pain seeps from her very essence. "It seemed absurd, like a violation or something, so we declined."

"It's a good thing they went against our wishes then, isn't it, Evangeline?" Abel murmurs, his expression indescribable as my gaze flickers between them.

"No, Abel. It only made things worse," she answers honestly, anguish quieting her voice.

"I still don't know what you're getting at," I grumble, my body wound tight with what they're saying. Someone looked at my magic? To what, learn I had none or…? Fuck.

Hope seeps into my heart and I can't take it.

"His parents had the seer look into your souls when they spent the day with you. It was our tenth wedding anniversary and they insisted we celebrate, so we took the opportunity. It was perfect." Her voice grows shaky as she lifts a hand to her mouth, a stray tear tracking down her face. "Until we returned home."

My chest is tight, my throat dry, and my pulse pounds in my ears.

The way she looks at my father in this moment, like the world was theirs, like the love that held them together was diminished by someone else's actions. I try to remember who she's referring to, a memory of spending time with someone other than my parents and Sebastian, but nothing comes to mind.

"What happened?" I think I might be sick, but I need to know.

"When we arrived home..."

"They learned of Sebastian's powers...and yours," my father finishes as the door he knocked on earlier finally swings open and an older man steps through.

My powers?

My powers...

I have them?

Mama smiles weakly at me, lifting her hand to my face, but she drops it before she reaches me. "They had your powers suppressed before we even returned home."

"My powers?" I whisper nervously and she nods.

Holy fuck.

"But in doing so, they also let someone else know what you would someday be capable of."

"What *great* things you would be able to do," Abel reiterates, which doesn't bode well for me.

"Which is what?"

"We can't be sure yet, the seer isn't always correct, but once the suppression is removed, we'll find out." My father encourages the man toward me and my adrenaline spikes.

"What does that mean?" I ask, lifting my hand to stop him from approaching, but he completely ignores me as my mother grabs my face, turning me to look at her.

"I thought it would be safer to hide you, but I was wrong. I thought those who loved you would only want the best for you, but I was wrong. I thought you would be safer without your powers, but I was wrong. If what the seer said is true, your best defense... is you."

"What does that even mean?" I plead, hating that they're still talking in circles instead of explaining everything to me.

"All that matters is that you trust no one. Not even me. You don't know what abilities another has, what hold they can have on another," she murmurs, her grip on my chin tightening.

Why does it feel like I shouldn't have whatever ability she's talking about? If it has them both so worked up, I don't want it.

"I don't want the suppression removed," I breathe, and she sighs as my father comes into view over her shoulder.

"As soon as we learned about the suppression, I had it removed. But the second your mother took you to Shadowmoor, you were draped in theirs," he states, running his thumb over my temple where my black ink once sat.

"The mark is gone," I breathe, flinching back away from his touch and he shakes his head.

"The ink was concealed, but the suppression still remains. That's what my friend here is for."

"I don't want it," I blurt, and my father laughs.

"When the time comes and your magic finds your soul again, they will either want to kill you or use you, there's no in between. You want the latter and that's what I'm going to be able to aid you with, Raven." He stands tall, almost proud of the fact that he wants to use me. But for what?

None of this makes sense. I thought I was at war with myself over whether I wanted to be here or not but that was only the surface problem. Now it stands between me and my power. A power I'm unsure I want, even though it's all I've ever wanted.

"I don't want this," I repeat, glancing at my mother, but she takes a step back.

"If I thought there was a safer alternative for you, I would take it. I might look like the enemy but I swear to you, I am putting you first in all of this," Mama promises, another tear trailing down her cheek as the stranger my father brought in nudges on my shoulder for me to lie down.

"Don't fucking touch me," I shout, leaping out of his reach and landing on the other side of the bed.

"I'm sorry, Miss. It won't take long."

That's not the reassurance I want. I'd rather be facing some bullshit Sebastian is throwing my way instead of this. I want to go back to the classroom and refuse to leave. I need the Bishops. I hate it. I hate that I can't survive in this room on my own.

"No."

"Raven, there really isn't time for this," Papa states with a sigh, glancing down at his watch as he circles the bed.

"Stay away from me," I grind out, inching backward, but there's nowhere for me to run and he knows it. "If you lay a hand on me, I *will* fight and I will scream," I yell, the rage inside of me bubbling uncontrollably until my entire body stills.

The fire that burned moments ago turns into ice, my

rage simmering to a placid sense of calm as I move against my will. My father's hand is aimed in my direction, guiding my rigid body to the bed. I scream, but no words come out, not a single sound, but it vibrates in my head so hard I'm sure I'm going to pass out.

Droplets of rain trickle over me and I have no idea where they're coming from, but the unmistakable sound of thunder rumbles in the distance. Mama's magic.

It doesn't save me though, it doesn't shield me from what I don't want, it just storms in the room until my world goes dark.

TWENTY EIGHT

Raven

Nausea swirls in my stomach, my head pounding as I try to open my eyes, but it's impossible.

What the hell is wrong with me?

Everywhere aches, my body cemented to the surface beneath me and panic rising in my throat like acid. I have no idea where I am and the brain fog I'm rocking isn't helping at all.

Taking a weak breath, I try to open my eyes again. It takes a few more attempts but, eventually, I can see the dim room without my eyeballs wanting to burn.

I'm in my bedroom. *How did I get here?* I'm still in my uniform on top of the covers, the late evening sun casting shadows across the room. Squeezing my eyes shut, I try to remember the last thing that easily comes to mind. Sebastian. He came to collect me from class to take me to…

It hits me all at once. Mama, Papa, the random guy, the medical department, the murmurs about abilities and suppression and crazy fucking grandparents that violated my mind as a child, which lead to… running? Hiding? Surviving? I don't really know what to call what we were doing in Shadowmoor, but my gut clenches with the thought. It was because of me, because of the magic the seer saw in me.

Panic morphs into dread and I feel like I can't breathe. Pushing up to sit on the bed doesn't make it any easier, my lungs constricting despite my efforts.

"Raven? Hey, calm down." I startle at the sound of Zane's voice, my heart lurching even more when I find him sitting on a chair beside my bed. How did I not even notice he was there? He reaches for the lamp on my nightstand and illuminates the room in a soft glow, highlighting the concern on his face as he moves closer. "Is there anything I can get you?"

I shake my head, unable to find any words. My stress must be evident in my body language because he's reaching for my hands in the next moment, taking big, deep breaths, encouraging me to copy him. I feel like an idiot, embarrassed at my panic attack, but I mimic his motions regardless. After what feels like an eternity, it starts working, my shoulders relaxing a little and a sigh finally falls from my lips.

"Better?" he asks, tucking my hair behind my ear, and I nod.

"Thank you."

"I'm just glad you're okay, Dove. What happened?" He looks deep into my eyes, his hazel pools practically touching my soul as he searches for answers, and I don't even know how to formulate words.

Rubbing my dry lips together, I glance around the room. "How long have I been here?"

He swipes a hand down his face, irritation tightening his jaw. "I honestly don't know, Raven. We searched the entire academy after you didn't come back to class. Over an hour checking every inch of the place. It was only after Brax cornered Sebastian that we considered coming back to the house. That's when we found you laying here, passed out, and that was at least two hours ago."

Fuck.

A knock at the door interrupts my response and Eldon's head peeks through the gap as he inches it open. "She's awake." He rushes into the room, Creed right behind him as Brax waits by the door, filling the space with his broad shoulders.

I expect to feel overwhelmed with them all barging in but it doesn't seem to bother me. Although, that's likely because I'm already sinking over something else. Over what my parents did to me... whatever that is.

I'm standing before Eldon can reach the bed, running my hands over my crumpled uniform.

"What's happening?" he asks, blocking my path to the door.

"I need to get back to the academy, back to them." My mind goes into overdrive and I can hear the mania in my voice, teetering on the edge of panic. They have to still be there. They can't have left. Not after this.

"Who's them?" Creed asks, his brows furrowing at my vagueness.

"My parents."

"Your parents were here?" Zane's expression matches Creed's as they stare at me in confusion.

Join the party, guys, I'm fucking confused too.

Wiping a hand down my face, I don't really want to explain any of it, but I have to offer them something. "That's where Sebastian took me, to them. To..."

"To what, Raven?" Eldon's tone gets sharper, not *at* me, but *for* me, but that doesn't seem to make a difference to the bubbling turmoil inside.

Locking eyes with Creed, a thought comes to mind. "I need you to reveal the mark on my temple again. Please."

I move toward him and he instinctively steps back. "I'm not doing that."

"I need you to, or one of you, please." I'm very

aware I'm starting to sound a little crazy, but he doesn't understand.

"Tell me why."

I shake my head. "Just please, one of you," I plead, glancing at Zane and Eldon, even chancing a look toward Brax, but it's Eldon who steps closer.

He swipes his thumb over my temple, my heart pounding wildly, but the second his nose wrinkles, I know it's not working.

Fuck. Fuck. Fuck.

"Nothing's happening, Raven. I don't understand."

Hiding my face in my hands, my breathing is coming in shallow bursts again, the panic consuming me once more as my father's words replay in my mind.

"When the time comes and your magic finds your soul again, they will either want to kill you or use you, there's no in between. You want the latter and that's what I'm going to be able to aid you with, Raven."

My mother's warning piling on top does nothing to calm me. *"I thought it would be safer to hide you, but I was wrong. I thought those who loved you would only want the best for you, but I was wrong. I thought you would be safer without your powers, but I was wrong. If what the seer said is true, your best defense… is you. All that matters is that you trust no one."*

No one. Trust no one.

I don't feel any different, I don't *feel* anything new, anything living inside of me, unsuppressed, not even a flicker. Yet her final words haunt me. I was always my own defense before I came here and learned to rely on them. *Trust no one.*

"Raven, you're going to need to explain to us what's going on," Creed states, his voice seeping through the fog I'm lost in, but I shake my head.

Turning to face him, I roll my shoulders back, a numbness washing over me like I've never felt before. "Actually, I think it's the complete opposite."

Zane grabs my arm gently, frowning down at me. "What's going on, Raven?"

"I need some space."

"Space from what?" Eldon asks, confused by everything unraveling, but it's better now than later.

"I just need you out of my room." I fold my arms over my chest, holding myself tight as they glance between each other.

"Why?"

"I just need to be alone," I bite, my anger not even remotely aimed at them, but after the events of today, they're the ones who are going to feel it.

"Raven, I don't know what happened with your parents, but whatever this is, pushing us away isn't going to help," Brax grunts, and I scoff.

"You've got some fucking nerve telling me that pushing people away isn't going to help. How's that working for *you*?" I hate the words as soon as I say them but there's no taking them back now.

"It's not the fucking same and you know it."

"Isn't it?" I stare him down, pleading with him to just leave so I can think, be alone, and figure out what my next move should be. I'm protecting us all, they just can't see that. Not that they would be able to without the bigger picture but I don't really know shit either.

"Dove, please just—"

"Just get out," I yell, hating the hurt in Zane's eyes as I point toward the door. I'm panting, steam on the verge of pouring from my ears as they all gape at me. It takes three short breaths for them to nod in reluctance, trailing toward the door one after the other.

My soul hurts with every step they put between us, every inch I ask for. It's a double-edged sword and I'm going to feel the sharp sting either way.

Brax stands to the side for each of them to walk past before he grabs the door handle. I'm ready to hear the door click shut but he fixes his stern eyes on mine. "Enjoy your space, Raven."

He slams the door with more force than I expect and I jump slightly. Flopping down onto the bed, I look down at my hands. They don't look any different. How can I look no different yet feel so constricted all at once?

I'm lost, alone, and uncertain. Just like I was in Shadowmoor.

I expect more of a challenge to get out of the house, but it seems my bitchiness and need for space pushed all of the guys into their rooms. So when I step into the lounge in a brown sweater and black leggings, with my boots fastened high, I'm met with silence.

Guilt twists in my gut but I double down on the numbness that likes to take hold of me as I quietly slip out the front door. I walk to the end of the path and wait a few minutes, expecting one of them to follow me, but no one comes and I take that as my cue to get on with it.

Marching down the pathway back toward the academy, I only come across two people. Everyone else is either in their houses or the shopping district. Even when I step into the halls I find them mostly barren. The few people I do run into don't pay me any mind, wrapped up in their own tasks instead.

My boots echo off the marble floor as I cut through the halls until I find myself at the medical center. Tension starts to creep up my spine and nausea threatens at the back of my throat again. I stop outside the same door as earlier, straining my ears to listen for anyone on the other side, but I get nothing.

I take a deep breath for strength before rapping my knuckles against the frosted glass panel. When I count to ten and no one answers, I try the handle and the door slowly creaks open. It's completely dark so I search for the light switch, but even the glow doesn't reveal anyone or anything.

They really just did that to me and left without another word? Maybe I shouldn't be surprised at this point. It's bullshit. All of it.

Closing the door behind me, I step further into the room before taking a seat at the foot of the bed again. The urge to scream and cry burns beneath the surface but I bottle it up. They don't deserve anything else from me, not after I pleaded with them earlier and they did it anyway.

I have no recollection of what happened after my world went black, no idea what the process entailed, how invasive it could have been; nothing.

With a sigh, I stand, hands on my hips as my chin dips to my chest. What the fuck am I supposed to do now? I need to go home. There's nothing for me here. Scanning the room one last time before I leave, my gaze focuses on a circular cut out card on the far cabinet.

I don't know what draws me closer, but I'm reaching for it without even thinking, and I gasp when I see it's an image of me with Mama. I must be four, maybe five, but I can definitely tell it's before Shadowmoor. The old house looms in the background. Lifting it closer, my thumb skims over the image, my heart aching, and I'm not even sure what for anymore.

"I knew you would come back... or I was hoping at least." I startle at the sound of my mother's voice and turn to find an astral projection of her sitting on the bed where I had been moments ago. Sadness consumes her features, her bottom lip trembling as she looks down at her lap. "It's done, Raven. The suppression has been lifted. It's not going to happen overnight, but your magic is coming. Now only time will tell whether the seer was correct or not."

If they could just tell me what the seer said to begin with then I would at least know what I'm up against.

"You're not a Void, Raven, and if what the seer says is true, you're far from it," she continues, still offering me nothing as I stand here helpless. But despite that, I know if she was here in the flesh, I would throw myself at her. "Despite all of that, you're my daughter, the purest soul I've ever known, and that's not going to change. I'm sorry this has turned into your world. Maybe I shouldn't have tried to prevent the inevitable, but I guess we'll never know and I'm sorry for that. I'm sorry decisions were made on your behalf without your input. I just felt like a harder, darker life was still safer than The Monarchy..." She shakes her head, cutting short the important facts once again. "I love you so much, sweet girl." She lifts her head, looking right at me even though she's not even here, but it's like she knew exactly where I would be.

"I love you too," I whisper, hating that today's events don't seem to change that.

"Remember that you are strong, brave, fearless, and resilient. Keep being you and everything is going to be okay. Follow your heart, find solace in the shadows, and take down the dawn."

She disappears with a blink, leaving me helpless with adrenaline coursing through my veins. All of this is based on an *if*, and I think that's what I hate the most. Now only time will tell, but one thing seems to be true.

I'm not a Void.

TWENTY NINE

Brax

I'm quite sure she thinks I don't know that she snuck out last night after she blasted everyone with her wicked tongue and banished the fools tripping over themselves for her. I'm not dumb and I can hear everything, including the creak of a door and her boots on the hardwood floor. I considered telling the others but decided that, if she wanted to sneak out, it was her prerogative. As long as she came back, that's all that mattered. Otherwise, I'd go hunting.

Just like I did when she didn't come back to class yesterday, but she doesn't need to know that.

I'm quickly realizing that's my obsession; hunting her, capturing her, rescuing her when she's a damsel in distress. But she's far from a woman in need. She's the alluring, wicked evil thrumming through my veins, unknowing of what creeps in my thoughts.

It's impossible to deny it to myself anymore, not after last night. The memory repeats in my thoughts as I watch her sway her ass in front of us. She thought it would be cute to try and sneak out this morning too, but Zane, Creed, and Eldon were at their wits end, desperate to get back into her good graces and they were ready.

I held back, though. Watching. Waiting.

Last night was revolutionary for me. The list of what I like about her quickly outweighs what I hate. Suddenly, my anger feels predatory, desperate, and almost sinister when I think of all the things I want to do to her.

Swiping a hand over my mouth, I slow my pace, putting a little more distance between me and the group so I can think and appreciate her.

I like that she pushed back last night.

I like that she didn't give a fuck that we were twisted up with worry over where she was or what had happened.

I like that she put herself first.

I like that she isn't so doe-eyed over the others that she relented to appease them.

I like that she was on the verge of delirium.

I like seeing her a little unhinged, even if I still don't know why. That's going to change.

But most of all, I like that she pushes me.

My hates are the issue, and she's going to hear all about it when we finally have a good talk—a talk that is definitely coming, whether she likes it or not. The others are going to pepper her with questions all day but I'm going to bide my time and learn everything there is to know for when she least expects it.

I keep my permanent frown in place and my gaze on her ass as we move down the academy halls. When we reach Professor Fitch's classroom, he's waiting outside for us.

"We're going to have a lake trial today," he announces, his voice gruff and sharp. "Everyone head to the locker rooms and change into your wetsuits. I'll meet you down by the lake." He shoulders through the crowd of students without another word, only offering a partial smile to his daughter before continuing through the masses.

Confusion and surprise seems to be on everyone's tongue as murmurs rise.

"What's this about?" Zane asks, leading the way toward the locker room.

I shrug.

"They seem to be upping the game preparations. In a little over a week we've had the Gauntlet, the swords from Figgins, and now this," I state as Raven slips past us with Leila to head to the girls' locker room.

"Are they worried?" Eldon asks, pulling my gaze from the sweet flare of Raven's hips. I bite back my irritation, acting unfazed.

"They're definitely trying to speed up our learning. For what though, I don't know." I press my thumb to the tip of the clothing hook, waiting for the wetsuit to present itself before I start to change.

"Maybe they should focus on our actual magical abilities then," Creed mutters, hanging his blazer up, and I nod in agreement. It's clear we're being left in the dark about a lot and the method behind their madness is yet to be revealed.

Nothing more is said on the topic as we finish changing and head back outside. Two seconds later and Raven is strolling out with Leila at her side. My cock is going to be prominent through the wet suit any second. I can't hide my reaction to her in this fucking thing.

That's another thing to add to my hate list.

We tail behind them like before, heading down the walkway to meet Fitch at the water. Excitement starts to buzz through the air when everyone sees the two-man watercrafts littering the shore.

"I'm going to call out names in twos and that will be your pairings. You'll share a watercraft to search for the coin linked to each of the wet suits you're wearing. Speed isn't the main priority today. It's all about following your instincts, listening to the connection and following it. The nets on the back of the jets will help you. Any questions?" He casts his gaze over everyone but no one raises their hand so he proceeds to call out the pairs. "Genie and Finn. Leila and Eldon. Creed and Zane. Brax and Raven."

Fuck yeah. It seems today is my lucky day. To be partnered with her after all of the revelations I've had, there's no escaping it.

Once he's reached the end of his list, he waves for everyone to find their own watercraft.

Raven glances back at me with a nervous glint in her eye and I smirk. "After you, Shadow."

Her eyes narrow and I'm not sure if it's at the nickname or the fact that she's paired with me. Either way, I like it.

We reach the closest one and she tosses a glare over her shoulder at me. "I'm driving."

"Okay," I murmur, and she gives me a suspicious look. I'm assuming she was waiting for me to argue with her, but sitting at the back sounds good to me.

I push the watercraft out into the water and hold it still as she climbs on. She mumbles her thanks, likely hating that she feels obligated to say it, and I swing my leg over the back of the seat and settle in behind her. I make a conscious effort to not sit flush against her. She doesn't need to know how affected I am by our close proximity.

A few people take off on their jets and Eldon makes Leila scream as he goes full throttle while Raven's eyebrows pinch in confusion.

"What do we do now?"

"Blast it. We may as well have a little fun while we figure out where it's trying to lead us."

Without another word, she hits the throttle, forcing me to grab on to her waist before I fall in the water. I feel her body tighten at my touch as the wind whips around us, but she doesn't tell me to move. The faster we go, the more distance we cover and I feel the tension inside her slowly ebbing.

Eventually, she slows, lifting one hand to her chest and I stretch out to grab the handlebar.

"What's wrong?"

"I feel something," she mutters, nibbling her bottom lip. "This way," she breathes, taking off again, and this time I keep my hand rested beside hers. "Could you pass me a net please?" she asks as she comes to a stop again. I reach behind me to grab one for her.

It almost feels odd, being civil with one another. Who knew?

She makes a conscious effort not to touch my hand when she takes it from me and slowly starts to swish it in the water to our left, getting deeper and deeper into the water until I'm sure she's going to fall in.

I grab her waist and she startles. "I've got you."

She rubs her lips together, considering my words for a moment before she nods and leans further into the crystal blue water. "I've got it," she says with a gasp, bolting up straight in her seat with a hand-sized coin in her net. The pleased expression on her face surprises me.

I unclip the small box at the back of the watercraft, taking it from her and storing it away. Now it's my turn to figure it out. Reaching for the handlebar again instead of her waist, Raven stops me before I get all the way, grasping my hand with a frown.

"What happened to your knuckles? Why are they busted up?"

Fuck.

"Don't worry about it."

Her frown deepens. "I can't help it. What happened?" she insists, meeting my gaze this time as her hand remains on mine. I shrug. "Wait…" she breathes, her eyes widening to saucers as she gapes at me. "I remember Zane saying something about you speaking with Sebastian yesterday to find out where I was. Does this have something to do with that?"

I raise my shoulders dismissively. "He deserved it."

Raven's jaw goes slack. I can't tell if she's mad or thankful. "I'm sorry," she finally murmurs, making me frown this time.

"What for?"

"Not being able to heal it."

"I wouldn't let you anyway. I like the sting, the bite of pain, and I relish in the damage I did to that fucker's face."

Her smile grows at my words, adding another thing to my like list. I'm so screwed.

Deciding to push my luck, I quirk a brow at her. "Since we're sharing, are you going to tell me about yesterday?"

Her hand quickly drops from mine and she faces forward in her seat once more. "No."

"Why's that?" I ask with a smirk, crowding her as I place both hands on the handlebars without actually touching her.

"It's not for anyone else to worry about." Hmm. That's not what I was expecting.

"Well, we both know I don't worry about shit so why don't you enlighten me?" I retort, and she peers over her shoulder at me, wavering slightly before she shakes her head. Inching closer, I bring my mouth to her ear. "How about you don't push me away and I don't push you away," I breathe, and she shivers.

"Fuck that, you're full of shit," she rasps, and I pull her back against me so she's flush against my chest, the press of my cock nestling between her ass cheeks.

"Try again."

She squirms against me for a moment before she finds her tongue. "The feel of your impressive dick isn't going to make me spill."

Fuck.

"Are you sure?" I push again and another shiver runs

down her spine. "How about you tell me what happened yesterday, and I won't tell the others how you snuck out."

"What the fuck? Did you follow me?"

At least she's not trying to deny it.

"No."

"Swear it?"

"Swear on what, Shadow? You left, you came home, the rest is your business. Unless it involved Finn or some other fucker, then the gloves are off."

"Of course it didn't," she grunts, sinking into my hold a little more, and I nuzzle my nose against her throat.

"Then tell me."

I know I'm pushing—hard—but the second she wavered the first time, I couldn't help myself. I know my chances are slim but I've always had a way with odds.

"When you guys concealed the mark when I got here, it didn't remove the suppression that it represented. So, that's what my parents forced on me yesterday."

What. The. Fuck?

"Tell me everything," I bite, my body vibrating at the fact she said *forced*. Much to my surprise, she does. She spills everything, about the seer and what her parents said, as well as the message she found when she went back last night, everything.

When she's done, it's like she's zapped of energy, her body limp in my hold as I prop her up.

"So, to clarify, you're being a bitch to be kind because you're scared you can't trust anyone, worried who might use you and why, but mostly petrified of the target that may be put on your head and those you care about?"

Slowly, she sits tall again, twisting in her seat to look at me properly. "Pretty much."

If anyone understands that, it's me. My parents died. The thought of being close to anyone ever again and feeling that loss or making someone else feel that way over me has driven me for as long as I can remember.

"You're crazy. Do you know that?"

She snickers as she shakes her head. "I don't know what the fuck I am." Her admission kills me. I can feel her pain, but more than that, I can sense her confusion and loss.

I don't even touch her this time and she nestles back against me, wiggling her ass slightly against my dick as she tilts her head to keep her eyes on me.

"Don't look at me like that, Shadow." I know exactly what she's doing and I'm not a polite gentleman like Eldon who will honor her under any circumstance. I want to defile and take while bringing her to the greatest heights.

"Like what?"

"You're playing a dangerous game. You won't like it when I get my hands on you, Raven. What I'll do to you," I breathe, watching her eyelashes flutter as she shivers for a third time. I'm hanging by a thread and I'm ready for it to snap.

"You don't want any of that," she mumbles, her eyes narrowing at me. But the lust floating in her irises only grows more prominent.

Banding my arm around her, I splay my fingers out over her stomach, wishing the wetsuit wasn't there. "What I *don't* want is the way you get under my skin without even trying. What I *don't* want is to admit how much you consume me. Actually, there are a lot of things that I fucking hate about you, Shadow," I growl, unable to stop the dam now that it's open. "I hate that you make me scared, terrified. I hate how fast you have me under your spell. I hate how quickly you're trying to make me fall. I hate how much I want you." My breaths are ragged, as are hers, and it spurs me on. "What I want is to chase you, claim you, take you. And I hate that too."

Her pupils are blown as her tongue sweeps out to wet her lips and she waits for the other shoe to drop, but there is nothing else. That's all of it. On the table for her whether she wants it or not. I've been holding it in for what feels like an eternity, but she started the eruption when she kissed me on Friday night.

If this is anyone's fault, it's hers.

"Fuck, Brax," she whispers, searching my gaze. But I'm done.

"I warned you what would happen if you continued to look at me like that, Shadow." My voice comes out darker than usual as I reach around her to grab the handlebars and start the jet up again.

Instead of clinging to the handlebars with me, her hands go to my thighs, her nails digging in as if to be sure that I'm real, that this is real. Rushing us to the shore, I make sure to get to the shallow waters before I cut off the power.

"Run." I lean back, giving her space, but she twists to look at me in confusion.

"What?"

"Run."

"But class," she breathes, looking around us, but no one is here. Fuck class, fuck my coin, I couldn't give a shit about anything else but her.

"Run, Raven. The hunt starts now."

THIRTY

Raven

R*un*.

    Run.

Run.

The hunt starts now.

I'm frozen in place, gaping at the most hot and cold man I've ever met in my life, trying to decide what I should do. I *should* say no. I *should* say anything other than what I'm considering.

The seriousness in his eyes is what's holding me captive, twisting my gut with a mixture of apprehension and excitement. One brown, one green, always digging beneath the surface and prying for more.

If I run…

If I let him hunt me…

Fuck.

But if I don't…

It's not even a question. The mere thought of it has my body alive. He must sense the decision in me because he leans back an inch, giving me a head start, and I slowly slip off the watercraft. The cold water does nothing to cool my heating body.

"You have a ten second head start while I sort out the watercraft. Make them count, Shadow."

My breath lodges in my throat, my pulse racing with a tinge of uncertainty colliding with exhilaration. I'm running for the shore before I can change my mind, and the second I'm on dry land I glance over my shoulder to check where he is. He's still behind me, pushing the watercraft up onto the sand.

Casting my eyes around the water one last time, I still don't see anyone else. It's just me and him. What would he do if he caught me here? The feral gleam in his eyes tells me exactly what he would do and my thighs clench at the thought.

I need to move, I want the exhilaration of the chase just like he does.

With my mind made up, I bolt up the hill without another glance back. The panic and adrenaline coursing through my bloodstream is euphoric as I bypass the locker room, not caring about my things. My main focus is putting as much distance between Brax and me as possible.

I'm still baffled where all of this is coming from but I can't deny that I like it, like *him*. I was snide and shitty with the words I threw at him yesterday but he doesn't seem to be holding them against me. I unloaded the events of yesterday on him, against my better judgment, and instead of telling me I was wrong for any of it or trying to shield me from the unknown, he admitted to hitting Sebastian and now he's chasing me.

It's fucked. Oh, so deliciously fucked.

Passing the academy building, I brace myself to run into someone, but it's as if the fates are working in my favor today because there's no one around. As I approach the pathway that leads down to our house, I can't stop myself from taking a peek over my shoulder and I catch a glimpse of him in the distance.

The fucker isn't even running, he's taking purposeful strides, yet he's still too fucking close for my liking.

Damn.

My bare feet burn with pain, but I don't care. I'm zoned in on our house and that's all that matters. Racing for the front door, I panic when I realize I don't have my key. Fuck. Trying the handle, I pray for it to open but, of course, it doesn't.

Think, Raven. Think.

Glancing over my shoulder, I spot him as he starts to turn down the path and I'm moving before he gets too close. Frantically making my way around to the back of the house, I leap over the small fence and barrel toward the patio doors, pleading with anyone who can hear me for the door to be open.

My heart races as I grab the door handle and I gasp in surprise when the door opens. Slipping inside before he can catch me, I quickly shut it behind me and turn the lock.

Holy fuck.

Panting, I swipe my hair back off my face, noting a slight tremble in my hands as Brax appears on the other side of the glass. I grin, victory humming in my chest, but it's short-lived when I realize all too quickly that he has magical abilities and I don't.

Panic kicks in. I should have said not to use magic to make it fair, right?

Dammit.

He tries the handle and doesn't seem too surprised that it's locked. Dark intent swirls in his eyes as he swipes his tongue along his bottom lip.

"Open the door, Shadow." I step back, shaking my head, and his palm hits the glass in the next breath, startling me. "Open the fucking door, Shadow," he repeats, but I retreat a little further. "Last chance before I come in anyway," he offers, and a frenzy of need sweeps through me.

Turning my back on him, I take two further steps so a sofa now stands between us. When I spin to face him again, he's shaking his head.

"Have it your way," he declares, swinging his left arm out at his side. It turns to stone before my very eyes, leaving me awestruck, before he slams his fist through the glass and the entire thing shatters.

I gulp, my breath lodged in my throat as I watch shards scatter across the floor between us.

Brax steps inside, ignoring the glass beneath his feet as he shakes his arm and it returns to normal. He's eliminating the distance between us and I'm locked in place, too stunned to move.

Instead of charging at me like I expect, he reaches for the zipper at the back of his wetsuit and slowly starts to open it. The sound of the metal mixed with my shallow breaths echoes in my ears until he pulls his arms out and lets the material hang at his waist.

"You got further than I thought you would."

"Is that a compliment?" The adrenaline seems to pound faster inside of me as he shrugs.

"It's something worth punishment," he quips, making my eyes widen.

"Punish how?" I ask as he rounds the sofa and I finally remember how to move.

Unfortunately, it's too little too late as his hand clamps around my hair, pulling me back to him with a yelp. He plasters my back to his front, his mouth finding my ear again as his breath caresses my skin.

"What happens when the hunter catches the prey, Shadow?"

Holy shit. I don't know, but I'm desperate to find out.

"Show me," I breathe, not truly knowing what I'm signing myself up for when his hand wraps around my neck in a choking necklace. His body is gone from behind me as he lifts my feet off the ground by my throat and pins me to the wall.

I reach for his wrists, nails digging into his skin as I fight against him, but he just smirks. He at least relents a little and I manage to place my toes on the floor, but his grip doesn't loosen. With his free hand, his index finger turns to stone, his nail sharp as he brings it to the top of my wetsuit, slicing through the material like it's nothing.

I'm completely bare beneath since no swimwear was provided, and I relish how wide his pupils go when he takes me in from head to toe.

"Fuck, Raven," Brax breathes, releasing my throat to drag the fabric down my arms. It flops to the floor, exposing every inch of me. His hand quickly lifts to my throat again before I can speak as he steps in closer.

Almost every part of my body is touching him and it's intoxicating. His nose drops to my jaw, slowly dragging over my cheek as he inhales and I groan. I'm not fighting him anymore. I can't even pretend. I want this too much, bruises and all.

Dipping down, he continues to drag the tip of his nose over my shoulders, collarbone, and down between the valley of my breasts. My eyes close, ecstasy zapping through me at the gentle touch, but it's a fleeting feeling when Brax's teeth suddenly sink into my breast.

Instead of recoiling from the sharp pain, my back arches, needy for more as my gasp evolves into a moan. He sucks on my skin and my hold on his wrists transforms into a squeeze of need.

He has me right where he wants me, ready to do and be whatever he desires. His hand drops from my throat again and I wheeze in a gulp full of air, but whine the moment he releases my breast from his mouth.

I slump back against the wall, trying to gather myself as he steps back, eyes fixed on my pussy.

"Now I make you mine, Shadow," he states, briefly flicking his eyes to mine before fixating on my core again.

There's enough space between us for me to make a run for it. Not because I want to escape, I just want that final rush of him hunting me down. It's addicting. *He's* addicting.

Taking a deep breath, I push off the wall and rush to the right, making it around the coffee table before he sweeps me off my feet, a growl tearing from his lips as I squeak in surprise. He drops me unceremoniously onto my knees on the sofa and I bounce twice before I brace my hands on the back, ready to react. But he's already splaying my legs open wider.

Colossal hands palm my hips, thrusting my ass into the air as I scramble to keep my balance. It's all futile though because in one swift move his cock is at my entrance, stretching me wide without mercy.

"Fuck, Brax," I pant, feeling a slight burn from the size of his dick, despite my wet folds.

"So. Tight. Shadow," he bites between shallow thrusts, working deeper inside of me.

I'm sure I'm going to pass out, it's all too much, too intense, too... "Brax, protection. Are you wearing—"

"Fuck protection," he grunts, fully seated inside of me as he lifts one hand to my hair, tearing the hair tie and wrapping the ends around his fist.

"You can't just—"

"I can do what I fucking want." He sounds savage, untamed, and wild. Enunciating each word with a thrust of his cock, my needy pussy clenching around him, which only adds fuel to his argument. "If I wanted, I could turn my dick to stone and let you feel me *that* hard for you. What do you say to that?"

My eyes slam shut, the vision flickering across the back of my eyelids before transforming into an array of fireworks as I come apart at the seams. I can't even scream with ecstasy, it's so intense as my body shakes with the sudden onslaught of my orgasm.

All too quickly, his hand is gone from my hair, his cock from my pussy, and his bruising hold from my waist. His grip is at my chin, twisting my face to him before I can open my eyes.

Brown and green. Green and brown. Both swirling with ferocity and surprise.

"You want to take me like that?" They're the calmest words he's ever spoken, like he's never considered actually saying them out loud.

I sink my teeth into my bottom lip. I can't deny it. The way I just came all over him from the thought alone is answer enough and he knows it.

"Say it, Raven." The use of my real name shows how serious he's taking this, and I nod.

"Yes." It's more of a croak than a word, my body trembling with need like I didn't just climax.

I'm sure anyone else would call me insane, but I don't care. If I can call him a savage, untamed, and wild, then I want to be painted with the same brush.

He rubs his thumb against his fingertips and a moment later the protection I was calling for earlier appears in his hand. I'm locked in position, in complete awe as his straining cock turns to stone. Somehow it's thicker, longer. Two things I'm sure couldn't have been possible.

His dick is sheathed in protection quickly and his gaze finds mine once more, silently asking for confirmation. I tip my hips up, showing him exactly where I want and need him.

He's back at my entrance in seconds, but more cautiously this time. Getting a better grip on the back of the sofa, I push back on him, hopeless for more, and he grunts, holding still inside of me as I adjust to the new sensation.

I don't know what I expected, but I can still feel his heat, even through the layer of protection between us.

"Are you okay?" Brax rasps, his restraint clear as he flexes his hands at my waist. Glancing over my shoulder at him, I nod.

"Fuck me, *Hunter*," I plead, rolling my core around his length.

The curse that falls from his lips is like music to my ears as he pulls out and slams deep inside me. It's too much and not enough all at once, but his pace increases. The precise and determined thrusts from earlier are gone though. In their place are jagged, consuming lunges that have me screaming at the top of my lungs.

His groans echo in my ears, sending me higher and higher until I succumb to the tingles zapping through my body.

My climax claims me, slowly at first this time, wrecking

every inch of me as I explode. My arms give out and my chest hits the sofa. That doesn't stop Brax though as he crawls onto the sofa with me, thrusting into my core in short, sharp bursts until I feel his cock pulse inside of me, even with the protection between us.

He doesn't stop until he's wrung every drop of euphoria from each of us. Only then do we completely collapse into a heap.

Perspiration clings between us, our breaths mingling as he stays plastered to my back. I'm going to be riding this high for days, my thighs already feeling the delicious ache.

"Is someone going to explain the broken glass?"

I startle at the sound, but it takes me a second to glance at the source of the voice through my sex-induced haze as Brax lazily lifts off me just enough for me to see.

It's not just some*one* though, it's three of them.

Eldon, Zane, and Creed stand in the garden in their uniforms assessing the shattered glass. And us.

"What are you doing here?" Brax asks, making no effort to move. The sofa is shielding us but it's still very clear what's happened here. The pleased look on Eldon's face tells me they're not mad.

"When you didn't show at the end of the class we panicked, even considered whether you could have been killing each other. Seems it was quite the opposite," Zane states with a smirk.

"Well, you can see we're good," Brax grunts, finally lifting up off me. His softening cock slips from my core and I startle at the loss.

"We can see that," Creed adds, winking at me, and I blush. "Are you going to be joining us for classes again or—"

"Nope. I'm not done with her yet."

THIRTY ONE

Raven

"**C**an we please go to the party tonight? Pretty please?" Leila asks as soon as I step out of the house on Friday morning. No good morning or other such pleasantries, just straight to tonight's plans.

Shaking my head, I focus on her question as she links her arm through mine and the guys trail behind us. "There's a party tonight?" I'm clearly out of the loop when it comes to anything fun.

"Yeah, and considering the week we've had, I'd say it's a done deal." She quirks an eyebrow at me, silently pleading for me to go, and I purse my lips.

Apart from Monday's mess with my parents and the turn of events between Brax and me on Tuesday, the rest of the week has been mellow. But Monday was fucked up enough for me to nod in agreement.

"Count me in," I say. She claps excitedly as I mentally start trying to piece an outfit together. Although a trip to the shopping district is more than likely in the cards.

"Count you in for what?" Eldon asks, tugging gently at my ponytail, but Leila answers him before I can.

"The party."

He nods once, releasing my hair and falling into step with the others again. "Boys, we're going to the party tonight." Groans echo from the other three, making me grin. It's on the tip of my tongue to state that they don't actually have to come with us if they don't want to, but Eldon continues before I have a chance. "She's going to look hot, quit your moaning."

"So true," Zane adds, and I feel my cheeks heat.

Assholes.

"They're so into you it's beyond amusing and all dreamy instead," she says with a wistful sigh

I roll my eyes at her.

"I don't know what you're talking about," I deflect as we step into the academy building.

"Please. Don't think I'm not completely aware of the real reason you and Brax disappeared from class the other day and faked an illness for the rest of your classes, only to be miraculously better the next day." She wags her eyebrows and I hip check her. "You know it, I know it, we all know it."

"Shut up, Leila."

She laughs louder as we step into the classroom, only to come to an abrupt halt when we see Professor Burton waiting to address everyone.

What the fuck?

"Good morning. Filter in, everyone, we have much to do."

I glance back at the guys, who look as confused and intrigued as I feel. We shuffle into the room but don't take our seats like the rest of the class. A few minutes pass, no one breathing a word as we assess him talking with the professor, before he finally turns to address us again.

"It's been brought to my attention by some of the parents that last week's trip into the Gauntlet was, indeed, not how we usually operate. We're aware it's not common practice for the first years to experience the Gauntlet and they did so without having a chance to practice before some unfortunately lost their lives." His gaze sweeps to Zane's, making it clear who has had an issue with the process. Zane doesn't falter under his stare and Barton quickly proceeds. "With that in mind, we're now going to incorporate Gauntlet training into the first year's schedule."

A gasp of worry flickers through the group and Professor Meade, the potions teacher, quickly waves her hand. "It will be in simulator mode so we won't lose any lives while practicing," she says in an attempt to reassure us.

Why the fuck couldn't they have done that last week?

"So your schedule has been adjusted to accommodate these changes, with Friday mornings now being allocated to Gauntlet training," Professor Barton states, a pleased smile on his face. "Professor Meade has offered to aid Professor Figgins while you're in there, so you will be in safe hands." He nods, more to himself than anyone here, before edging toward the door. "Follow the sun, destroy the shadows, and survive another dawn."

He's gone in the next breath, not even waiting to hear the chorus of students say it back.

"I'm sure by now you all know where the locker rooms are," Meade says with a knowing smile. "I'll meet you all at the Gauntlet in a few minutes."

The second we're back in the hallway, I spin to the guys. "Why is this even happening?"

"I don't know…" Eldon ponders, rubbing at his chin.

"They're trying to prepare us for something. They've never done this shit before, but fuck knows *what,* exactly, it is that's causing such a stir," Brax adds, his words making a lot of sense. He's right, we don't know the whole picture.

"Has your father said anything about it, Leila?" Creed asks, and my friend shakes her head nervously as she nibbles at her lip.

"No, and I'm going to assume he wasn't aware of this last minute schedule change because he definitely wouldn't have kept it to himself." My chest tightens with worry.

"What's this about simulator mode? Why couldn't that have been used last week?" I ask, my earlier thoughts playing on repeat in my mind.

"Fuck knows, but that's twisted," Zane states, his hand mindlessly lifting to stroke over his now-healed shoulder.

We part ways at the locker room like we've done far too many times in the past two weeks. Leila is silent as we change, as are most of the girls in here—Genie included—then we're back out and quickly heading toward the arena.

The Bishops are waiting for us and we move to the entrance as a unit. It feels weird with no other years in here, like it's bigger than it was before.

Following the crowd down to the bottom of the steps where Figgins waits, she wastes no time getting straight to it. "Today, I've split the Gauntlet into eight sections. This is how you're supposed to train in it, not what happened last week," she comments, and I'm surprised she's so openly irritated by it. Leila's eyes widen in shock too. "Today it will run as a simulator, which means if you happen to die at the hands of the monsters inside, you'll find yourself waking up in the medical center. But, let's hope it doesn't come to that, okay? You'll also be entering in groups of six and not alone, so choose your team and we'll get the ball rolling."

All I'm hearing is last week was a complete clusterfuck

and they're just not telling us why, even among the professors. Fun.

Turning back to the guys, I stumble on my feet when someone shoulder checks me from the left. Leila manages to stop me from falling and I whirl around with anger to find Genie stepping up to Eldon with her eyelashes fluttering.

Bitch.

"Hey, Eldon baby, do you want—"

"Fuck off, Genie," Brax grunts, interrupting her.

She turns a snarl his way, "I wasn't talking to you."

I'm almost sure she's going to stomp her foot. Her hands are clenched so tightly at her sides I'm shocked her palms aren't bleeding but, to my surprise, she turns her attention back to Eldon like nothing was said.

"There's five of us already, and I was hoping you'd take the sixth spot."

Eldon snorts, shaking his head at her and firing back before I get a chance to put an end to her. "Genie, my dick only gets hard for one girl and it's not you. When are you going to learn that you're not wanted around here?"

I gape at him, almost impressed, but annoyed that I can't just beat the shit out of her like I want to. Her mouth opens and closes a few times but she still doesn't move.

"Get the message and fuck off. We've got some big, bad monsters to fight," Brax snarks, waving his hand dismissively, and Leila snorts while I try to hold it together.

Genie snaps her gaze to his again, her lip quirked with a sneer. "Maybe the monster in there will be a fucking gargoyle. Maybe you might know them."

Oh this bitch. Fuck that.

"I'll show you a fucking monster," I bite, lunging for her, but I'm caught mid-air. Even with me restrained, she darts down the remaining steps with a yelp as I thrash in Creed's hold. "Put me down. That bitch needs to be taught a lesson."

"Save your rage for the pit, Shadow. She's not worth it," Brax mutters, and I relax in Creed's hold. Turning to look at Brax, Creed slowly lowers me to my feet. He's acting completely unfazed but there's a slight darkening to his green eye, a shade I haven't seen on him before, and I know that she affected him more than he cares to admit.

Cutting the distance between us, I look up at him from the step below. "You're not a monster."

"I am." His eyes dip down, avoiding my gaze, and it pisses me off that she managed to hit such a sore spot with him.

"No, you're not," I insist, reaching for his hand. "If I thought you were a monster, I wouldn't have wanted…" My words trail off, the memory hanging between us as he squeezes my hand back before wrapping his arms around me and pinning me to his chest.

I hug him back, basking in his heat as he holds me

tighter. "You're going to be the death of me," he whispers against my ear, and I lean back with a grin.

"You're welcome."

He lowers me to the floor, and I quickly remember we're not in our own little bubble. The guys grin at us and Leila wags her eyebrows like a fool while Genie and her friends all glare in our direction.

"Do you see why she didn't get any kind of handbook, Dove?" Zane asks, a wry smile on his face and I smirk back.

"It makes total sense."

The six of us wordlessly form a group and follow Professor Meade's direction into our section of the pit.

"The Gauntlet will run simultaneously for everyone, and we will be here to oversee it all. Remember, deaths are not final in here today, but we highly recommend you learn about your group, understand their strengths and weaknesses as a whole, and piece together a plan for victory," Professor Figgins announces to everyone before a horn sounds and everyone makes their way into the Gauntlet.

The unsettling feeling of stepping through the barrier washes over me and I note that the surroundings are completely different than last time. There's no small pool of water or stacked boulders filling the space. In its place is a cave at the far end with a field surrounding it.

"Everybody keep your wits about you. It's going to be impossible to devise a plan until we actually know what we're up against. Since your magic works opposite to one another, Leila should hold to the right and Eldon to the left," Creed orders and they nod in agreement. "Brax, you need to hold front and center since you're the more durable one, and your invisibility might come in handy, Zane." They all nod in sync, which leaves me and Creed. "Since we're not as hands on, we're better hanging back, otherwise we could be a major weakness to the overall group."

I hate how my gut clenches knowing he's covering for the fact that I have nothing to add to the team, but I appreciate his efforts to not out me. I squeeze his arm as I step closer and the others fan out a step or two, readying in their positions but still holding together until we see what we're up against.

A scream echoes from another section of the pit and my heart gallops at the sound. Gulping hard, I try to relax my body, but it's harder than just willing it to happen. A screech reverberates from another section of the pit a moment later, only this time, it definitely doesn't belong to a human.

"What the hell is that?" Leila yelps, eyes wide as she looks to each of us for an answer, but I have no fucking clue.

The sound rings out again and Creed frowns. "I think it's a—" his sentence is cut off as his gaze is drawn to the cave, and I follow his line of sight to see what has his attention.

I stifle a gasp, eyes locked on the monster we're up against. Half lion, half bird. I thought they were a myth, a thing of legends, but the one standing before us, with its talons scratching at the ground, is very fucking real.

"It's a griffin," I breathe, standing in awe of the majestic aura in the air around it.

"Everybody take their positions. I'll use my mind if necessary, but I'm unsure how to penetrate it, so it's going to take a second," Creed orders and the others spread out, powers flicking over their skin with every step they take.

"You can't hurt it," I shout, drawing a frown from Creed.

"That's the whole point of the assignment, Raven."

Turning my attention back to the creature, it tilts its beak up and locks eyes with me, captivating me. Its golden feathers and tan fur shine despite the lack of direct sunlight, the white stripe down its chest ruffling with a nonexistent breeze.

The griffin's head tilts to the side, its stare penetrating my own, and I swear I can hear its heart beating from here. Ever so slowly, it tips its head down, and before I can even process what's happening, I take a step toward it. Then another and another, until Zane calls out my name.

"Raven, what the fuck are you doing? Stay back."

"You can't hurt him," I repeat, creeping toward him one small step at a time. I don't know how I know it's a male, I just do.

"Raven, get back," Creed shouts, but I ignore him too.

It's out of my hands. I couldn't stop myself even if I

wanted to. The closer I get, the bigger he looms, but my feet keep on moving until I'm standing directly beneath him. The sound of his heart still echoes in my ears.

He's at least three times my size and when he crouches down, the ground vibrates beneath us. I can hear my name being called but the heart beating in my ears blocks it all out as the griffin lowers its beak.

I don't know what I'm fucking doing, but I lift my hand to his beak before stroking through the feathers down his neck. He croons at my touch, making me smile despite having no clue how this is happening.

"What the fuck is going on?" Eldon yells, breaking through the fog as the griffin nuzzles its face into my stomach. I gently stroke my fingers over its head, bewildered and in awe as a whistle sounds from somewhere in the distance.

"Professor Figgins, someone needs to help us."

"You don't need help with anything," she says calmly, and I manage to tilt my head to see her staring at me, delight dancing in her eyes as she waves Professor Meade closer. "It looks like Miss Hendrix may have found herself a familiar."

THIRTY TWO

Raven

Everyone's looking at me and I can feel my skin crawling from all of their gazes washing over my body. My shoulders are tense, my hands clenching, and my breathing hitched, but I still manage to put one foot in front of the other as we circle around the Silvercrest Memorial mausoleums.

It's like a scratch I can't seem to itch and I have to voice it even though it makes me cringe. "Everyone's looking at me."

"No, they're not," Leila replies too quickly and with an extra dose of perky that's not the norm for her, which only confirms I'm right.

"Yeah, they are," Zane states from behind me, and I give Leila a pointed look.

She sighs, relenting to the madness and admitting

it. "It's not every day someone gets a familiar, Raven. Nevermind a fucking griffin, of all things. That's hot gossip, girl."

I grimace. I feel like there's been enough hot gossip and I'm really not excited for another dose of it. The connection I instantly felt with the griffin is incomparable and the second the professor confirmed it, I knew it was true.

Ari. That's his name. I don't know how I know it, but I do.

Professor Figgins insisted he will be released from the Gauntlet and I'm going to go and meet him after classes on Monday. That sounds weird as fuck. *I'm going to go and properly meet my familiar, Ari the Griffin, in a more neutral environment instead of in the Gauntlet where I was supposed to kill him... a simulation?* But I guess it's my new normal. Understanding anything at this stage seems beyond my capacity.

"Raven?" Leila calls my name, breaking through my thoughts, and I quickly shake them off. "Like, a griffin? The coolest thing ever."

I smile. "Go big or go home, right?" I say with a smile, trying to brush over it and she, thankfully, smirks and leaves it at that.

"They might be looking at you for how hot you look in

that dress," Eldon declares as he comes to a stop with us at the makeshift bar. Zane nods in agreement with him and I scoff. "What? It's true," he insists, earning himself an eye roll as well.

After Figgins declared Ari my familiar, the class ended. They didn't want to startle him by harming the others. One class led into another before the day was over, then I was hitting up the shopping district with Leila. She insisted on the dress I'm wearing and I can't deny that she definitely has good taste.

It's a pale-blue, puff-sleeve mini dress that clings to me in all of the right places. I opted to get some strappy white sandals to go with it and kept my make-up light with my hair loose. But the guys are delusional if they think that's the alternative. If they're not staring at me because of the griffin, it *has* to be because of them.

"Maybe it's because the infamous Bishops have shown their faces at another party?" Leila states, cocking a brow at them. It's their turn to be flustered.

"Looking as hot as you all do, she definitely has a point," I add with a grin.

As the drinks line dwindles, I heed my own statement and give myself another moment to take them in. Brax is dressed in black, which is no real surprise. Fitted black tee, black jeans, and black boots. He looks hot as hell, with his muscles flexing beneath the material.

Creed is rocking similar boots and jeans with a black fitted shirt instead of a tee, and I'm desperate to flick open the top few buttons. Zane and Eldon are both in gray shorts. While Zane wears a white tee, Eldon wears navy, and all I can think about is how easy the access is to their dicks.

Damn, I need a drink because I'm working up a sweat just thinking about them.

As if sent here to answer my prayers, Leila hands me a bottle of pearl shine and I take a big gulp. It's so sweet and fruity, I love it. I'm about to ask if we're doing any moon dust shots as well, but she offers me one without me uttering a word.

"We'll meet you at the table over there," Eldon murmurs against my ear as he points to the right. I nod, unable to find words to respond since my body is obsessing over his close proximity.

Leila leads the way and I finally take stock of my surroundings, realizing yet again that I'm easily letting my defenses down. Music plays in the background but it's not so unbearably loud that I can't think. There must be at least a hundred people here and that number will likely grow the later it gets. It's set up the exact same as last time: the mausoleums framing the open space, a few high rise tables scattered around the edges, and a dance floor in the middle.

"Is that familiar girl with the Bishops?" Someone murmurs as they walk past me talking with their friends, and I hold back another eye roll. Apparently the hot topic of gossip is, indeed, the griffin and the Bishops. At least I can say I was right.

Placing my drinks on the table, Leila wastes no time hinting at the shots. "We so deserve this. Ready?" I nod and she counts us in before we down the liquid and it burns my throat in the most soothing way.

Damn. We should have gotten two of them.

"We are definitely having more of these after we do some dancing," Leila states with a hopeful smile on her face.

"I'm down for that." Her smile spreads wider as I take a sip of my pearl shine.

Turning my attention toward the bar to watch the Bishops, my view is quickly obstructed by an unfortunate sight.

"Nice familiar choice. But I must say, I'm surprised you're still here after Monday," Sebastian sneers, tucking his hands into his pockets as he tilts his head at me.

It's hard as hell to act unfazed by his presence, but I force it anyway. "Didn't you hear from Papa? He wasn't sending me away after all," I retort, hoping he'll fuck off. What Papa did feels worse somehow, but I don't say that. That's definitely not information Sebastian needs to know.

I turn to look away from him, giving him a silent dismissal, but he grabs my shoulder and turns me back to him. "I don't know what game you're playing, but griffin or not, you're not going to survive here, Raven. I don't know why you keep trying."

Placing my drink down on the table, I shove at his arm, forcing his hold on me to drop. "What is your problem, Sebastian? I'm quite happy staying out of your way, pretending you don't exist, yet here you are, getting in my face. Again," I bite. I've had enough of his bullshit.

He glares at me, a carbon copy of my chocolate brown eyes piercing into me. "I wouldn't even waste my fucking time on you," he sneers, making me scoff.

"So what the fuck are you doing here?" Brax's grunt comes from behind Sebastian, who stiffens at the menacing tone.

He quickly shakes it off, back to his unfazed bullshit, as the rest of the Bishops circle around the table. "If it isn't the almighty Bishops. It seems that some time with your new housemate has you a little confused on how things work around here," Sebastian snarks, clenching his hands at his sides.

"We haven't forgotten anything," Eldon states, stepping closer to him until they're shoulder to shoulder. "We just protect our own, and you're treading, unwanted, on territory that isn't yours. Maybe it's your turn to take an unwanted trip to the wastelands."

I gulp at the memory of being lost out there and the

thoughts of what could have happened if they hadn't found me try to consume me, but I push them down.

Before Sebastian can respond, Brax steps up to his other side. "How's your face?" He lifts his drink to his mouth, revealing his busted knuckles, and my core clenches.

I should not be getting turned on right now, especially not by some mostly-healed knuckles that were busted from hitting my brother. Apparently in the face too. Extra saucy.

"Sebastian, I've been looking everywhere for you. I got you a drink." Everyone's attention slips to Genie, who joins the mix, and I'm already past my limit of assholes for the evening. She links her arm through Sebastian's, preening up at him with her eyelashes fluttering, and I think I'm going to be sick.

She moved on from Eldon quickly. I glance in his direction, not sure what I'm expecting to find, but he's completely placid. I'm just pleased she's not still clinging to Eldon, really, but of all the people in this place, it had to be him?

"I was just coming to find you anyways, baby," he purrs back, licking her cheek, and the bile burning the back of my throat threatens to rise.

They saunter off without a backward glance, the whole interaction weirding me the fuck out, but I'm just relieved that they're out of my space.

"Did that just actually happen?" Leila asks, her face

scrunched up in disgust, reflecting how I feel on the inside, and I chuckle.

"I wish my eyes were deceiving me, but it seems I'm going to need to wash them with acid," Zane muses with a sigh.

"You know, if that actually becomes a thing, they're going to think they're a power couple for sure," Leila adds, and I fake shiver.

"They can be whoever the fuck they want. Those two deserve each other." I raise my bottle in salute to the group and take an extra large swig. Leila was right, we *definitely* deserve this.

Attempting to enjoy the presence of the people I like, I finally start to relax, my hips slowly starting to sway with the music as Zane grabs a few more bottles of pearl shine from the bar. The carefree vibe of letting go that I've been chasing suddenly feels possible.

Brax smirks at me from across the table, heating me from the inside, when Creed's frown catches my attention. He's looking off into the distance and I follow his line of sight to see a group of ten or more people entering the party. They look older and I don't recall seeing them before. It's startling how none of them are smiling, laughing, or joking around. They're all wearing solemn looks as they head toward the bar, and the other students seem to give them a wide berth.

"Who are they?" I ask, turning back to the table to find everyone else also watching them.

"Fourth years," Eldon explains, and my eyebrows shoot up.

I turn to watch them again, this time looking a little deeper. There are bags under their eyes, exhaustion written on their faces, and a tension rippling through them that I've never physically seen on another person before.

"Do you think they're the ones from the attack?" I ask, still watching as they each down a shot before reaching for another.

"The way they're downing those shots, I would guess so," Zane answers, my stomach twisting into knots. I can't even imagine how they're feeling. They're only three years older than me and they've already experienced battle and loss like I can't even imagine.

I turn away, feeling guilty for staring, and my gaze locks on Creed's for a moment as he offers me a soft smile.

"Nope, you're not allowed to lose your good groove," Leila states, reaching for my arm. "We're dancing and having fun whether you like it or not."

I quickly down the last of my drink before I relent.

Smiling at the guys, they seem amused by the fact that I'm being bossed around. Exhaling, I try to shrug off the funk trying to weigh me down as we slink into the middle of the dance floor. The music seems much louder here and

I let my inhibitions go.

Fuck the drama with my parents, fuck the worry of what my magic may be, fuck the added pressure of suddenly having a familiar, and fuck Sebastian and Genie.

Fuck all of it.

THIRTY THREE

Creed

With every sway of her hips, another ripple of tension eases from her limbs. It's intoxicating to watch. I can't look away, I can't even blink, I can't stand to miss a single second of her.

I have no idea how she has managed to land in our laps like this, but thank fuck she did. I sense that she's still holding us at arms length, which is understandable, while Eldon, Zane, Brax, and I are already in too deep to deny it.

Mere weeks ago, Eldon was slipping his dick into anything that could hold his attention for more than five minutes, Brax grunted and growled at anyone that wasn't one of us, and Zane wouldn't have been seen dead hanging off a woman's every word. And now, here we are. Brax still pulls off a killer caveman impersonation, but there's another person in our tribe now. Raven.

"She's too fucking pretty, man," Zane murmurs, scrubbing a hand over his mouth as he takes her in, and I hum in agreement.

"That doesn't seem to sum it up," Brax states.

"That's very fucking true," Eldon adds, taking a swig of his drink as the four of us continue to watch her every move.

She's carefree around Leila, who seems to lighten up around Raven too. They're like oil and water on the exterior, Raven harsher around the edges than Leila, who usually seems more composed and timid, but there's something deep inside of them that connects them on a level that can't be explained or questioned.

Blindly reaching for my drink, I lift it to my lips, but when I tip my head back, no liquor comes out. "I'm out, I'm going to get another." I wave my empty glass at them and they nod in acknowledgment but barely tear their gazes from our girl.

I almost bump into two different people on my way over, my focus repeatedly returning to her. Muttering my thanks as I take my fresh drink from the server, I pause when I turn to find a fourth year leaning in close to murmur in Leila's ear first, then Raven's.

Glancing toward my brothers, I find each of them glaring in his direction and quickly rush back to them.

"What's going on? What's he saying?" I ask, earning a

glare from Eldon, who rapidly turns his attention back to Raven.

"How the fuck are we supposed to know?"

"She's fine. She can handle herself," Brax states with a shrug, but I sense the tension rolling off him in thunderous waves from him as he watches. He's not as unaffected as he thinks he is.

Turning back to Raven, I watch as the fourth year places his hand at the base of her spine and she finally stops dancing. That's my cue.

"I don't give a fuck," I grunt, leaving my fresh drink on the table as I head toward them.

Irritation rises from my toes all the way to my chest, swirling with determination with every step I take. Leila sees me first, eyes wide as she watches me approach, but she doesn't try to stop me. If anything, she makes room for me to slip in beside my girl.

"Are you saving this dance for me, Raven?" I ask, draping my arm over her shoulders and pulling her firmly against my chest. My voice is calm while my blood boils beneath the surface.

"Hey, man, we're dancing," the drunk fourth year slurs, and Raven instantly wags her finger.

"No, I'm dancing with my friend. You just aren't taking a hint."

"You heard her, back off," I grunt, my free hand

clenching into a fist, ready to do whatever is necessary.

"Whatever. No pussy is worth this bullshit," he grunts, stumbling back a step before disappearing into the crowd.

"He's clearly never tasted your pussy, otherwise he would know that's not true," I murmur against the shell of her ear, earning me a shiver.

"Creed Wylder, you're a menace," she says with a smirk, wrapping her arms around my neck as she continues to sway.

"Don't you fucking forget it."

Her laugh is infectious as she throws her head back. The pearl shine has definitely worked its magic on her. The harsh exterior she usually hides behind has a little crack in it, just wide enough for a glimmer of her sweetness to shine through.

When she doesn't let go, continuing to dance against me, I can't help but move with her. It's like there's no one else here, just the two of us, the music getting more and more sensual with every song that passes, working up a sweat between us.

Raven spins in my hold, pressing her back to my front, and my cock nestles perfectly between her ass cheeks.

"You're ruining me," I breathe against her ear, and her tongue flicks out to trace over her bottom lip.

"I'm already ruined."

Shaking my head, I take her hand and she follows

willingly. "Not yet, you're not."

I'm not sure if she's going to argue with me on the matter, but when I get to the edge of the dance floor, she's right beside me, eager to see where I'm going to lead her. Not fucking far, that's for sure. I won't survive the walk home.

I want to race off, drag her along with me, but I can't bear even that much distance between us. So I take my time, keeping her plastered to my side as we sneak behind one of the mausoleums and through the scattered bushes until we reach a large oak tree.

Need takes over when I'm sure we're alone and I spin her around so her back is against the bark. In her sandals, I'm still taller and she almost feels delicate in my hold. Looks are deceiving though, because I know it's her that has me in her grasp.

Gripping her waist with one hand, I lift my other to her cheek, running my thumb across her soft skin as she looks at me with wide eyes. No words spill between us as our breaths mingle together and my mouth gets closer to hers, inch by inch, until there's no coming back and we collide in one final swoop.

She tastes like coconuts and pineapple, a sweetness to her lips that isn't usually there, but her essence still comes through. Desperate to dominate her mouth, she puts up a fight, vying for control until I grab her throat, running my thumb over her pulse and tipping her head back further. Only then does she concede.

Her hands run up my shirt, her fingers slipping between the buttons to try and feel my bare chest until she gives up completely and untucks it from my jeans.

Fuck.

Her palms are scalding against my skin and I tighten my hold on her, pressing my lips more firmly against hers as I try to bite back the groan. Certain she's going to make me self-combust, I release her throat to grab her hands, but she must sense my move because she drops them to the outline of my cock, squeezing my length through the denim.

"Shit, Raven," I grunt, tearing my lips from hers as I stare down at her. I can barely breathe and she's grinning up at me with a pleased expression.

Instead of removing her hands, I opt to skim my fingertips over her thigh, hitching her leg at my side. The gasp that parts her lips is a direct prayer to my dick, forcing me to bite back another groan.

"Do you want to be caught, Raven?" I ask, my lips brushing against hers as her eyes pop open, but she doesn't glance around in a panic. If anything, her breaths become shorter and sharper. "Are you excited by that, Raven?" I tease, inching my hand further up her thigh, beneath the hem of her skirt and closer to the warmth I'm desperate to feel explode around my cock.

"Maybe," she admits, and my cock pulses against my jeans, begging to be freed.

"What do you want to get caught doing, Raven?" I nuzzle my nose along her throat, down to the crook of her neck, before pulling the puffed strap of her dress aside to trail kisses over her skin.

"I want to get caught with your dick in my mouth."

Holy. Fuck.

Leaning back, I instantly miss her presence and her hands whip behind her to clamp against the bark to keep her balance. I don't glance around, I don't make sure we're alone, I just keep my gaze locked on hers as I unbutton my jeans, slowly lowering the zipper before letting my cock spring free.

"Get on your knees for me."

My words hang in the air for two whole seconds before she drops to her knees with force, not even wincing at the thump of the ground beneath her. "Are you going to take a step closer, or are you going to make me crawl to you?"

I squeeze my length, liking the sound of the latter, but that might be best saved for another day. Today, I cut the distance to her. Tugging at my length, she hungrily wets her lips as she lifts her hands to my thighs.

Making sure she has my attention, Raven doesn't lean closer until our gazes are fixed on each other. She flattens her tongue, running the heated pad against the base of my dick before sweeping it up to my tip excruciatingly slowly.

I can't be sure who groans first, both sounds swirling in the air between us before she wraps her sweet mouth around the tip of my cock and swallows me whole.

We're too far away for me to lean against the tree, so I grab her hair instead, wrapping the ends around my fist as she tests the weight of my length on her tongue. I'm going to come too fucking soon at this rate, especially when she hollows her cheeks out, repeating the motion again and again until I'm about to crumble.

Yanking at her hair, I pull her off me, gasping for breath as she stares up at me with bleary eyes and a wide smile.

"I'm not coming in your mouth, Raven," I grunt, releasing my dick to encourage her to her feet. The second she's standing again, I shuffle her back a step so she's pressed against the tree again. "Hold on to the branch," I order, nodding at the closest one, and she instantly does as I say while I lower myself to my knees this time, my cock still hanging out of my jeans, whimpering at the lack of contact. "Has anyone caught you yet?" I ask, and she startles, glancing around the area before looking back at me with a shake of her head.

Running my fingers under the hem of her skirt, I lift it with a single, quick motion, her skin pebbling beneath my touch as her pussy comes into view. Bare. Completely fucking bare.

"I didn't want panty lines with the dress," she mumbles, like I need an explanation.

"One less barrier between us, baby," I breathe before throwing her thigh over my shoulder and pressing the lightest kiss to her clit. My reward is a gasp. Trailing my tongue between her folds, her gasp transforms into a groan, then another, and another until I tease two fingers at her entrance. "Anyone looking yet?" I push, and it takes a second for her gaze to focus before she glances around us, my fingers still circling her core.

"No."

"That's a shame. Let's see if anyone can hear you." I thrust my fingers deep into her pussy as I clamp my lips around her clit and her cry of pleasure rings in my ears. Fucking *yes*. I relish in it, her euphoria, as she rocks against my fingers, her tight nub desperate under my tongue.

I'm going to fuck her out here, claim her as mine for anyone to hear, but first, she's got to come on my face. Doubling down my efforts, I rake my teeth over her clit as I add another finger to her pussy and her groans get louder.

It's such a fucking turn on.

I can feel her starting to clamp down on me more and more, her hands dropping to grip my hair as she rides my face.

"Fuck, Creed. Fuck. Fuck. Fuck," she chants, offering

a moment's notice before she topples over the edge of ecstasy and falls into a pool of desire as I lap at her climax.

I sense her relaxing back against the tree with a sigh and only then do I relent on her pussy, pressing one final kiss to her clit before dropping her leg and standing in front of her. "Still no one?"

She shakes her head, barely glancing, no longer caring. She's just as caught up in this as I am.

Reaching for her face, I cup her cheek, stroking my thumb over her lips as she pants with every breath. "Want to find out if you'll get caught on my dick, baby?"

"Yes." It's a mixture between a prayer and a sigh and I don't wait for any further comment as I grab the back of her thighs and lift her into the air. "Protection, Creed."

I pause, her back pressed against the tree as I stop myself from thrusting deep into her core. "What if I want to feel you bare?"

"You can't," she replies as I let the tip of my cock nestle against her entrance.

"What if I want to feel you come on my dick with nothing between us?"

"You can't." I nudge inside of her and she makes no effort to stop me as she strokes her fingers through my hair.

"What if I want to come inside you, plant my seed inside you, fill you with every ounce of me?"

"You can't." I thrust in the rest of the way, filling her

pussy until she can't take any more, and the cries that rip from her lips make me even harder.

"What can't I do, Raven?" I push, grinding against her as I rest my forehead against hers.

"I-I don't know," she rambles, her core desperately clenching around me as I hiss back my own needy moans.

"Do you want me to stop?"

"Don't you even think about it," she snarls, tightening her hold on my hair as she glares at me.

I pull out until only the tip remains before I slam deep into her core again, repeating the motion harder and faster every time until she's on the verge of screaming.

Movement to my right catches my attention and I spot Eldon watching us. I'm not sure if the others are there and I don't care to find out because everything is about her. Focusing on her eyes, I channel my magic.

"Fuck, Creed. I can't see. I can't fucking see. Is that you?" she pants, still managing to roll her hips with every thrust I give her.

"Someone's coming."

"Fuck."

"You can't see so you don't need to worry. All I need you to do is come, baby," I purr. She doesn't need to know it's Eldon, she just needs the mystery of it.

"Oh my... fuck, Creed," she cries, her heated center clenching around me as she climaxes. I have to hold my body still as she wrings out every ounce on my cock before I slip from her folds and paint the tree with my release. She clings to me as my veins thrum with adrenaline.

Reeling my magic back in, I clear the darkness from her eyes and she sags against me.

Nothing gets better than this.

Nothing.

FALLING SHADOWS

THIRTY FOUR

Raven

Coming to Silvercrest Academy was never what I wanted. At least, I don't think I did. I guess I relented because I was trapped between a rock and a hard place, and there was a small glimmer of hope inside of me that an alternative future was on the horizon.

After this weekend, I hands down know it was the best decision ever made, even if it was forced upon me. The happiness I feel with the Bishops and Leila outweighs the negativity leading up to my arrival. Including the fact that I was unsuppressed against my will.

It almost feels like a distant dream now, a week later, and I'm sure I'm going to have more problems to face between my mother's warning and Sebastian's mere existence. But after the relaxing weekend and fun I had on Friday night, I don't feel so caught up about it all.

Besides, as much as I might want to stay in bed today instead of getting my uniform on, it's also Ari day and I can't deny how excited I am. I've tried to explain to the guys what it feels like, but it's impossible. It's not like I can feel every inch of him in my body, but he's there, a part of me, and me a part of him. Like he's my family. It sounds insane, but I'm desperate to see him. Three days is definitely too long. Hopefully, the professors will offer me some more insight when I see him later because I surely can't be expected to go this long every time.

I've got so many questions ready on the tip of my tongue that I don't know how I'm going to make it through the rest of the day first.

"Let's go, Shadow," Brax hollers, knocking on my bedroom door. I slip into my school shoes and grab my bag, tossing it over my shoulder as I reach for my sheathed sword and greet him in the lounge. "You have a little something…" he lifts his hand to his cheek, hinting for me to do the same, but shakes his head at me when I do, leaning toward me to help instead.

I spot the grin spreading across his face as he inches closer a second too late, leaving me no time to react as he presses his lips to my cheek. "There, I got it."

"Oh, you're full of slick moves this morning, huh?" I fail to bite back the smile teasing my lips as he throws his arm around my shoulders and leads me to the door.

"You love it."

I don't know who this calm guy is standing in Brax's shoes, but he's just as hot as the broody asshole that still pops up too.

"I love to irritate you," I grumble, stomping my foot down on his in hopes of inflicting a little pain, but he doesn't even grimace. He just gives me a pointed stare as he leads me outside to where the others are waiting.

"Are you excited about seeing your griffin today?" Leila asks as I squeeze between Zane, Eldon, and Creed to walk beside her.

"I honestly can't wait," I admit as we head to the academy building. It feels weird seeing us all with our sheathed swords, every week adding something new into the mix, and, as daunting as it might be sometimes, it's also exhilarating.

I'm practically bouncing all the way to Professor Figgins's class this morning, taking everything in my stride. I don't even react to Genie's sneer as she boasts about being with my brother in the girls' locker room. I'm too focused to deal with her shit.

Heading out to the field with Leila and the Bishops, our swords in hand, I'm eager to learn.

"Miss Hendrix, may I speak to you before we begin please?" Figgins asks, waving me closer. She walks me a step or two away from everyone, offering a little more privacy as she smiles at me. "With regards to this afternoon, I've arranged for you to meet us out here. I've never witnessed anyone have a connection with a griffin before so I'm not sure what it's going to look like, but you just need to be patient and open to what it's offering."

"He," I correct, wincing a little in embarrassment at the interruption, but she smiles.

"He, sorry. But if you'll meet us out here after your last class, that would be perfect. After we're done here I'm going to escort him out here so he can get a feel for where you are, but I'm assuming you're more than ready to meet him."

Tilting my head at her, I smile. "Do you have a familiar too?"

"I do. It's a rare and sensational feeling, but I can't imagine going so long without seeing her. She means too much to me." I eagerly nod in agreement. That's exactly how I feel. "I thought so. You might be best coming alone though, or having your friends hang back so you can get acquainted with him first."

"Thank you."

I rejoin the group, even more ready for the end of the day to roll around.

"Okay, we're going to start by learning about our connection with the sword before learning the most basic, yet most important, practices when wielding a weapon,"

Figgins states, reaching for her own blade as she stands front and center of the class.

"What did she want to talk about?" Eldon asks, quirking a brow at me.

"Ari. She was keeping me in the loop of what's going on today," I answer. That seems to satisfy his curiosity and we focus on the class.

"As I'm sure you're all aware, when we selected the swords, it took a drop of our blood as payment. Did anyone not bleed?" I glance around to see if anyone makes themselves known, but it seems like we all got the sharp bite of momentary pain. "Excellent. That means your connection with the weapon is superior. The sword in your hand will literally be yours until the day you die."

"What benefit does that have for us?" Creed asks, running his thumb over the handle of his sword, and I clench my thighs, thinking of those same hands soothing me.

"Excellent question, Mr. Wylder. If you die with this sword in battle, it will disappear when you take your last breath. We're going to learn the language etched into the blade. You each have something different to wrap your tongue around, but saying those words will summon the sword when needed. Next week, I plan for you to come to class without your weapon so you can summon it when asked." I nod along, impressed at the bond you can have with such a seemingly-simple object. "Now, everyone unsheathe your swords."

The zing of metal escaping its confines echoes through the air, sending a shiver down my spine as the blade shimmers in the sun. Intrigued by the passage she mentioned, I bring it closer to my face to find elongated, cursive letters etched into the sword's blade.

I read each letter but I don't have a clue what I'm supposed to be saying. It's undeniably heavy in my hands, a definite weapon when needed, but the thought of summoning it without access to my magic has me excited.

"Hold the sword downward, like this, a firm grip on the handle, without letting the blade touch the ground," she orders, and everyone takes a second to get it in place. "Now, let a hint of your magic free, allow it to wrap around the sword, let it touch and learn and the words will come to you. Be patient though, it can take a few tries for some."

My stomach instantly sinks. I can't fucking do that. That shatters my hopes. I can't just say that though. I'm going to have to act like I have my shit together like everyone else.

I don't look up, worried I'll lock eyes with one of the Bishops and find pity flickering in their gaze. I can't face that, not when I'm hyped up for today.

Holding the sword as she instructed, I close my eyes and focus on the sword. Maybe if I tried... maybe with the suppression being lifted there might be something. Exhaling, I try to clear my mind, channeling all of my thoughts on the sword, but... it feels like just that—a sword in my hands.

Frustrated, I glare at the weapon in my grasp, hearing others around me murmur words that almost seem like a different language. I hear Brax murmur beside me, the handle on his sword glowing at his words, and my eyes widen in surprise.

"Struggling, Raven?" Figgins asks, walking among the group, and I nod. "You're probably too worked up over your familiar. It has a way of getting under your skin like that. But I'm sure if you keep practicing through the week, you'll get there." I take a deep breath, nodding in understanding as she gives me a reprieve and a viable excuse.

I spend the remainder of the lesson slightly pissed that pretty much everyone I can see has the hang of it. It takes a lot longer than I assume she predicted because there's no time to learn the basics, which means I've spent longer than I care to admit failing at connecting with my sword.

Let's hope Ari isn't as difficult later.

The usual slump to my shoulders is back as we make our way to the locker room. The Bishops stay close while still giving me the space I need to sulk for a minute, but the tightness of Brax's jaw tells me I won't get to carry on with this mood for much longer if he has a say in the matter.

The thought calms me a little and I appreciate how well they seem to be able to read me, knowing what I do and don't need at any given time.

"Are you doing okay?" Leila asks as we get dressed.

"Yeah, I just get frustrated when I can't connect with my magic so easily," I admit, omitting the truth but not barefaced lying.

"I know what you mean. Honestly, before the Gauntlet, my father pulled me aside to train because I really do struggle sometimes. Besides, my father always says just because you're struggling, it doesn't mean you're failing, and that always gives my heart the jolt it needs."

Her words coil inside of me, making my shoulders fall back and my chest relax. She's right, struggling isn't failing, and I need to remember that. Taking another deep breath, I finish getting changed and head out.

The Bishops are waiting for me like usual but the look on Zane's face has me a little concerned. "Is everything okay?"

"Did you guys hear the news?"

"What news? We were gone for like five minutes," I grumble, glancing at Eldon, Brax, and Creed too.

"They've cleared a spot for another outpost visit."

"Wait, so soon after we've had an attack?" I clarify and he nods. "At the same one?"

"No, we're heading to Shadowmoor."

My heart sinks. "I didn't even know there was one."

"It's off the shore and nowhere near the actual place, really. Are you going to be okay?" Zane asks, reaching out for my arm. I nod, despite the worry gnawing at me. "Okay, well, Brax is going to drop our swords off at the house and we'll meet him at the main entrance."

Brax takes my sword from my hand and I try to force a smile to my lips, but I know it falls flat. I hate that I'm such a rollercoaster of emotions today. As soon as I think I'm over something, I have another obstacle to face. It's exhausting.

Eldon slips his arm around my shoulders as Brax rushes off, likely sneaking away to create a portal, and we head through the corridors to the main entrance where Professor Fitch is waiting with a few other professors that I haven't had lessons from yet.

His gaze settles on Leila's for a moment but he doesn't say anything of concern and that makes me feel better. If he's happy for his daughter to be going then everything will be fine. Pleased to have pulled myself back off another ledge, I lean more into Eldon's hold as we stand together, waiting for the next order.

Brax appears at my left, just in time for Fitch to address us all. "I'm sure you're all familiar now with the gateways. If you can gather in the same groups you were in last time, we'll get this trip underway."

Fuck. I forgot about that part. Grimacing, I go to find the right group I assigned myself to, but before I can even take a full step, Eldon is claiming my mouth with his. He leaves me breathless and disoriented in the best way possible before nudging me forward.

"We're not letting you out of our sight with these gateways around, even if Sebastian isn't present," he grumbles, and a fleeting flicker of panic washes over me. Even though he said Sebastian isn't here, I still have to glance around to be sure.

I find the right line, and Finn is thankfully further in front this time. When I'm ready to go through, Eldon places his hand on my shoulder. "Let Zane go through first." He points to the gateway to my left where Zane waits. He offers me a wink before disappearing. A few seconds pass, and Eldon kisses my temple. "Your turn, Little Bird. I'll see you in a minute."

Shaking the nervousness from my limbs, I step through the iridescent center of the gateway, my shoes hitting the ground instantly on the other side. Myriad memories flood my thoughts as the constant darkness that casts over the sky comes into view.

There are two towers, one to the far left, the other to the right, and a border that wraps around the exterior acting as an extra barrier from whatever lurks on the other side.

There are no cute turrets and walkways like there was on the last outpost trip. There's not even any grass beneath our feet. Just dried out soil.

We may not be in Shadowmoor, but we're close enough. It's like the sun's been blocked out forever. I wrap my arms around myself, the chill in the air a bitter reminder of the contrast between here and Silvercrest.

"Are you okay?" Zane asks, and I nod, smiling at him as I join my group.

"Apparently, it's always this dark," a guy in front of me murmurs to his friend, and it hurts my chest knowing the people of Shadowmoor know no different. I hate that I feel guilty that I was offered a way out, an alternative life. Even the fools I hated there deserve more. They're simply a product of their surroundings. Nothing more, nothing less.

"Students, gather round as quickly as possible and we can begin the tours," Professor Meade states, wrapping her thick coat around her body.

"What is there to even see? It's all black, grim, and filthy. Excellent, we've seen it. Let's leave," the same guy grunts, sparking anger in my veins as I bite back my remark. He's also a fucking idiot; a product of his elite surroundings who wouldn't survive a day in Shadowmoor, with or without his powers.

Professor Meade rattles off which group is going where

and I fall into step, ready to give Shadowmoor the respect it deserves and learn everything there is to know. By the time we're halfway around the outpost, it's embarrassingly clear that there's nothing to be proud of here apart from the fact that it's still standing and doing its job.

Every room holds gallons of blood staining the walls, the names of the people it belonged to unknown, as all remains are cast out at sea. It doesn't make sense, it's like they send people to this outpost to die. It's a suicide mission, but why?

We move from one dreary room to another in the left tower, careful not to touch anything as the wind whistles through the broken roof. No one speaks apart from the professor guiding us, which only adds to the eeriness. "That's everything from the west tower. If we make our way back down, we will hopefully get a moment to speak to the people on guard before we travel over to the east tower."

I don't see what the point is. It's beyond depressing and I hate that the guy with his shitty comment was correct. Once we've seen one room, we've seen them all. I take the spiral staircase two steps at a time, ready to get the hell out, and I find Zane and his group at the door when I get to the bottom.

He smiles when our gazes lock and I rush toward him with added urgency, hoping to suck up some of his warm energy before I have to endure any more. I'm two steps away from him when a boom ricochets off the walls around me, the ground rumbling beneath my feet, and panic starts to kick in.

"What's going on?" I yell to anyone who will listen, but everyone is as clueless as me.

"Stay there, Raven," Zane orders, rushing back outside, but there's no fucking way in hell I'm just going to stand here.

"What's happening?" Finn hollers, but I don't answer, chasing after Zane.

Horror washes over me as I step out under the dark sky to see a huge ball of flames hurtling toward us. I'm frozen to the spot as it soars over my head before it crashes into the top of the tower and everyone inside cries out with fear.

"We're under attack," someone screams at the top of their lungs as another burning orange light shoots through the sky.

The ground continues to rumble beneath my feet as I call out to Zane. He spins to face me with panic shining in his eyes as he screams my name. I follow his gaze and watch in slow motion as another fireball smashes into the tower, knocking slate and brick in every direction as an explosion sounds out.

Then everything goes black.

THIRTY FIVE

Zane

Raven falls and time slows around me as I race to catch her. I barely manage to stop her head from smashing into the ground as I collapse to my knees with her in my arms. Blood trickles down her face from where the brick hit her head.

Fuck.

My heart thunders in my chest, my pulse ringing in my ears, muting the chaos around me as panic sets in. I need to get her out of here. I need her safe.

Grunting, I rise to my feet with her in my arms, looking for the best escape from the fire now consuming the west tower.

"What's happening?" Finn asks, frowning down at Raven's limp body in my arms.

"You, come with me," I bite, turning away from where

the attack is coming from. To my surprise, Finn stays at my side, not saying a word as a professor yells over the commotion.

"There are trolls on the other side of the wall. The guards are holding them off but everyone must take cover."

This is fucked up. *So* fucked up.

A familiar flash of black hair catches my attention in the distance. "Creed, over here!" He freezes at my yell, spinning to face me, and panic consumes his features when he sees Raven in my arms.

He calls out over his shoulder and, moments later, Eldon and Brax appear too.

"We need to get her to safety," I state when they all gather around us.

"What happened?"

"The tower. We need to get her to safety so Finn can heal her."

"I can?" Finn says with a scoff, and I turn my glare in his direction, but Eldon speaks before I get a chance.

"If you want to fucking live, then yeah, you'll heal her." He gulps, nodding in response.

Now that he knows his place, I turn to Brax. "Can you transport us somewhere away from the battle?"

He thinks for a moment, spinning around before he looks toward the building at the back of the outpost. "This way, quickly. The entire place is compromised." He rushes to the closest tree and creates a portal. I don't glance back as I step through, finding myself in an office. The view from the window confirms we're on the top floor of the building at the back, as far from the trouble as possible.

Let's hope it stays that way.

Creed and Eldon are right behind me, followed swiftly by Finn and Brax, who closes off the portal.

"Wait, if you can get us here, why don't you just transport us home?" Finn asks, wiping a hand down his face, smearing the soot already coating his skin.

"I can transport within the outpost but only the gateways work in and out," Brax grunts in response, moving to the large desk at the back of the room. He pushes everything to the floor, the clattering barely heard over the explosions going off in the distance.

I lay Raven down on the table as gently as I can, running my thumb over her cheek before I take a step back.

"Do you think we need to summon our swords?" Creed asks, and my gut clenches.

"Yes," Eldon answers immediately.

"You guys all get yours, I'll get mine once I know Raven is okay." I take a step back and wave Finn closer. "Do your thing."

Thankfully, he doesn't argue, but I still hate the way he strokes his fingers through her hair to find the injury. My spine is stiff, my hands are clenched, and my jaw is so tight that I'm sure it's going to snap if he doesn't move away from her soon.

"She'll just need a second. The wound is healed, the concussion eased, she just needs to break through the fog of it all," he informs us, stepping back.

Come on, Raven. Come on.

"Get your sword, Zane. It's a fucking mess out there and you're going to need it. I'll watch her while you do." Brax shoulders me out of the way and plants himself at her side.

Sighing, I give myself some space as I try to remember the words I learned earlier today. *"Aut cum scuto aut in scuto."*

I hold my hands out, not really knowing what to expect, but the sudden weight of the blade is undeniable on my palms as it appears in front of me.

Holy fuck.

"I can't summon mine yet. What the fuck am I supposed to do now?" Finn whines, and I shrug, trying the weight of the blade in my hands. We've had no training with the weapons gifted to us, but I'd still rather have it than be without.

"Not my problem," I grunt, while Creed seems to go for the gentler approach.

"Save yourself."

Panic takes over Finn's features as he paces in front of

the door but my gaze is locked on the carnage unfolding outside. "The trouble is getting closer. We either move or guard her."

"We guard her, that's all that matters," Eldon declares, and the three of us nod in agreement. "I don't know where Leila is though and we all know that's going to be her first concern when she wakes up," he adds, but Brax quickly steps in.

"She's with Fitch, I saw them before I came through the portal."

"Then it's settled, we stay and defend her with our lives." My heart races as my words echo around the room.

"Fuck that, I'm out of here," Finn grunts, spinning toward the door, ready to run. But the door opens to reveal three faceless men dressed head to toe in forest-green cloth with curved swords at the ready.

Finn stumbles back a step, but it's futile. The blade has already penetrated his stomach and retreated, leaving him to crumple to the floor in a lifeless heap.

They get that one kill, but no more.

"You're sure as shit not a troll," Brax bellows before charging at the closest attacker. The rest of us fall into step defending Raven from any and all danger.

A curved dagger comes toward me and I swing my sword to block the attack, using a little too much force and knocking me off balance, but I manage to catch myself before I fall. Clinks of metal on metal rumble around the room, mingling with the grunts and growls of anger charged between us all.

I block two more strikes toward me but the fourth manages to slice along my arm. Sweat clings to me, anger boiling beneath the surface as I lunge my sword toward my attacker, but it's impossible without the precision needed to control the weapon.

Sinking into my magic, I know trying to go invisible will be pointless because he can still attack me, but if I could aim something at him too, that would make a difference.

"Flames," Eldon shouts, giving little warning before fire flickers between us and the enemy I didn't know existed.

I use the distraction to let my magic consume me and I'm no longer visible a moment later. Stepping out of arm's reach, I search for what I can control, but the best option is my sword that clattered to the floor when I channeled my magic.

As much as I try to focus on the sword, there's too much going on around me to make it happen.

"I can't get in their heads," Creed grunts as he stumbles back a step, the faceless men moving through the flames without care.

We're screwed.

"Brax?" I whirl around to see Raven sitting up on the

desk. Confusion flickers in her eyes, and I'm not the only one to see it, either. Brax isn't looking at the attackers, he's glancing at our girl.

"Brax!" I yell, my magic dropping from my limbs as I rush toward him. He reacts to the urgency in my tone and his entire body starts to turn to stone, but the blade penetrates his back before he's completely solid. A burning bellow rips from his lungs as he falls to the floor. The impact rocks me to my core as I gape in horror when Brax doesn't move.

"Nooo!"

THIRTY SIX

Raven

I scream at the top of my lungs, my throat burning as I watch the sword pierce Brax's body.

Please, no.

No. No. No.

I'm helpless as I watch him become weaker and weaker before my very eyes. The struggle shatters Zane, Creed, and Eldon too. Rising to my feet, I try to move closer, very aware of the green men attacking us, but nothing matters except protecting Brax. My legs give out before I can take two steps, my body still not able to withstand the knock I've already taken.

The second my knees hit the floor, my face falls into my hands and I scream. Not just a sound, though, a name.

"Ari!"

The cords in my neck tense as the scream consumes

me, the plea for help hanging heavy on my tongue.

Creed, Eldon, and Zane all keep pushing the attackers, but we're outmatched, unprepared, and struggling. I've never felt more helpless in my life. The flames at the doorway grow bigger and wider, slowly taking up more of the room as sweat clings to my skin. It's not affecting the men dressed in green, but it's proving difficult for *my* men.

Creed stumbles, falling to the floor with an attacker hovering over him and my heart splits in two. I can't lose him too. I can't.

"Ari!" I yell, but it's not as long this time as an almighty wail rings through the air.

My eyes sting from the flames as the attackers freeze at the sound, watching the windows as a flicker of gold flashes on the other side of the glass.

He came...

Ari came.

"Please, Ari. Please."

The fire crackles, wood splintering around us as the room becomes thick with smoke before everything goes silent. Eldon and Zane don't waste the distraction, drawing their swords on the assailants and driving them straight through their hearts.

I weep with hope and relief, but one still remains. He inches back a step, then another, and another. He thinks he's clear to escape, but he trips over what looks like a body by the door and Creed somehow manages to scramble to his feet to take aim with his blade.

Silence echoes through the room, each of us waiting for the next hurdle, but after a few seconds pass and nothing startles me, I crawl on my hands and knees to get to Brax. The smoke makes it difficult, my heart galloping in my chest as I roll him over to his back.

"Brax... Brax... Please, Brax," I beg as a squawk rings through the air from outside. Ari can feel my distress, I can sense his too. "Guys, please, help me with him," I plead, turning to Zane, who looks down at me with a solemn and pained expression on his face.

"I can't, Raven," he rasps, and I shake my head in disbelief.

Running my hands over him, I search for his pulse or his heartbeat, but I can't get anything with the tremble in my fingers. "Where's his sword? Find his sword," I cry, desperate for anything that will confirm that he's going to be okay.

"I can't find it," Eldon states, looking around frantically as Creed curses under his breath.

"Raven, it's gone."

"No. It can't be. It can't. No, please," I sob, my heart aching beyond words as anguish consumes me. "I can't breathe. Please, Brax. Please." I can't shake the distress from my tone, but I'm desperate. I just need to see him, hear him, *anything*.

"Raven…"

"No. No! Nooo!" A gut-wrenching cry tears from my lips, ringing unbearably in my ears as my heart bleeds and despair consumes me.

I lower my forehead to his chest, my cry still burning my lungs, a sob desperate to calm the quake in my chest as I burn from my toes all the way to my head.

"Raven."

My eyes widen, the pain unbearable as I straighten, blinking in confusion, but the scream continues.

"Raven?"

The cry stops, the flickering of flames stops, everything stops.

Everything except the fluttering of a heartbeat as I come face to face with two colors.

One brown. One green.

AFTERWORDS

I don't even know who I think I am dropping another fantasy romance as casually as this, but I'm obsessed with Raven and her men. I think I was even more scared to start another fantasy series than I was with Saints Academy, I don't know why, but it hit so well I was left scared of high expectations. So I hope this story does them justice. I'm beyond excited and dedicated to telling their story.

I can't wait to dive head first into book two and see where this crazy story takes us!

THANK YOU

Michael, thank you for always holding my hand and being my best friend. Together we can achieve anything, and I wouldn't have it any other way.

Thank you to my Queen Bee's; Tanya, Nicole, and Jen. I'm not even sure this series would exist without you guys.

A million thank yous to my beta's; Monica, Lorna, Kerrie, Marisa, and Krystal! You rock! It's one hell of a journey and I'm thankful that you're here with me.

Kirsty. What a queen mate. Thank you for running this ship and letting me pretend I know how to steer it haha

Thank you to Laura for making this book look as pretty as ever. You're a superstar!

Sarah, and Sloane. I love you. Thank you for working your magic and making me look like I know what I'm doing haha

ABOUT KC KEAN

KC Kean began her writing journey in 2020 amidst the pandemic and homeschooling… yay! After reading all of the steam, from fade to black, to steamy reads, MM, and reverse harem, she decided to immerse herself in her own worlds too.

When KC isn't hiding away in the writing cave, she is playing Dreamlight Valley, enjoying the limited UK sunshine with her husband, children, and furbabies, or collecting vinyls like it's a competition.

Come and join me over at my Aceholes Reader Group, follow my author's Facebook page, and enjoy Instagram with me on the links below.

ALSO BY KC KEAN

Ruthless Brothers MC
(Reverse Harem MC Romance)
Ruthless Rage
Ruthless Rebel
Ruthless Riot

Featherstone Academy
(Reverse Harem Contemporary Romance)
My Bloodline
Your Bloodline
Our Bloodline
Red
Freedom
Redemption

All-Star Series
(Reverse Harem Contemporary Romance)
Toxic Creek
Tainted Creek
Twisted Creek

(Standalone MF)
Burn to Ash

Emerson U Series
(Reverse Harem Contemporary Romance)
Watch Me Fall
Watch Me Rise
Watch Me Reign

Saints Academy
(Reverse Harem Paranormal Romance)
Reckless Souls
Damaged Souls
Vicious Souls
Fearless Souls
Heartless Souls

Silvercrest Academy
(Reverse Harem Paranormal Romance)
Falling Shadows
Destined Shadows

Made in the USA
Coppell, TX
10 February 2024

28852677R00288